ZERO HOURS
ON THE
BOULEVARD

TALES OF
INDEPENDENCE & BELONGING

PARTHIAN

Literature Across Frontiers and Parthian Books gratefully acknowledge the support of the Arts Council of Wales.

Parthian, Cardigan SA43 1ED
www.parthianbooks.com
Published with the financial support of the Welsh Books Council
First published in 2019
Edited by Alexandra Büchler and Alison Evans
© The contributors 2019
ISBN 9781912109128
Typeset by Alison Evans
Printed by 4edge Limited, UK

CONTENTS

LANDS OF MINE

HANAN ISSA

Mae hen wlad fy nhadau[1] occupies my thoughts.
Blood, cries, and bullets pierce my dreams of Baghdad.

Al Askari[2] is gone. I roll up paper, twist out the middle,
then crumple it to resemble the damaged *Malwiya*[3] –

even the spot from which a lovesick girl jumped to join
the deaths
of Mongol hordes and scholars that lie forgotten in the dust.

Baba, you promised we would eat at the rotating restaurant.
But, someone like my son, yet nothing like my son, comforted
himself

that he was following orders. And, as the structure collapsed,
palm trees extend heavenwards, afraid to look at the painful
detritus

below that lights a blinding *hiraeth*[4] inside me
for *mae hen wlad fy mamau*[5] – the home I have loved halfly.

I often think about my great grandfather who breathed out
kindness
as he breathed in coal dust – *mishtaqeen*[6] gentle George.

From the dark wood drawers of my nan's Welsh dresser
stories emerge of loyal dogs and betraying flower princesses.

Kan yawma kan[7] there was a woman who felt neither here nor
    there.
Although it is here I have bled and brought forth a child

of more than two places. I gift him with the names
of legendary princes, and share the stories of my people:

of Fallujah, of Aberfan, of Baghdad, of Caerdydd.

---

[1] the land of my fathers

[2] A Shi'a mosque in Samarra that was severely damaged in 2006 by ISIS.

[3] An ancient minaret that is part of the Great Mosque of Samarra – damaged
    in 2005 by ISIS.

[4] A homesickness; nostalgia for a place

[5] The land of my mothers

[6] I miss you

[7] Once upon a time

THE INFINITE DEMONSTRATION

ALBERT FORNS

TRANSLATED BY JULIE WARK

The situation is this: we're in the middle of nowhere – or maybe I should say in the middle of everyone – and we have an emergency. Guillem's looking at me and yelling, 'Wee-wee! Wee-wee!' just as Martí, the other twin I'm looking after, slips between my legs and is running off in the other direction. I look up, trying to find some support from the adults but Gemma and Noe don't even see me as they need to get up to date with things after three days of not seeing one another, and Miquel is in the midst of a passionate discussion with some nuns about whether what we're doing is a sin or not. And beyond us, the multitude: two million people packed into one single avenue. It's 11 September and today, as happens every year, Catalonia is demonstrating.

*

I'm not sure that I can explain very well how we got to this point. Well, yes Guillem's 'Wee-wee! Wee-wee!' is clearly the result of an overdose of water because, with this heat, Noe's worried about the twins getting dehydrated. What I do know is that, when I was the same age as these boys, only a few loonies came out onto the streets on 11 September and even the protests against bullfighting were more numerous. For the last three hundred years we Catalans have been remembering 11 September, 1714, the day we lost the War of the Spanish Succession, the day they banned our language and our

1

institutions, but since the thing of celebrating a defeat looks a bit pathetic (we must be the only country that does this) most people used to make the most of the holiday by going to the beach for the last swim of summer.

But all that's changed and now every good Catalan knows that, on 11 September, you have to demonstrate. Every country has its thing: the Russians have their vodka, the Scotch have their whisky and, lately, the Catalans have had a fondness for the really big show. Since 2010 when the whole thing blew up, we haven't stopped making a spectacle of ourselves, getting more complicated every year, upping the ante, *más difícil todavía*, as they say in Spanish. First, we filled one street. The next year we filled another but that day, everyone had to wear white, for a touch of colour. Then we filled an avenue and, depending on the section they were in, people had to wear T-shirts of different colours in order to make a huge rainbow which would be visible from the sky. Then, tired of that, we decided to form a four-hundred-kilometre-long human chain crossing the country from end to end. It was brilliant for the villages, which made their summer that weekend, serving veal and mushroom casserole to thousands of city slickers. That show was inspired by the Baltic Way which linked up Estonia, Latvia and Lithuania in 1989. They got their independence two years later but it didn't work so well for us. But there are still more shows so, in 2015, we were back in Barcelona making a 'V for Victory' with the colours of the Catalan flag which meant filling the roads with a T-shirt mosaic: red-yellow-red-yellow-red-yellow, et cetera. And let's not forget last year's effort when we once again gladdened the hearts of regional restaurateurs with six decentralised demonstrations, the usual two million scattered around the territory. And so on and so forth through to today when we're doing the first massive demonstration in human history that will change its colour. Look it up for yourselves. You'll find it in *Guinness World Records*. Check out the category 'Catalonia' to discover the most absurd demonstrations.

It's also true that, if the politicians had smartened up their act, there would have been no need for this crazy escalation of North Korean-type extravaganzas but, in recent years, we've been stuck in a time loop, our very own groundhog day, with the government here demanding more powers and the government there cutting them back, the government here demanding a referendum and the government there banning it. Everyone was on tenterhooks watching the tug-of-war until, tired of all this zero-sum, we decided to go ahead anyway. With this infinite demonstrationism but also a thousand and one ballots, authorized and non-authorized referendums, plebiscites, multi-referendums of every kind, not to mention the lip dub for independence, the flash mob for our own state, the giant sovereignist casserole, and lighting candles for the referendum. I think it was the writer Roberto Bolaño – Chilean by origin and Catalan by adoption, and I am sure he'd be out demonstrating today – who said that you can invent the most original way of killing someone but someone will certainly have tried it before you. The same thing happens with pro-independence originality: invent whatever you like but you'll definitely be too late. And the whole thing without advancing as much as a millimetre, stuck between a votophobic state and a votophiliac people. So, here we are, in the middle of the last demonstration (Did I say the last? It's always the second-last!) trying to find a loo as a matter of urgency.

*

Before setting out in quest of a loo, I think it's worth making a plan. Heading out with no fixed destination into the wilderness of this multitude could be catastrophic so I try to make

Guillemet understand that I've registered the 'Wee-wee! Wee-wee!' and we'll start moving in a moment. I could take him to pee in the shopping centre right next to us but it might be closed today. I think about hotels, which always have decent toilets but, oddly enough for Barcelona, I can't see any around here. This must be an Airbnb neighbourhood. I raise the matter with the ladies because the father of the kids has finished his theocratic debate and is now glued to his radio, trying to discover whether the head of the march has begun to move. He rebroadcasts to us that there are so many people that it will be impossible to do the route, which means yet another year of forgetting about marching anywhere. And, this year, among the big shots, the organisers have recruited a Barça footballer who has already been duly lynched on Twitter by Spanish followers. Finally, Noe sorts it out. 'Don't make a big deal out of it. Just take him to the bar over there.' Bar Paredes. Looks good.

We set out through the human wall, making our way through the tight-packed crowd. It's a non-stop 'sorry, sorry, excuse me, excuse me', touching sweaty bodies, asking them please to move aside, squeezing through big families who've come equipped with baby buggies, boy scout types, pensioners, and groups of friends bearing flags and other paraphernalia. People with the *estelada*, our starred separatist flag, draped round their shoulders, people with *estelades* on their heads, people with *estelades* as skirts. And, of course, *estelades* waving high. Everywhere you look there are pro-independence flags, unstarred Catalan flags, Scottish, Basque *ikurrina*, and European flags. We've even gone past one enthusiast with three different ones waving on a very long fishing rod. We do a side-step because someone's brought along a ninety-year-old lady in a wheelchair. They've decked her out in a Via Catalana 2013 cap – typical past-sell-by-date merchandising – and her granddaughter is taking a selfie with her ('That's lovely, darling. Maybe I won't see it, but when you're independent you'll have a nice memory of your old gran!').

I must say that seeing people of this age roasting in the sun for the patria brings a tear to my eye. They are the proof that these demonstrations are transversal, and you'll find Catalan speakers and Spanish speakers of all origins and social conditions shouting together that we want to vote, we want a referendum. It's also true that demonstrating might have become fashionable and we just come along to be part of a group and not feel excluded. Getting out into the street for something to do, to break monotonous routine, to be able to say 'I was there' and talk about it authoritatively at work on Monday. Guillem suddenly tugs at my hand. What do you want, treasure? Yes, I know, 'Wee-wee! Wee-wee!' But no, he's changed the monosyllables because he's saying, 'Woof! Woof!' pointing at a little terrier whose owner has draped him in an *estelada*. Thousands of people mean thousands of doglings for independence. Finally, I pick Guillem up so we can move faster, praying that his mini-bladder will hang on a bit more since we are now nearing the Bar Paredes. We circumnavigate the din of a batucada – the child's eyes are popping out of his head – and push through a group of Miquelets, long-suffering patriots dressed up as troops from 1714, complete with blunderbusses, the gongs of the time, and Louis XIV wigs in this blazing sun. But they have a secret. I just heard the magic click of a beer can and now I see they've come with a full cool box. They're right: demonstrating has no quarrel with being well prepared.

*

Ask anyone you like: we're all tired of this statutory demonstrating but, as happens every summer, the utterances of Spanish opinion makers and pronouncements by the Madrid politicians end up convincing even the most reticent. With insults, especially the insults. This year the usual gang have called us 'Nazis', '*Polacos*' (why on earth they use 'Polish' as some kind of insult is beyond us), 'terrorists' and 'coup plotters', simply because we want to vote, but the Spanish pundits have come up with still more ingenious terms for pro-independence Catalans, among them 'Hobbits', 'pothead junkies', 'Taliban' and 'carnivores', quite apart from the delightful 'Catalan crap', pet moniker of Spanish roughnecks. They've devoted other friendly words to us, like one of former Spanish Prime Minister Aznar's ministers who suggested that the Catalan president should be executed by firing squad, and those of Aznar himself demanding that the army should be called in to put an end to the disorder in the Generalitat, the Catalan government. With all this fuel being flung around how could there not be flames?

Apart from this morbid daily checking of the press, the weeks leading up to 11 September always have the same rituals, starting with acquiring the uniform of the year, one of those thousands of T-shirts which, at the precise moment we all don together. In nearly a decade we've sported official T-shirts in almost every possible colour and now we're clearly running out of ideas. Someone suggested that we could go shirtless but the idea of a semi-nudist demonstration wasn't very well received – 'Catalonia will be Christian or nothing' – so finally, at the last minute, the organisation decided on fluorescent T-shirts so the whole world can see us, even in the dark. Like every other year we're running late, and like every other year the quarter of a million T-shirts have to be bought from Made-in-Taiwan suppliers. Needless to say, the Spanish newspapers have had a field day: 'The Catalan textile industry can't even make pro-independence T-shirts'.

To simplify things, I arranged with Miquel that I would buy

them for all of us and I must say they made it easy: on the promised day, they were on sale in the kiosk right outside my street door. Well, ninety euros for six T-shirts is daylight robbery and especially when I'm absolutely certain I'll never wear it again. Miguel de Unamuno, one of the few Spanish intellectuals who understood us, said 'Levantines, aesthetics is your downfall' but now precisely the opposite happens with us and our demonstrations. They are the anything-goes of vulgarity and not just because of the fluorescence. Bermuda shorts are omnipresent and a rubber-thong dictatorship has been decreed. That's when people don't turn up equipped for an expedition, with a safari waistcoat and Quechua canvas mountain boots: the classical traveller's uniform, as if when going to see the Champs-Élysées you need mountain boots.

This year I had to get a new *estelada* because my old one had faded after being out in the sun all year, going mouldy on my balcony. Because independence is also won on balconies. Today the street is ours and we pro-independence warriors are winning hands down but, during the year, things aren't so easy and the psychological war is fought on the facades. Each block has its own guerrilla war between those who hang out the four-barred Catalan flag and those who display *la Rojigualda*, the Spanish flag, between the Spanish bull fans and the Catalan donkey fans. One day, the history books will say, 'Before Catalonia was independent, every balcony was a trench'. Finding a flag these days is always complicated and I made a pilgrimage through three Chinese bazaars in my neighbourhood. 'Indentist frag? All gone!' On my fourth try I finally found one.

The final logistics headache was deciding on our spot. By definition, a demonstration is a spontaneous event but, since we Catalans are a well-behaved people, we've invented the 'prior-registration' demonstration as a way of getting organised. This means that some weeks before the demo you have to put your name down for a specific section, the so-called 'stretch', choosing the exact street and corner where you are to be located. It's like buying a numbered seat for the cinema or the theatre. We got stretch 77, but I have relatives in 63 and 19, colleagues in 21 and friends in 103. I'm fed up with conversations about stretches, the whole summer arguing about which is the best stretch and which the worst, and which stretch the people from Berga go to. Don't know. Don't care.

*

After the megaphone man, the kid with the GoPro on his head, and the Finns for independence with their banner saying '*Halauamme päättää tulevaisuudestamme*', we reach Bar Paredes. I can assure you they were the longest twenty metres of my life. There's a terrifying crush of people. The place is bursting at the seams, both in front of the bar and behind it, with a dozen waiters hard at work. From the aesthetics, decoration and signed photos of Cristiano Ronaldo you might say we're in the local Madrid circle hangout but they've made sure to put out a couple of impressively sized *estelades*. After all, business is business – *la pela és la pela* – and you've got to make the most of today. Most of the people near the bar are oldies, resting, perking up in the air-conditioning. The cafeteria section provides the box seats for the demo and a space for recovery. There are women breastfeeding, half a dozen of them side by side, probably a pro-independence lactation club. The bar's chock-a-block too. Guillem's whining that he can't hang on any more and I'm starting to despair until I can see that one of the waiters has taken pity on me with a unibrowed upwards glance from the fridges he's been looking at.

'What will it be, mate?'

'Listen, this boy's about to piss everywhere. Can we use the toilet please?'

'Toilet's for clients only.'

Bloody hell shit shit shit, I hadn't thought about that, should have gone straight there like Gemma always says, just go straight to the loo, the fait accompli policy. But I forgot about it and Guillem keeps tugging at my trouser leg.

'Right. So I'll have a water.'

'Four euros, mate.'

'Four euros? If it's four euros I'll drink from the tap in the toilet!'

'Great, but the toilet's clients only.'

'OK, I'll have a beer. No, I'll have two.' Yeah, I thought, I'll make Miquel happy.

'Great. Twelve euros, *mate.*'

The kid's yelling 'Wee-wee! Wee-wee!' with an I'm-not-mucking-around-and-you're-pushing-your-luck look on his face, so I decide, right, have your twelve euros, sweetie, 'for Catalonia', I think. We finally go to the toilet and find seven people waiting, all of them with water, Coca-Cola or croissants in their hands.

*

When I was a kid, the 24-hour news channels devoted the whole morning of 11 September to repeating the floral tribute to Rafael Casanova, the commander-in-chief of Catalonia who defended Barcelona during the Bourbon siege in 1714 (the same Bourbons we're still trying to get rid of). In those days, this untelegenic spectacle was the most important event of the day: hours of an incredibly boring, endless line of people leaving flowers at a statue. Nowadays, 11 September is a journalistic orgasm, the Big Bang news for Catalonia. First, because of Bin Laden, who wrecked our day, and then thanks to a heap of jolly events cooked up in the pro-independence stew. While having breakfast today, I learned about the Catalanist-crank-cum-marathon-runner who left Amposta at the arse-end of Catalonia first thing this morning with the aim of joining the demonstration at fourteen minutes past five (yes, 17:14), and we've also had pedallers for our own state, on a kind of spontaneous bike tour which ends in Barcelona, as if there weren't enough of us already. We've also discovered 11 September cakes, invented by the Pastry Chefs Guild, and are informed that Independence One, the sailing ship of a loaded Catalan, is en route from the Balearic Islands to the city in order to support the march. And the morning news gave a slot to some Spanish military men who, true to form and as required by custom, offered to bring on the tanks to crush the demonstration, and we were given a taste of what was to come this afternoon with Catalans demonstrating abroad, thousands of émigrés, wrapped in the *estelada* and photographed in Times Square, Piccadilly Circus or the main squares of their cities of residence. To top it all off, the programme presenter has cobbled in the last hour of the demonstration and connected up with toll collection points around the country – queues of cars and coaches with *estelades* – as well as the Barcelona city centre, interviewing the early-bird demonstrators who have tried to avoid the traffic jams and made the most of the time to do a bit of shopping or take the kids to the zoo.

Precisely in order to steer clear of the country bumpkins, we decided not to go out for an aperitif and to have lunch at home. By two we were on our way. This might seem very early for a demonstration beginning at 17:14 but everything is complicated on 11 September. First, you have to forget about public transport: the Metro's on the point of collapse, buses can't use city-centre routes, the Renfe railway service, since it is state managed, will do everything possible to thwart you. Last year, they called a strike, yes, even on 11 September. Luckily the Catalan government railway service is reinforced: as I said before, the perennial stalemate. Since nobody wants to rely on the train, people from outside Barcelona arrive by private car early in the morning, or come by coach. They say that more than 2,500 coaches will park in the city today, turning Avinguda Diagonal, the main entrance to the city, into a mega car park. Some friends of mine wanted to get married on 11 September last year but they finally gave up the idea. Most people said they wouldn't go to the wedding, and they couldn't find a coach for hire in all of Catalonia. We arranged to meet Miquel and family at the Metro station, thinking we had plenty of time, but when we arrived it was swarming with people. We found a couple of octogenarian volunteers – when we speak of the 'organisation', this is what we mean, an army of hyper-motivated pensioners – and they suggested we should go on foot, taking our time. 'And forget about the stretch that was assigned to you. There are a lot more people than we expected. When you can't go any further, stop where you are.' And that's exactly what we did. The mass was rock-solid long before we got to our stretch and we've been camped here for more than two hours.

*

Since the wait at the pissodrome is going to be a long one, I open my beer to kill time. The telly in the bar, with the sound turned off, is showing images of the demonstration. You can see an indeterminate mass, families, families and more families, millions and millions of people from the air. You can also see murals showing well-known faces, portraits of world leaders, Merkel, Trump, Macron and the Dalai Lama, with the words 'We want to vote' in their respective languages. Every year we do the same thing. We're so convinced we're the good guys that we swaddle ourselves in friendly messages and use slogans from Gandhi or Martin Luther King to prove we're right and we're the victims of a huge injustice. I check out my fellow toilet queuers. That ironic gentleman just in front of us, for example, with his Guardia Civil *tricornio* and the *estelada* draped round his shoulders like Superman's cape. He might be the human resources director for a big multinational and maybe he's going to sack half a dozen workers tomorrow, but today he's a soldier of the Catalan republic. Or the girl who's keeping Guillemet entertained, clowning around and showing him her fingernails and toenails painted with twenty *estelades*. Tomorrow, she'll be in the theatres of the Sant Pau hospital, assisting in life-and-death operations but she's here today, wasting her afternoon for a political ideal. Each and every one of us here in the bar, like the bovine mass of the multitude now appearing on the telly, we're all respectable people and we have a life.

The queue's dwindling. It seems that everyone's done what had to be done and at last it's our turn and we enter hell. It's a Dantesque toilet swimming in a couple of centimetres of brownish water on which are floating bits of paper and a few pellets of shit. And the stench, the stench, this revolting pong of nappies left by mums who've changed their babies, the cemetery of nappies now overflowing the bin meant for sanitary pads. In this sea of liquid crud, I bolt the door, wondering whether or not it's worth going to another bar but Guillem's too quick and, before I realise, he's got his willy out and is happily emptying his bladder, standing on tiptoe, aiming into the toilet bowl but soaking the seat. Without giving it too much thought, I forget about hang-ups and decide to go too. So here you have us, side by side, pissing together. It reminds me of when we were kids at summer holiday camp, playing at who could piss the furthest.

*

Our mission accomplished, getting back to base is equally as tortuous as the way out, but more relaxing. Guillem has calmed down and now his tank is empty I decide to lift him onto my shoulders so he can see everything better. Trying to avoid the batucada we found on the way in, I had the great idea of going further north but that took us into the orbit of a bunch of Catalan shawms, possibly the planet's most horrible musical instrument. Take a look on YouTube and you'll see that we Catalans are capable of the best and the worst. They're playing the bloody human castles music and, needless to say, a pillar four humans high rises with the kid at the top holding up the letter E. A few metres along, another pillar is topped by a kid waving a huge letter D. Now I see it: every pillar's holding aloft a letter from the word independence. We love people looking at us. We love to stand out. We dodge – excuse me, we need to get through – a lot of families, dodge some girls in traditional dress – sorry, sorry – leave behind a gentleman in a DIY hat looking like an altar in honour of the memory of our executed president Lluís Companys – sorry, excuse me – edge around a photographer who's got a ladder with him, I suppose to climb up for panoramic shots. Suddenly Guillem cries out in fright and, turning around, I'm looking at a face painted in the colours of the *estelada*: one of our Bravehearts. I'm trying to get my bearings but can't see the others anywhere. Maybe they've been dislodged from our spot. Despite the apparent immobility of the crowd, it's impossible to stay still in any one place because the mass is slowly flowing, pushing on, and we're mere leaves floating on the flood, so the swell must have swept them further downstream. There are so many of us that, if there was an avalanche of people, we'd all be squashed. Okay I know, I must be the only one in the whole demo who thinks like this but I can't help it, can't get the idea out of my head. Around us, there are more people than in a war and among the banners wielded by the infantry are all kinds of proclamations; 'We want to vote', 'Freedom for Catalonia' (this one in English), 'Independence NOW!', 'We want the alternative route for Balaguer'. (There's always some smart-arse with extraneous demands.) I put Guillem down and make him walk. He was destroying my cervical spine – his dad must do killer workouts at the gym – and, after moving a little ahead, I smell something familiar. A chap in a traditional red Catalan peasant cap is barbecuing meat, right in the middle of the avenue, and another shepherd boy is handing out haricot beans to their gang of hungry pals sitting on folding chairs. We pass a choir singing traditional songs, people lugging enormous cardboard ballot boxes, and a family with green *estelades* on which they've written 'The colour-blind for independence'. No luck, we can't find them anywhere and Guillem's getting tired, so I open the second beer – shh, Miquel needn't know – and we rest for a moment.

I try to call Gemma but no go. I'd forgotten that this is like the Barça stadium. With so many people connected at once the phones stop working. The Internet's not working either so I can't find out where they are or even send a pathetic WhatsApp. I remember the photographer with the ladder and think he might lend it to me so I can find our little retinue from the air, but I've lost sight of him too and there's no way I can find him. People and more people all around us, posters saying 'Sarroca de Lleida for independence', 'Linyola for independence', 'Monistrol for indepenence' (every year you see this error). People and more people but not our people. Luckily Guillem's staying calm. He's having a ball in the pandemonium, which is very different from the panic I'm starting to feel. Suddenly there's quite a hullabaloo and the crowd, hitherto compact, starts moving. Shit, the human avalanche. I knew it, the National

Intelligence Centre must have done their thing, the panic is spreading and we're all going to die trampled flat as pancakes. But, no, the crowd has opened up like when Moses parted the Red Sea, to make way for the bikers for independence, a hundred or so chaps built like brick shithouses, who you'd never even dare to ask the time of day, are grinning at everyone today, kissing babies, revving up their Harleys and waving Catalan flags, or they have them painted on their helmets or tattooed on their arms with phrases like '*donec perficiam*'. One's carrying a black *estelada* resembling the Jolly Roger, saying 'We'll be free or we'll be dead'. When the last one's gone by, plus the Catalanist Vespa which closes the parade, the sea closes again. Guillem's playing with some kids who've come with a – for-independence – pony, while a couple of tourists just in from the airport, suitcases and all, take selfies with the demonstration in the background. I decide to move on, but after the Barça granddad and a chap with a blow-up doll – Guillem loves it – we land in the midst of an improvised concert. I see it's the Brams – the lead singer's inimitable – and the whole thing's one great big shindig complete with groups of swaying giants, frisky big-heads, and Guita Xica (as Small Mule from the Berga Patum festival is known), and we're all jigging about, shaking up our bones. Guillem's clapping his hands and I have (very briefly) joined a conga line.

*

I can't find them and I'm starting to get pissed off. I'm sure they were here before, just opposite this real estate office. I'd say the crowd's not moving but maybe it's an optical effect. Or they must be the ones who moved. And, if they think we've taken too long, have they come looking for us? I wonder whether we should turn around and go back to the bar but it's too far away and I don't feel up to it. So we keep moving. But now where?

Guillem's having a whale of a time. He doesn't care. Now a young lad's letting him touch the *estelada* he's got shaved on his head. I'm noting a gradually rising tension in the atmosphere, with louder and more frequent chanting. Things are hotting up and I see on my phone that it's nearly H-Hour. I lift Guillem onto my shoulders again and ask him to look for them. 'Can you see mummy, Guillem?' But no. Then I decide to try myself so I find a lamppost, wrap myself around it to climb up a couple of metres, sweating like a pig, and I've barely gone a few centimetres when an old gentleman who's been watching me from a distance starts to shout and wave his walking stick around. 'We don't want vandals. We Catalans are peaceful people!' Guillem's watching it all from below without understanding much, and now the gentleman's wife and a couple more oldies join in the protest, moving closer, brandishing their walking sticks, as if they want to thrash me down to the ground, but luckily something distracts them, an excited roar of the crowd and ding-donging of all the bells that have begun to toll. And with the bells comes 17:14. The crowd, as one, dons the fluorescent T-shirt, and now comes the afternoon's loudest shouting. The usual roar, 'WE WANT TO VOTE! WE WANT TO VOTE!' and 'I/IN-DE/IN-DE-PEN-DENCE', the classical 1990s sovereignist shout, although then it was 'IN/IN-DE', out of respect for the rules of Catalan syllable separation, but the first N's been dropped with the new century. People are yelling in chorus, as loud as they can, bellowing till they're hoarse, like the lads raising hell in the Barça stadium but without the usual varicoloured invective hurled at the referee. Now we're all yelling our heads off, hyperventilating like mad and the shouts of the people around us are making us shout louder in a mad deafening spiral. Adrenaline's pumping through my veins. There's something cathartic and reassuring about these demonstrations.

You come out of them invigorated, more convinced, stronger and therefore more stubborn, more fanatical. The shared shout conveys a false sensation of truth, of power, of victory, which makes the depression of the next few days even worse when we can see that the politicians are carrying as normal, not lifting a finger. But collectiveness is a beautiful thing and we don't have many opportunities to see ourselves like this, united and at one, so when it happens it's always special. There are no differences and it doesn't matter whether you're Barça or Real Madrid, black or white, left or right, because today we're together and when we come together as one our power is infinite. This is perhaps the drug of these demonstrations, why we're so hooked: you feel the power, you feel the strength of this 'we'. Today we can do anything, we could make a revolution, we could even lynch someone and, when it's all over, we'll embrace each other, full of emotion. We're addicted to the joy of being part of all this, of belonging and experiencing this exceptional moment. We all live our lives and have nothing in common with 99% of the demonstrators but today everyone's talking to everyone else because the cause unites us and we're all sparking with the collective electricity.

*

It's twenty past five and we're still shouting, as if nothing's happened, but the climax has passed and the show will slowly deflate. You can tell by the chanting, which is scattering and overlapping. And the intensity's falling. Until now we've been one single being. We didn't care if the guy standing next to us doesn't use deodorant. But the people around us are starting to get annoying, those wailing babies, those kids chasing each other, are a non-stop irritation. We've still got a good hour of shouting ahead of us, yelling our demands in case Madrid hasn't heard us, or their clocks are slow, especially because the avenue's packed tight as a cork and it will take a while to uncork it, but it's evident that the job is done and some people have kids to bath and washing to do. Moreover, a demo's like football: you can see it better at home. We're still smiling, still shouting but we all want to get the hell out of here and go home. We have more or less long trips to get there but after 17:15 the couch is our only *patria*. Naturally, we're all going to watch it on Catalan TV, which does the most complete report. This is the day when you only watch the Spanish channels if the doctor's prescribed that you must get pissed off. The demonstration's always the last news of the day and they only show a few hotheads who've set fire to the Spanish flag and the Madrid politicians saying that demonstrating means a rupture of cohesion, and a ballot is an attack on democracy. On Catalan TV, however, we can revel in our own human performance, and we'll see splendid advertorials about the march, with drone images and *Gladiator*-style epic music, followed by an endless line-up of interviews with participants in which you always see someone you know. We also keep an eye on how the demo's doing on Twitter, where the hashtag #CatalansVote is always a global trending topic, even though those of us actually at the demo can't tweet, and they also show us – we love this – what the BBC, *The New York Times*, and the media around the world have to say about us. It's always headlines with photos. It's such a pity the English or French reader is left with, 'yet another nationalist demonstration' when the image is just the tip of the iceberg. Finally, the icing on the cake of this TV night is when they start talking numbers which, year after year, swing wildly depending on who's counting: organisers and traffic cops go for the high ones and count us by millions, while the Spanish Government Delegation in Barcelona waters down the wine and talks about half a million 'at the very most'. But whether the count of the night is to be high or low, we're still stuck here. The atmosphere of the demonstration has changed and I now see that the colour of the thing has changed too. The crowd is now fluorescent green, as if we were extraterrestrials making a gigantic pool of snot. That reminds me that we haven't put our T-shirts on. I take mine and Guillem's out of my backpack and see I've still got the other four, which means the rest of our contingent couldn't get transformed. And I realise that it will be easier to find them now, knowing that they're the only specks of colour in the green tide. And that's how it is. A minute later I spot them in the distance, downstream, thirty metres away.

*

'Hey! At la-a-ast!' I shout, holding up Guillem who's giggling happily. I park the boy with his mum and hand out the T-shirts. 'Come on, get your uniform on. Let's show off the ninety euros, at least for a while.'

'Where the hell were you, lad?' Miquel removes his transistor earphones.

'Taking Guillem to the toilet, but with all those people ...'

'Okay, right, because now Martí needs to piss. You don't mind taking him, do you, since you know where to go?'

The Garden

Uršul'a Kovalyk

Translated by Peter Sherwood and Julia Sherwood

There was absolutely nothing exceptional about the flat. Crammed full of commie-style furniture, reeking of citrus air freshener that always made her nauseous. The only thing that was attractive about the place was the walnut-coloured parquet flooring as it sparkled in the cold March sun. 'Another boring flat,' Ela grumbled. The estate agent, who was rushing up and down the living room in a state of agitation, raised her eyebrows. Ela was getting fed up. Of viewing flats, of moving from one place to the next, of prattling estate agents determined to foist upon her flats furnished in the most appalling taste, at prohibitive rents and located in the worst parts of the city. She walked into the hallway boasting a tatty old palm tree mural wallpaper and an old wardrobe. The estate agent took a deep breath and began to spew forth a stream of information about the advantages of the neighbourhood: several bus stops just a stone's throw away, the health benefits of a naturally-breathing brick-built block, the friendliness of the neighbours and the endless sunshine the flat would get from one-thirty in the afternoon until six in the evening. Ela didn't say a word as she looked around the living room dominated by an antediluvian settee that must have been home to an army of starving dust mites. The kitschiest painting of Jesus Christ she'd seen in her life graced the wall, though it had a fairly tolerable frame. She preferred not to open the bathroom door, to be on the safe side. She shrank back from the smelly black sink plugholes full of fermented bits of hair, skin and other biological matter, repulsive remnants and residual smells left behind by a previous lodger. That is why, whenever she moved into a new rented flat, she would start by disinfecting the bathroom. The estate agent waxed lyrical about the tall ceilings, pointed out the benefits of living on the second floor and rhapsodised about the huge savings due to the independent heating system. Ela didn't react. She asked no questions, made no comments, but that only encouraged the agent to bombard her with more and more information. Ela felt a headache coming on. She switched the sound off in her head and continued walking around the flat as if she were deaf, just observing the agent's gestures and facial expressions. This was quite funny at times, like watching a silent movie. When Ela got to the kitchen, she opened the balcony door wide, although it was cold outside. She went out on the balcony, or rather the 'loggia' as the estate agent called it. It was quite large, with peeling plaster and a frozen rubber plant in the corner. She leaned over the railing. A huge terraced garden stretched out below. The sight nearly took her breath away. The garden was filled with ornamental trees and shrubs. She recognized cypresses and thujas, sprinkled with hoarfrost that hadn't melted in the feeble winter sun. The ground was green with saxifrage and assorted alpine plants she couldn't name. It seemed as if she wasn't looking at a garden at all, but at an illustration in a lifestyle magazine, too perfect to be found in this town. A sensation unlike anything she'd experienced for ages washed over her. It was relief of the kind you feel when, after a long, long time, you suddenly find yourself somewhere that makes you feel good. 'I'll take it,' she told the estate agent who was struggling to open a wardrobe door with a cracked mirror. The agent stopped rattling the wardrobe and without saying a word produced a contract. 'You'll get the keys as soon as you've paid the deposit.

The landlord lives abroad so if you need anything you can speak to me. Our bank account details are in the contract,' she announced and glanced at her mobile nervously. Ela closed the door to the balcony and, smiling for the first time, said:

'You should have started the viewing on the balcony.'

Ela forked out an astronomical amount for the deposit. She borrowed money from a loan company at an extortionate rate of interest. Her job as a crisis centre counsellor didn't pay particularly well. When she left her native city to move to the capital she had hoped she would be able to get on her feet financially. Persuaded by tales of the fat pay packets in Bratislava shared over a couple of beers by two fortunate fellows, she took a train and got off at the main station. She was aghast at the state of the station. This shabby open-air museum of communism was the last thing she had expected to find. Ticket queues stretched all the way to the station entrance. People were pushing and shoving, those meeting passengers getting in the way of those catching trains. Winos guzzled cheap wine in front of the station, cackling and shouting. A homeless man was asleep with a cardboard box on his head as if he were reading it. She didn't dare take a cab. She'd been warned that the taxis parked outside the station would rip her off. She lugged her suitcase along the station piazza. On a crumbling block next to an ultramodern building a giant advertising hoarding, aglow above dirty, tacky food stalls, caught her eye. A cosy café where she stopped for a cup of coffee helped improve the overall impression slightly. Things couldn't be all that bad, she told herself. She was determined to connect with this city, to learn to love it even.

But the city made it difficult, showing her an angry face more often than she would have liked. On the very first day, as she walked across Freedom Square, she chanced upon some kind of a rally. She'd never seen so many Neo-Nazis in one place before. Some were standing on a rostrum, railing against Jews, immigrants and other traitors to the nation. Her stomach turned when she noticed that a simulated execution of the President, Soros and Merkel, was being enacted on the stage. She couldn't believe this was really happening, that it wasn't just a bad movie. So much aggression and hatred. A terrifying image haunted her for a long time: a shaven-headed young man ushered a veiled woman onto the stage and pretended to choke her to death with a black scarf. The crowd chanted angrily: 'String 'em up! String 'em up!' There was in this rage a kind of animal fervour and a delighting in death. Like young predators learning to break the neck of their prey. They begin tentatively, training until they can do it for real. One day these people will do it for real, too. 'Have you all lost your mind, have you really lost your mind?' she kept repeating but the crowd wouldn't listen, busy tearing an EU flag to shreds. After this experience Ela lost her confidence. She could feel the suppressed hatred spreading around the city like a fetid cloud. She sensed the animosity blazing from people's eyes, in the graffiti scribbled on the walls, and in the angry curses screamed from the cars. The hatred had the pungency of mothballs in an old fur coat in a wardrobe. She started to suffer panic attacks. Something inside her had crumpled, her sense of inner security was gone. She steered clear of large-scale public events, crowded pubs and, above all, demonstrations. She began to doubt herself. She used to believe she could handle anything. She would find a good job and take out a mortgage on a small flat in a quiet neighbourhood. But life was taking a different course. Her job kept her constantly busy but didn't pay enough to make her attractive to a bank. And so she moved from one rental to the next. When she celebrated her forty-seventh birthday she had to admit to herself that she was, in fact, homeless. The meagre salary coming into her bank account each month formed the thin line separating her from life on the street.

After a while she consciously started to suppress this knowledge for fear of going round the bend. The strain of her work counselling abused women, the uncertainty and tiredness of the endless packing up and moving, drove her to flee reality for reverie. She was capable of spending hours daydreaming. She'd freeze and stare at an invisible point in the distance. She'd picture herself in exotic locations she'd read about or seen in films. The place to which she returned most frequently was the Roca Blanca coast she'd seen in a documentary. The film featured the fauna populating the mouth of a river emptying into the ocean. A deserted beach, the freshwater river running over glittery black boulders, languidly flowing into the salty sea. White egrets sitting on mangroves, strangely twisted cacti and pelicans catching fish amid the rolling waves. The place had cast a spell over her. Sometimes she would imagine herself sitting there in the sand, watching the waves ebbing and flowing along the coastline and listening to the roar of the Pacific. She wished she could be there for real. Ela wasn't naive. She knew she'd never be able to afford it. She was stuck in this country, tied to her job, ageing, locked into her clients' problems. Maybe that was why the garden behind the new house gave her so much joy. The view gave her strength and offered an escape. The garden had a calming effect on her and offered, if only for a brief moment, the illusion of a safe paradise on earth. She felt as if she owned it a little bit. Sometimes she'd sit out on the balcony until midnight.

Spring had arrived with a vengeance. A warm front from the

Mediterranean forced the flowers out of the ground. Ela would count them every day and every day she'd find some new ones. She would sit on the balcony sipping hot coffee and couldn't take her eyes off the yellow crocuses. She had never realised how fast flowers could grow. They would make a sudden spurt overnight. Like adolescent girls. After two days of copious spring rain the garden was bursting with colour. It attracted a timid redstart, and from now on it would come regularly and perch on the lightning conductor by her balcony, gazing at her. At times she expected it to start talking. It seemed to have something urgent to tell her, so much so that she began seriously to ponder the kinds of problem redstarts might have. Fortunately, she caught herself in time and realised that she was starting to lose it and that she was just an ordinary counsellor on the verge of burnout.

Ela had no idea who looked after the garden. She would come home late in the evening and never saw anyone out there. She assumed a professional gardening firm did the job for an extortionate fee. It wasn't until after Easter that she finally met the 'firm', busy replanting tulip bulbs and bearing an uncanny resemblance to Mrs Králková, a lady she used to know in her home town. Actually, to call it resemblance would have been an understatement, the woman was the spitting image of Mrs Králková. Ela was tempted to say hello the way you greet an old friend, shout out something jokey. The woman had the exact same pair of blazing black eyes and facial expressions, was of the same small stature, and even wore hair curlers, covered by a thin kerchief, with the same grace as Mrs Králková. Ela watched her, joyfully and affectionately, hoeing, replanting and deadheading the plants. After a while the woman stopped, stretched out and took a cigarette from her pocket. She lit up. She put the lighter away with a hand grubby with soil, inhaled and then exhaled. Blue smoke curled around the dwarf thujas like rising mist. Mrs Králková's doppelganger stood majestically amid a cloud of smoke admiring the fruit of her labours. She inspected beds of tulips, daffodils and grape hyacinths, the precious works of art she had created. It occurred to Ela that she could never examine the results of her work in this way. Her own work was undetectable. Endlessly repetitive, full of horror stories of violence and abuse of power. She was often aware of the futility of her endeavours, of trying to stop running water with a spaghetti strainer. No sooner had one client managed to ditch her tyrant, the next one would turn up, then the next. Thinking of her professional future, all Ela could see was an endless queue of battered women. She realised how much she missed the sense of liberation that comes when every problem has been resolved and every wound healed. Just a brief respite. Just one week without a horrific case. But in her job there was never any respite.

Ela sat on the balcony as still as a mouse so as not to disturb the woman who seemed to be gripped by some creative frenzy. She didn't even stir the coffee she'd brought out onto the balcony. She just drank in the precious intimate moment slowly rising towards her balcony, taking it in with the cigarette smoke. Just then Ela's mobile rang. The silly ringtone a colleague had downloaded on her phone for a laugh ruined the silence. The early morning artistic idyll was wrecked. Startled, Mrs Králková's doppelganger looked up at the balcony that had been empty for a long time. Now this woman sitting there had the cheek to spy on her. Ela flashed her a guilty smile and lifted the phone to her ear. A colleague announced reproachfully that she had a client waiting in the office. 'Got to dash to work,' she said in a friendly way, as if they had known each other for ages. The woman waved to her from the garden. Ela realised how long it had been since someone had waved to her. The last time it had been her dad, who'd waved her off as she boarded the coach on her way to the young pioneer camp. And it occurred to her that she hadn't waved to anyone for ages either, so she raised her hand and shouted: 'You've got the most beautiful garden in the world!' Mrs Králková's carbon copy cracked up laughing. 'But I keep thinking something's still missing to make it perfect!' Ela would have loved to respond, to say something like: there was no such thing as perfection. The most wonderful thing in the world was natural variety. She would have loved to tell the woman what she thought of her creation, but called by duty, she got up immediately.

Later that night, after a hard day's work, she went out onto the balcony again. The woman was gone. The fragrance of spring was in the air, even here, in the middle of the city. Scattered among the stones she spotted a few new garden lights. They looked like white dumplings of yeast shining a magic lantern over the garden.

From now on Ela saw Mrs Králková's doppelganger from her balcony on a regular basis. She learned that the woman's name was Boženka and that she had been living in this block for donkey's years and knew all the tenants. 'Everyone except for you, that is,' she said. 'Where are you from?' Ela was unnerved by the question. She knew the locals looked down on country bumpkins. She was an immigrant, one of those who had no idea know how to behave, as it said on some blog. These easterners form cliques and drive rental prices way up, the blogger had said. 'I'm from Košice,' she said quietly, expecting the woman to unleash a stream of complaints and stories about impertinent females from the eastern metropolis. And their funny clipped accent. 'So you're from Košice!' Boženka exclaimed. 'How nice! I used to go there to visit my aunt in the old days. She lived on

Southern Avenue, in one of those prefab highrises. We used to go for ice-cream to Yusufi's place, do you know it?' Ela was relieved that Boženka was so forthcoming: 'Of course I know Yusufi! He was a legend even back then, people used to queue up for his ice-cream all the way to the High Street!' Boženka went on reminiscing about visiting her aunt in Košice. 'But when she died I stopped going there. You know what it's like – hotels are pricey and what was I to do there on my own?' Boženka gradually told Ela everything there was to know about the house they lived in. It was the last of the brick blocks built in the 1960s for the top managers of Hydrostav, a state company. 'Only the finest people from the building trade could live here. My father was allocated a flat because he was a brilliant construction manager!' she confided. 'Know the grey-haired chap who lives on the ground floor, the one with a walking stick? He always tosses his fag ends into the garden, thinks I'm stupid and don't notice.' Ela scoured her memory for a neighbour with a walking stick and eventually remembered an old codger she'd once met on the stairs. 'You mean the sweet grandpapa in a checkered fleece shirt?' she asked. 'Sweet grandpapa my foot,' Boženka guffawed and pulled a cigarette from behind her ear. She looked around as if someone was spying on her, lit up and whispered: 'Why don't you come down from that balcony of yours? It would save me having to yell.' Ela put on her shoes and walked down to the garden. It was a festive moment. Seen from down below the garden was even more magnificent. Ela noticed things she couldn't see from the balcony. A strange conifer with blue cones, marigolds planted in an old shoe, nettles and something that looked like a birdhouse in a tree. 'Is that for the little birds?' she asked but Boženka just grumbled dismissively: 'Oh no, it's for bats.' She grabbed Ela by the sleeve and it all came tumbling out: 'That sweet grandpapa in a fleece shirt used to be the greatest snitch! He grassed on my dad, too, nearly got him sacked. If it hadn't been for an engineer, a big shot who stood up for him, who knows where we'd have ended up. We used to play out here when I was little. It was just an empty lot covered in thistles. When we played ball and it happened to land on his balcony he'd get a knife and cut it to pieces. And the names he used to call us! He'd steal doormats from outside our flat, just to spite us! Let me tell you, that sweet grandpapa is a nasty old piece of work. Watch out for him!' Ela was barely listening. She was walking up and down the garden, thrilled to bits. She felt she wasn't in the heart of a concrete city jungle but in a botanical garden. The plants were arranged in delightful colour schemes, shrubs alternated with creeping ivy and cultivated grasses with rocks, creating distinct, if tiny, spaces. Boženka stood beneath a magnolia tree. A mantis had landed on the scarf covering her hair curlers, its elongated metallic body gleaming in the setting sun. The mantis waved its long arms as if praying, as Boženka solemnly initiated Ela into the block's history. She told stories of fabulous barbeques that used to take place here, joint birthday parties, weddings and children's competitions they had organised. 'And the fabulous New Year's Eve parties we used to have! Now I'm the only person who ever comes down here. Ever since they've been showing soap operas on the TV rather than Husak's speeches everyone's been stuck at home.'

Summer came early and unexpectedly. Heat enclosed the city like a lid covering a boiling pot. Without air-conditioning in her office, Ela was suffocating. Everything seemed to have slowed down and got covered in sweat, many of the officials were away on holiday, and she couldn't get through to anyone. Court hearings were few and far between and getting hold of any official document took ages. Even her counselling sessions seemed to go around in circles. The heat exacerbated her clients' Stockholm Syndrome. The last vestiges of their self-preservation instinct were absorbed by their T-shirts and they were drowning in powerlessness like flies in syrup. Ela, too, had run out of ideas. She stared absent-mindedly at the open window where not the even a slightest breeze would stir and couldn't think of any advice to give. The city turned into a red-hot furnace. The tarmac in the streets was melting, as were the heels on people's shoes. People walked on the shady side of the street. Despite the heat and her non-functioning brain Ela loved the summer. It was so much more carefree than the other seasons. Every problem suddenly seemed unimportant. She could go around wearing very little, just a T-shirt, a pair of shorts and flip-flops. She enjoyed walking. The city had put on a much friendlier face. Foreign street musicians played in Hodžovo Square, water finally spurted from the fountain. You could go to evening concerts by the Danube and buy fresh vegetables cheap in the market. Summer was the only time Ela was really able to relax. The sun didn't appear on her balcony until late in the afternoon, by the time the heat became more bearable. The garden was now in full bloom, the plants had grown, filling every available nook and cranny. There was was lush green as far as the eye could see. Ornamental plants mingled with hemp nettles and stinging nettles, creating a vivid, fragrant jungle. Boženka had given her some curious climbing annuals that spread along the entire balcony wall. The ceiling was covered in akebia, an amazing liana with purple flowers, and Ela, lounging in a hammock, could spend hours watching the insects crawling around it. She succumbed to a languor that gradually turned into summer torpor. She stopped cooking for herself, she didn't clean, sometimes was even too lazy to pour herself water into a glass.

When the temperature rose above thirty-five degrees Celsius, Ela took to sleeping on the balcony at night. She would lie there listening to the sounds of the city. Shrieking ambulances, echoing car horns, an Affenpinscher yapping furiously, drunken girls laughing as they walked home from the disco. The thrush's evening song melded with the noise of a TV in an open window. She stared absently at the slowly darkening skies, which would never get completely black in Bratislava. One by one, stars began to come out, the odd aeroplane would blink above her, a bat would fly past, chasing woozy flies. A hot wind licked the garden like a thirsty dog lapping up the last drops of water with its dry tongue. One evening Boženka turned up with a long hose. Clumsily she spread it on the ground. She got out of breath as she tried to position it properly. 'Wait a minute, I'll come and give you a hand!' Ela shouted and ran down. Between them the two women managed to subdue the stubborn hose, Boženka turned on the tap and the first drops of water spurted into the air. 'So how do you like living here?' she asked. Ela dabbed some water on her sweaty neck: 'I think this is the best place I've ever rented in this city. Thanks to this garden of yours. If I could afford it, I'd buy the flat straight away.'

Boženka told her what it had been like in the old days when the garden was just a neglected plot of land, full of weeds, plastic bottles and carrier bags. 'You see, my old man, may he rest in peace, he couldn't take it anymore and one morning he started digging up the slope. He hauled up some rocks and built the terraces. It nearly killed him! First we planted some alpine flowers, then ornamental shrubs, and that huge magnolia tree over there he lugged all the way from Hungary. We kept telling ourselves we wouldn't overdo it with new plants. But every time we saw something nice we'd buy it. And we'd be planting like there was no tomorrow. That was over twenty years ago now.

And just when the garden was almost finished my husband died. He didn't get to enjoy it for very long.' Ela stared at the water gushing from the hose. Boženka noticed and passed her the hose without a word. Ela pinched its end between her fingers to create a delicate stream of water. She directed it at the roses and asters, letting a gentle rain fall on them. The leaves trembled under the drops of water and she could smell the soil mixed with chlorophyll and rotting plants. The garden came to life. 'So tell me about yourself. You live alone? No husband or boyfriend?' Boženka inquired. 'I'm an old maid,' laughed Ela and gave a faded zinnia a good splashing. Boženka lit a cigarette and put the box away. 'So you never got married. Mind if I ask why?' Ela thought of her clients. 'To be on the safe side,' she said laconically. The other woman fell quiet and stopped asking questions, perhaps wondering what Ela had meant. 'Would you mind hosing me down a little?' asked Ela, breaking the silence. Boženka grinned, took the hose out of Ela's hand and started to spray water all over her, holding the cigarette in the other hand. The water glued Ela's T-shirt to her breasts and ran down into her shorts, leaving wet marks. 'Isn't it too cold for you?' Boženka asked. 'Oh, no! When it's this hot I wish I could sleep in water. How about you? Let me freshen you up a little.' Boženka giggled: 'All right, but only a little bit, I don't want to catch a chill.' Ela turned the tap down and gave her a gentle splashing. The woman whooped. The burning cigarette in her hand hissed and went out. With her eyes closed Boženka let Ela wash down her sweaty back, legs and elbow. 'My turn now!' she ordered. They started splashing each other. The water squirted every which way, leaping out of the hose wildly. Sometimes it hit them in the face as the hose turned, slithered and heaved. It looked like a water serpent surrounded by crazy dancing women. Their whooping attracted the attention of the neighbours. A few faces she had briefly glimpsed at the entrance leaned out of the windows, curious. 'Good evening, neighbours!' Boženka yelled. The heads vanished instantly. They withdrew like sea anemones startled when a diver touches them. 'Here we go! Now they'll have you down as crazy, too,' Boženka commented, wringing out the hem of her dress. 'They have thought I was crazy for a long time. Actually, when my husband was alive, they thought he was was crazy, too. They used to badmouth us, saying we were dumb to plant the garden at our own cost. "*What are you doing it for, you don't own the plot, so why put so much money into it!?*" Cultivating a piece of land that belongs to the city for no money, that's not considered normal these days, right?' Ela turned off the tap on the wall. 'If you like, I'll help you water the garden regularly.' Boženka sat down on a low wall. She scratched the odd mosquito bite on her leg: 'But it has to be watered every night, you know. And it needs lashings of water, especially the hydrangeas, they're so delicate they might die.' So Ela would water the garden religiously. The water intensified the blue of the hydrangea blossoms. It was as if they leaked colour like ink, colouring the snow-white ox-eye daisies in the beds below. Ela watered the garden every night, day after day, all through the summer, which was unusually hot. She went on watering it until the arrival of autumn.

Pouring rain formed a grey wall outside the window, imperiously pounding the earth. It flushed the city dirt into gutters along with the last remnants of summer. The city filled up and accelerated. Constant traffic jams returned. People were in a miserable mood. Rain streamed down the tarmac and into the drains, vanishing from the city. Overcrowded buses regularly treated the pedestrians standing on the pavements to a shower. Ela, too, was miserable. She could feel in her bones the winter looming ahead, that most unpleasant of seasons. Even as a little girl, she had never much liked the winter and the older she got the more difficult she found it to bear. She was extremely sensitive to the cold, her feet were always frozen, her nose running. Thick tights gave her eczema on her legs and under woolly hats her hair became greasy faster than usual. Spending all days in overheated rooms made her feel claustrophobic. That was why why Ela couldn't stand the autumn either. 'Autumn is basically just winter in disguise,' she muttered under her breath as she turned on the heating for the night. Boženka, on the other hand, relished the autumn. She would hoe the flaming red chrysanthemums that suddenly appeared in the garden, singing and holding her face out to the autumn wind. 'Goodness, isn't it lovely, just look at these colours!' she shouted one Saturday morning. Ela was sitting on her balcony bundled up in a thick jumper, reading. 'But this is winter sun, it's got no warmth at all!' she snapped and went back to her article. She was in no mood for Boženka's cheery talk today. She felt drained. Three new women had come to the crisis centre for help, all victims of brutal violence. Listening to the litany of things their husbands had done to them over the years she thought she might be sick, in a completely unprofessional way. It was as if someone had hit her in the solar plexus. From an early age she'd been blessed with a lively imagination and during counselling sessions a film would start rolling in her head. A film full of punches, broken glass, screaming, threats. She could no longer remember how many medical reports she had read. Sometimes, instead of letters on the page, the worst injuries she'd ever seen would surface before her eyes. More and more often she would bring the films home with her like an accountant taking unfinished work home from the office, and she couldn't stop the screenings inside her head. She had to put a stop to it somehow, so she would read, read, and read some more.

Ignoring Ela's annoyed response Boženka flashed her a lovely smile. As always, she lit a cigarette. She went on clipping the dried up leaves off the shrubs and said amicably: 'Been reading anything interesting? Care to share it with a curious old woman?' Ela sighed. She realised there was no point fighting Boženka's good humour. 'Oh, just one of those National Geographic-type mags. You know this one?' she turned the magazine cover towards her. 'Gosh, what's that skeleton there, why is it all painted?' Ela explained that this was La Catrina, made of paper. She represented death, something that was a custom in Mexico. People display these skeletons on miniature altars to mark the Day of the Dead. 'Never heard of the custom?' Boženka took two quick drags and shook her head: 'What kind of holiday is that?' Ela offered to read her the report on *Día de muertos*, the most beautiful celebration of death on earth. Boženka listened intently and quietly. Only when she heard something unusual would she mumble: 'Gosh, really?' By the time Ela finished reading, her mood had improved. Boženka was rubbing her forehead, lost in thought, and then commented that although it sounded rather over the top, it might actually not be a bad idea to commemorate the departed in such a cheerful way. 'When you're dead you feel no pain. Personally, I think both heaven and earth are just a Christian invention, so what's the point of all the praying and grieving?' She loved the idea of Catrina street parades and especially graveside parties. 'Is it really true that they leave cigarettes on the graves as gifts for their dead relatives?' she inquired until Ela showed her a photo showing a grave covered in flowers, fruit, cigarettes and tequila. 'Paul, my husband, would have loved that. He was fond of *pálenka*, he liked his drink. As for me, I prefer a cigarette. Well, well. Mexicans, who'd have thought it,' she muttered under her breath as she picked up a few tiny grey stones that had been washed by the rain down into the terrace. A few days later, Ela went out onto the balcony with a cup of kidney-cleansing tea and nearly fell over the railing. What she saw in the garden must have been Boženka's work. A section of the terrace had been turned into a miniature altar. A plastic skull towered over it, decorated with something akin to folk embroidery from the village of Čičmany. Candles flickered in grave lights and oranges were strewn around withered torch lilies. Next to a huge rock a box of Mars cigarettes, a bottle of liquor and shot glasses had pride of place. 'Surprise!' a voice called from the far end of the garden and Ela saw Boženka dressed in a black skirt. 'Just like in Mexico,' she laughed. Ela ignored her painful bladder, put down her special tea and went out into the garden. It smelled different. A mixture of rotting leaves, moss and the gentle fragrance of heather was in the air and the sky was the colour of dark denim. Ela happily accepted Boženka's offer to be on first name terms. 'I'm Božena but everyone calls me Božka,' she said, giving Ela a wink and poured her some slivovitz. 'That tequila of theirs was far too expensive, I hope Our Lady of the Holy Death will forgive us for drinking our own local stuff.' They clinked glasses. 'It'll be weird calling you Božka now. Have I ever told you that you look like someone I used to know in Košice? In fact, you could be her twin,' Ela said and took a sip. Maybe her dad had stopped in Košice on a business trip, Božka joked: he had been a big womaniser and, for all she knew, she might have half-brothers and half-sisters all over the world. 'Fortunately, my husband wasn't like that, he just liked his drink and would start hollering songs. It was awful, he was cloth-eared, but he really had green fingers.' 'And what do you do, Ela?' Božka asked. Choosing her words carefully, Ela explained about her job. 'Really? I haven't heard about that, in the old days nobody used to look after the poor women who got beaten up at home,' said Božka and, turning serious, continued. 'My Paul never so much as a raised a finger to me, I guess I was lucky, my husband was a good man.' She downed her shot and poured herself another. 'Even these days there aren't many people who care about these women, they have nowhere to go and the police often don't give a damn either,' Ela said. Božka seemed sad all of a sudden. But making her miserable by talking about her work was the last thing Ela wanted. 'What's that growing next to the fence, the thing with the white flowers over there?' she asked, to change the subject. Božka stared at the spot Ela's finger pointed at for a while because it had turned almost completely dark in the meantime. 'Oh, that's viburnum, can't you tell? A wonderful shrub, it stays in bloom well into winter.' It had gone dark. The women sat on the stone parapet looking at the garden. The moon was as round and white as a skull and in the candlelight their modest little altar looked like a real *altar de los muertos* somewhere in Oaxaca.

There's nothing more disgusting than a dry winter, thought Ela, rubbing the eczema on her hands. 'Only a silly-billy like me would leave home without her gloves in this chilly weather,' she told herself off as she tried to turn the house key with her frozen fingers. After struggling for a while she managed to open the door and run inside. She darted up to the second floor and unlocked her flat door.

The familiar palm tree mural in the hallway looked so inviting she wished she could just lie down beneath it. She was frozen to the marrow and and at the end of her tether. A woman had been shot dead by her partner, the murder sending shockwaves through the crisis centre and the city as a whole. It was all over the news. Everyone was horrified. A search was launched for the culprit. They always start looking for the culprit only after something terrible happens. It had been public knowledge that the man had a gun. But the police and the authorities had turned a blind eye, nobody had done anything about it. They had all made light of the situation. Ela didn't know the woman. She was a client of her colleague's and Ela had never met her, but the tragedy affected her profoundly. It could just as well have happened to a client of Ela's. For example, the one whose husband liked to go hunting. He kept a gun at home, after all. It could have happened to any one of her clients. There are so many ways to kill a woman. You don't even need a weapon. Ela was really scared. She was physically aware of her powerlessness. Her stomach started to churn. She accused herself of being a failure. Then she got very angry, and by the end of the day she just felt drained. She had lost the energy to keep helping others. She threw a pair of sausages into a pan and as she watched them bobbing up and down in the boiling water, she recalled the mock execution. All of a sudden the city, the whole country, seemed full of violence. There was violence wherever she turned. She wished she could run away. But where could she go? Some other country maybe, somewhere warmer, Ela thought. She put the sausages on a plate. While they were cooling down she massaged some cannabis cream on her eczema. She sat down at the table by the balcony window offering a view of the last rays of daylight. She looked out at the garden. Slowly, she began to calm down. Order, sobriety and stoic calm. The branches of the trees bereft of leaves reminded her of the photographs of hairs under a microscope magnified a thousandfold.

She knew the plants in the garden so well by now she could spot them without really looking. The magnolia, a linden tree and an ornamental maple on the right, one terrace further down a rhododendron and the hydrangeas. Rows of lavender alternating with rose bushes. In the far right corner by the fence a dwarf pine, next to it a viburnum and honeysuckle, which she used to confuse with juniper. Mosses, alpine plants, heather, and tulips, daffodils and wild garlic, asleep, buried in the soil. Boženka had covered everything with gunny. Like a caring mother tucking up her sleeping children.

Before Ela managed to finish her first sausage, two gentlemen in dark coats appeared in the garden. They spoiled her view of the calm evening landscape. One of the men gestured agitatedly, explaining something to the other. The latter found a mobile in his pocket and started taking pictures of the garden. Ela couldn't understand what this meant. But she knew it had to mean something. Her social worker's alarm started to flash at the back of her head. A week later she saw an excavator parked in the garden. A shabby yellow JCB 3CX, it resembled a piece of crumpled metal more than a machine. It was like a sore thumb that disfigured this sacred place and threw her off balance. Ela put on her windcheater and went out to the garden. 'Božka! Božka!' she shouted at her neighbour's closed window as if she had lost her mind. The curtain shifted and a head covered in curlers appeared. Boženka made a face. Something to the effect of: 'What is it now?' Ela hollered: 'Someone has brought an excavator into the garden!' Boženka shrugged. She opened the window and leaned out so far that she nearly fell out and said: 'I know. I know everything. There's nothing we can do about it. It's terrible but it's been approved by the local council. The plot is city property. They're going to build a car park here.' Then she closed the window and disappeared into the depths of her flat. Ela stood there for a while, staring uncomprehendingly at the abandoned closed window, at the garden that pretended this had nothing to do with it. Then she noticed a sheet of paper sealed in a plastic that said: 'Construction approved.'

Ela had always thought that all good things took too long and bad ones happened too fast. Like the worker with a chainsaw, who took just one afternoon to chop down all the trees in the garden. Boženka had spent twenty years cultivating them. She had planted them, hoed them, talked to them until they finally grew and suddenly – chop chop! A single chainsaw, a single afternoon and the trees were gone.

Christmas was getting close, yet Ela didn't feel like smiling. The holiday season was just an extra burden for her clients. They were exhausted by all the housework and resorted increasingly to the crisis line. Ela's heart sank every time she picked up the phone. In the evenings she watched the garden die. She couldn't begin to imagine what this meant to Boženka, who followed the massacre from behind her curtains. Ela was sure she stood there chainsmoking as her soul died along with the garden. After the trees it was the turn of the shrubs to be taken to the slaughter. The Judas tree gave them the most trouble. It put up real resistance. Boženka had told her it was toxic and during breaks from work at the centre Ela imagined the workmen ending up in hospital. The dying garden was constantly on her mind, distracting her from work. She couldn't take proper case notes, stuttered during conversations and caught herself not listening to what the clients were telling her.

On the second Sunday in Advent a pit appeared in the garden. It looked like a burnt-out wound or a black hole that was about to suck in Boženka, Ela and the whole block. The garden was gone for good. Tree stumps and roots jutted out of a pile by the road like imploring hands rising to heaven. A few days later a lorry came to take the pile away. A garish sign attached to the fence announced that a car park was being built there. In the mornings she woke up to the noise of the excavator. She no longer looked out from her balcony. She no longer sipped her morning espresso there or chatted with Boženka. In fact, she no longer felt at home here. The flat suddenly seemed boring, trashily furnished and alien. Boženka gave up leaving her flat altogether. Or at least Ela never saw her again. She rang her doorbell a few times but nobody answered. She put an ear to the door but all she could hear was the whirring of an old fridge. She couldn't shake the nasty feeling that the woman had vanished along with the garden. Just like the brightly coloured redstart that stopped visiting Ela's balcony. She felt betrayed and lonely. She kept buying more and more magazines and would read them over and over. She forbade herself from looking in the direction of the balcony. She had nowhere to relax after her exhausting work. The car park had moved right into her flat. It now formed an everyday part of its tawdry interior. She knew when cement was being delivered and was forced to listen to the workmen's vulgar jokes.

The day a grey concrete surface appeared under her balcony the first frost arrived. The air tasted of mint as she stood on the balcony watching the grey concrete pancake. The car park had changed the place beyond recognition. Concrete kerbs made the space look smaller, flattened and dead. The white lines on the tarmac reminded her of an old computer game, in which you had to make a little green man jump over hurdles. It was exactly the same kind of car park you could see in front of any block of flats in town. She imagined cars parked there, dozens of shiny expensive vehicles, and their irritable owners getting in them in the mornings. It occurred to her that at night, instead of the chirping of cicadas, she would now hear the howling of car alarms set off by mistake. That's when Ela gave up. She glanced at her watch. She packed her stuff into her huge suitcase, washed the dishes, switched off the fridge and threw the remaining food into a bin bag. She found the kitschy painting of Jesus Christ in the wardrobe and hung it back on the wall. The estate agent didn't pick up her phone. She left a message on her answerphone. She called a colleague and explained everything. For a moment she stood in the hall looking at palm tree mural, then put on her coat and turned off the lights. She locked the flat and dropped the keys into the letterbox. The ticket queue at the station inched forward like a slimy slug. People were pushing and shoving, those meeting travellers getting in the way of those catching trains. She bought a magazine and a baguette. She brazenly jumped the ticket queue and had to endure a lecture about country bumpkins with no manners. As she boarded the train the first snowflakes timidly wafted onto the platform. She checked her reservation number, pushed her suitcase under the seat, took off her coat and sat down. The train started to move. The world outside the window accelerated. People on the platform vanished, the snack kiosks were gone, the station was left behind somewhere, while cars, houses and pylons sped past the window. Ela gazed at the villages and fields flashing past. She opened her magazine but didn't feel like reading. She started looking out of the window again. The first snow was falling, whirling in the air like scattered feathers. It settled on the village houses, disguised the rubbish dumps, cleaned the dirty suburbs. Suddenly the landscape seemed pure, delicate and innocent and she couldn't take her eyes off it. The conductor checked Ela's ticket without a word. The woman sitting in her compartment greedily began to chomp her baguette. Ela smelled a mild whiff of mustard. She took off her boots and loosened her trouser belt. An inexplicable calm fell upon her. Somewhere deep within her soul the snow-covered garden lay fast asleep.

Autumn in Springtime

Llŷr Gwyn Lewis

Even under the strip lighting of the *parrillada* restaurant, this looked like a real feast. We would never have ventured in by ourselves: the tables with their red oilcloths all packed tightly together and already full to the brim, and the walls filled too with posters of old Quilmes adverts, fading and bluing maps and charts of the country, and gold-framed portraits of people we didn't know, next to flags bearing the colours and insignia of the Boca Juniors. The place was full of smoke and steam and the smell of meat and frying and loud chatter and clinking glass. But as Ciana and Marcos had insisted that we come here to try a real, authentic parrilla, L. and I had indeed ventured. It took a few seconds for us to get used to the light after the darkness of the street outside. It was warm in there too, and we had just started to feel it getting colder that night. It was the end of May, and autumn was upon us. The papers were full of talk of a swarm of moths – the word they used for them was *polillas* – which had descended upon Buenos Aires over the summer, capping off a turbulent season of police strikes and unsettled weather. By now the residents were glad to feel things beginning to cool, and to find that the moths had disappeared back to Uruguay from whence they came.

Earlier, L. and I had enjoyed a cold Quilmes in an ancient-looking bottle on the hostel's roof. We looked out over the towers and bright lights of Buenos Aires and the rush of traffic on the Avenida de 9 Julio as Eva Perón watched over it all from her tower. A half-finished building hung above us on one side,

43

as the day darkened early and quickly. Then we left the wooden doors and floors of the hostel and the chatter of the Spanish game shows on the television, gathered our pesos and ventured out onto the checked, cracked pavements of San Telmo, to be greeted by a large poster on the other side of the road which advertised, in harsh light, a film called *Muerte en Buenos Aires*.

It was still hard to find our way between the city's ordered grids. More chaotic, higgledy-piggledy or winding streets would, somehow, have been much easier to remember and to know. Even the pavements themselves had all been laid down in the form of small squares, as though the person who had put them there had also been trying to work out, as they did so, where exactly they were at the time. Or maybe they were trying to leave a hint for those who would come after them over these pavements, as they inscribed a small microcosm of the city onto every slab. We felt with each step that we were walking into a map. And just like the grids of the city on the map, I couldn't quite decide whether these were squares or diamonds either. Maybe we had lost our sense of direction in the midst of all this newness; maybe it all depended on your way of looking at it. L., if she had been conscious of these thoughts, might have told me to stop worrying and to get on with it.

But we had found the place eventually, with Ciana and Marcos waiting for us outside and we were glad to see them. Then after a vast dinner of provolone, morcilla, chorizo, steak, and various other suspicious but delectable pieces of meat, washed down with plenty of Malbec and cold water, the four of us went out once more to tread those grids, with the map by now beginning to form in my head. There are few things more terrifying than finding yourself for the first time in a strange city without idea or notion of where you are, without any kind of map in your head. Walk around the place for long enough, and that map will form and fill your head street by street, grid by grid, gradually. But then you can never get back that terrifying, pleasant innocence again, that feeling of being lost halfway around the world. We can only be thankful, perhaps, that there are more cities in which to get lost than we will ever have time to visit in one life.

I was familiar enough with the area by now to realise that the path taken by Ciana and Marcos towards our next destination was not quite direct; we tended to turn back on ourselves or go past two blocks when one would have got us there sooner. It would have been rude, of course, to mention this to two who had been raised in the city and who knew it as well as those little tiny grids of skin in the palm of one's hand. My work and L.'s was to follow obediently. Rounding one corner, we emerged to a slightly broader street, and saw on the pavement a tall, wide character standing askance and perfectly still. We approached him from behind, and as we came nearer we soon saw that this was a kind of model or plastic statue, wearing a suit and a chunky tie, and with a cartoonish face, his arms folded in some gesture that was a mixture of laughter and surprise. I insisted on standing next to him to have our photo taken.

It turned out that there was a number of these statues dotted about San Telmo. They were characters from a cartoon called 'Mafalda', a fairly childish cartoon at first glance but which in fact offered a satirical and scathing view of the country's intricate politics. The model of Mafalda herself (a six-year-old who is a source of constant frustration and exasperation to her parents because of her astute and impossible-to-answer questions regarding issues such as Chinese communism, but who also holds a deep-seated hatred of soup) sat on a bench directly opposite her creator and artist Quino's flat, in some sort of permanent homage to him, almost like a dog faithfully awaiting an owner who would never arrive home.

This was why, we later realised, Ciana and Marcos, her boyfriend, had been leading us seemingly astray, though these models didn't really mean much to us at the time. As we walked northwards later, after L. had also begrudgingly had her photo taken on the bench next to Mafalda, I thought of those cartoons and of how their characters had somehow stepped out of their stories, quite literally larger than their own lives, to lay claim to the city's streets and to its realities, and how people flocked to see them though they knew very little of their history, and like us insisted on having their photos taken with them, almost as though they were flesh and blood celebrities. But then what was the difference between them and the giant stone statue of Mendoza that we had seen in the park? These were the future's historic monuments.

Later, after the long walk along the busy, wide, never-ending Avenida de 9 Julio, the four of us reached a high block of flats and were greeted by the owner before being led to a shaky, cramped lift that whisked us up to the highest floor. We were greeted by a kiss on each cheek by complete strangers, and there was dancing and smoke and cumbia music and a peculiarly strong green drink that tasted like toothpaste, and a balcony where all the busy, wide street's lights shone beneath us. There were children running riot around the flat whilst their parents danced around them. A spliff was being passed around the room and we were cornered, out on the balcony, by a young man who thought that his friend was the funniest man alive, because he had dropped everything and moved to Spain, only to be deported less than two months after arriving.

When L. and I left some three hours later, the walkways had

grown quiet though the traffic still roared by as we made our way back to the hostel in San Telmo, and the grids of the pavement were empty once again. In truth, if L. and I had cared to admit it to one another, we had independently of each other begun to feel a little afraid as we returned along the Av. de 9 Julio, and each dishevelled wretch who now passed us seemed to have a surly look about him, and a threatening manner. We quickened our steps and grew quiet, and were glad to reach the door of the hostel in one piece but glad also to have had a tiny taste of the bright lights and murky corners of this half-finished city.

The next morning it was raining lightly, almost the only rain we had whilst we were in the country, and you could only just see the ends of the streets through the mist. L. and I meandered through the streets of San Telmo again, which were unfamiliar once more in the light of day, and the map of the previous night more or less ruined. We were aiming for the museum of El Zanjón de Granados.

By Defensa we came across some big, wooden doors in the shape of a grid, at the front of a building that appeared much like all the others on the street. We rang the bell, and waited for quite a long while, so long that we considered leaving. But the door was eventually opened and we stepped into a wondrous space. We stood in some sort of old house that dated back, according to what we with our old-world standards could gauge, to around 1800. We were greeted by a young man, who appeared as though from nowhere, and he was very sorry indeed and apologised profusely, but if our wish was to be guided through the building in English, then he was duty bound to inform us that the lady who usually gave these tours had fallen ill and was currently in hospital receiving treatment. But he would make every effort to find someone who would be able to guide us. Perhaps, he suggested with a peculiar hint of excitement in his voice and his eyes lively, perhaps indeed that the 'director' himself would be willing to show us around. He had pronounced that word not in the English way, but in Spanish. L. and I could sense, from this young man's peculiar tone, that this would be a privilege indeed if it were to transpire. I suppose that is how the chasm between continents, and between two cultures from two sides of the world, reveals itself when they meet: in the hint of a raised eyebrow and a trace in the voice.

The young man vanished and we were alone again in the splendid space; some sort of atrium without floors above, which meant that we could see all the way to the ceiling. The red bricks were bare and had been lit artistically so that we couldn't decide whether we were in a tenement from the 19th century or in an art gallery. We stood in silence until, in a while, and again as though from nowhere, a bald man appeared, white moustached and in a dark blue pullover, corduroy trousers, with round spectacles. He smiled at us and at once we felt that we were in the company of some gentle old man, a grandfather, but there was also something in his smile and in his steady grip when he insisted on shaking our hands which suggested some determination that bordered on severity. Without much ado he began to lead us around the building with no small amount of mastery and thorough knowledge. As he spoke he had many idioms and turns of phrase that seemed to me somehow magical or spectral: the sort of characteristics that could only stem from possessing English truly as a second language, not as a kind of other-first-language as it is for us. We almost felt that we were simply hearing him speak Spanish through a filter. As we passed a window high up in a wall that had once separated two parts of the building and which had been intended for a shop that had never been built, he described it as a 'love letter to a marriage that never happened'. It's a shame that I can't recall the many other turns of phrase that peppered his conversation.

He asked us where we came from and what our backgrounds and lines of work were. This was important, he said, so that he could decide which stories and which details to share with us, because 'there are many ways of looking at a stone'. As we wandered among the various levels of the *conventillo* and climbed between different layers of the building, and learned through this of the various roles for which the building had been used over the decades and centuries, the man described to us the many pieces and artefacts, such as the ceramic water tank which had later been used to store flour. At one time, the building had been a block of flats which housed a number of poor families, and when the place had been bought – the man was careful always to use 'we' when discussing his involvement with the project – it had been in a pitiful state. He then took us down, into the bowels of the place, beneath street level, and led us through a series of tunnels, again all brick and artistic lighting, which stretched away far further than we could see, until we reached one spot where the paving on the floor split into two paths, like a fork in the road, with two tunnels stretching on into the darkness in different directions. The old man explained to us that this was the place that gave its name to the museum, the Zanjón de Granados, and that *zanjón* meant some sort of ravine or gully. This was the ravine where two rivers, at one time, had met, and the place where it was believed that the first settlers had occupied when the Spanish, under Pedro de Mendoza, had come to establish the city of Saint Mary of the Fair Winds. In fact the two small rivers continued to flow beneath this pavement, eventually flowing into the Plata, some tens of metres east from here.

By the end of the tour, though nobody had told us this directly, we had sensed that this man was, indeed, the 'director' himself. I wanted to make sure so I asked him, and he answered immediately, 'I am the man who did it'. He spoke of a letter he had received some years ago from an old lady who used to live in the tenement building when it was still divided into slums. She was incredibly grateful to him for his work in transforming and conserving the building, and she had sent him detailed descriptions of the manner of life there during her childhood and of the building's condition and form at the time. Though she had wished and desired to be able to return and see the place once more, however, she had been killed in a car accident before she could do so. This had much to do, explained the old man to us, with something with which we weren't yet necessarily very familiar, and that thing was 'destiny'. 'Destiny' was what had led him, as a young architect and businessman in the early eighties, to buy this building and to begin to turn it into a luxury restaurant and hotel, before discovering the *zanjón* beneath the place, and the tunnels, and all the various items, in the process, and had decided to turn it into a museum of a world that had disappeared. He had devoted his life and his work to this building ever since, to its restoration and conservation, with the aid of a team of architects and builders, in order to become, in his own words, 'the archaeologist of memory, the custodian of this house of destiny'.

Little did he know, however, that this word and the things he would say afterwards, almost as if by 'destiny', would colour and direct all that we saw over the following days and weeks. He tried to explain his feelings for this peculiar house and the way in which it had changed the course of his life by using the two words 'history' and 'story', and by explaining that there was only one corresponding word in Castellano, *historia*, which covered both, and that there was indeed no real way of drawing a distinction between them always. Come to think of it, he could not be entirely sure what had happened to him over the last thirty years, whether it had all happened in reality, nor indeed whether this house itself, with everything that had happened within its walls over the centuries, was the result of story or of history.

This brought to my mind something I had studied some years before, and the way I had discovered that our way of drawing a clear distinction between fact and fiction, between history and story, or indeed between *historia*, *argumentum* and *fabula*, is a fairly modern phenomenon or mode of thinking. I recalled that I had read a volume by a scholar named D. H. Green, who argued that medieval audiences did not much care whether some story or other was 'true' or not – that is, whether it was factually and historically accurate. No, for them, 'truth' had much more to do with the question of whether something was believable or not: the question therefore was not so much whether the story had really happened (*historia*), but more whether it could, within the realms of possibility, believably have happened (*argumentum*). Beyond that, however, audiences could also accept that there were some stories which contained characters and events that could never have been believed to have occurred in real life (*fabula*). That did not do anything to impair their enjoyment nor their ability to accept these various and contradictory elements within one story, without having to ask 'which parts of this story are true' and which are the fruit of the imagination. To me this suggested that they were, in their own way, a much more mature audience than we are today, as they accepted happily that every good story is really a patchwork of truths and lies, and were still able to enjoy the story, to recite it and to hand it down regardless.

As we bade farewell to the gentle 'director' and as we took leave of the Fair Winds some hours later, I could not shake off what he had said to us that morning, and the way in which they had reminded me of the thin and ultimately insignificant line between true and false, between the real and the product of imagination. With his words in our ears L. and I flew onwards, rising from the half-finished city of the fair winds towards the endless completeness of the plain.

It would be impossible by now to try to comprehend fully what effect the fact that we had first visited Buenos Aires had on our subsequent journey to the Welsh Colony in Patagonia, where the whole place was so much emptier and more desolate, and Gaiman like a grave. It was impossible to erase that order, and the links and associations it created in our minds, or to undo it. The fact, for example, that we had visited the massive cemetery in Recoleta, with its monumental palaces of crypts for the rich dead, before getting a chance to meander between the desolate, bald, almost Puritanical headstones of Gaiman. It seems odd to think that it was these, and not the grand gaudy creations of Recoleta, that seemed to us old-fashioned and timeworn, almost kitsch. In a town like Gaiman, where it felt that time had stood still to the extent that this new world felt so much older than ours, I could not help feeling that the amiable moustachioed old man, with his mixture of story and history, had not been too far amiss.

I don't really know what we had expected from the place. Wales wasn't here, or at least the Welsh weren't. But the autumn was more insistent, the leaves already brown and gold, and we felt the cold biting. It was one never-ending siesta, and the two of us were the only customers buying cheese and meat and bread and wine from the small supermarket, with love, in the afternoons where there was no-one. The sun was searingly cold.

We were disappointed many times during that journey: the mill in Dolavon was closed, and the owner away on his annual holiday with his daughter in La Plata; in the (dead) poet's house the woman who opened doors was in town on her errands; in the (living) poet's house in Trelew we were told that he had moved some years ago to Bariloche. There was no question of going up to Ffos Halen without our own car, and it was only through Anabel's kindness and generosity that we were able visit Bod Iwan. After walking all the way from Porth Madryn's bus station, along the broad beach with the wind whipping, we found the museum where the first settlers had come ashore, but it was closed and no-one around to open for us. It was *temporada baja* all about, and all attractions closed. Why, however, the two of us had expected all these places to remain open just for us, as though we had some right to visit them, I don't know.

One thing that struck us was how quickly it got dark in the Gaiman when night fell. We had just come from Buenos Aires which seemed almost constantly lit (at least in the long, broad, busy boulevards if not in every corner). Of course, that city was also several hundred miles nearer the equator, though I was not adequately meteorologically equipped to say whether or not that made a discernible difference. How could such a natural phenomenon, namely the fact that it grew dark sooner as autumn closed in, have appeared so unfamiliar to us? Because we had, I suppose, just landed there in the middle of our May, just as everything at home was about to spread and open. When someone lives somewhere, and goes about his life there every day, little does he notice the day slowly lengthening or shortening, because of its gradual nature; but by being thrown into the middle of this autumn and all of a sudden finding it getting dark, not around nine or ten at night but at five in the afternoon, its effect on us was so much the deeper. Added to this was the way in which the whole town seemed to fall into a deep slumber around one o'clock in the afternoon, and where everyone in Wales in autumn, for example, would be thinking around six of getting home, drawing the curtains, putting a nice pan of something on the stove and settling in for the night, here people were at that time beginning to stir and to emerge, going from to shop to shop on their errands.

There was nothing for it but to conform, of course; sharing a bottle of wine over lunch and allowing it to send us to sleep for an hour or two, then waking to a town on the brink of night, and beginning to think about going out. As a result, a number of my memories of the Gaiman play out in my mind as though in some half dusk, or otherwise harshly under a yellow-white electric light which constrasted with the darkness framed in the windows.

The place was already quite dark outside as the bell rang and we stepped in from the street. L. and I were visiting Lisabeta's, or Bet's, clothes shop on the high street. We had been encouraged to venture there by a friend who knew what was what, so that we could hear a mouthful of Welsh. But who in their right mind would step into an unremarkable, slightly old-fashioned shop on a long dark street in the depth of South America in order to hear a few words of the old tongue? And what on earth were we supposed to say?

As it was, the thing that struck me above all else as I stepped in was the layout and look of the shop itself, with a large counter that had built into it a long ruler for measuring out and cutting fabric, and along the walls there were white metal shelves full of boxes and clothes all higgledy-piggledy in see-through plastic bags. The whole shop was not that big, but most of it was filled with flimsy-looking wheeled metal racks, creaking under the weight of clothes. There were piles of old catalogues on the grey carpet in the corner, and the women on the covers were all makeup and big hair, straight from the eighties or the early nineties; and in the midst of it all, busying herself and tutting slightly under her breath, was an old woman in a gilet of blue fleece. Such was the strong effect of this place on us, and the way in which it had, somehow, managed to transport us somewhere – some old shop in the mind's eye that we entered in our mothers' hand – straight from our childhood, that to greet this woman now in Welsh, and to tell her full of apology that we had meant to call for a long while, was simply the most natural and instinctive thing to do.

She stood still when she saw us and heard us, staring at us, and we could see her trying to discern whether she knew the two young people in front of her, or whether they were someone from *draw*, from 'beyond'. Did she perhaps feel herself to be a relic, stood there before us? But her welcome was warm and if she felt like that then she certainly didn't display it in her face or her voice. She cross-examined us on our homes, our parents, our work, our reasons for coming over, adding every now and then how nice it was to be able to converse in the old tongue, and gossiping about every poor soul in town. She was eager, she said after learning that we were friends of Siwan's, who had come over to teach at the local Welsh school, she was eager to find her a husband in order to keep her here. She complained that by now the *Bolivianos* were everywhere, had taken over all the farm labour, were a plague throughout the town and refused to respect the area's Welsh heritage or learn the language. From the outside, we could see the absurdity of this statement: why would a person who has travelled hundreds of miles to find scarce work and feed their children, to build some kind of life for themselves, give one damn about a language from the other side of the world, especially when everyone could speak Spanish anyway? The *Bolivianos*, according to Bet, claimed – no, demanded – milk from the state for their children, and then drank it themselves instead.

We soon steered Bet away from this topic and to the safer territory of her memories. She had been brought up on one of the Chubut Valley's farms, but had moved to the town after marrying, first to teach and then taking up the clothes shop. It was so nice, she reiterated, to be able to speak Welsh with someone new. She had lost her husband some years before: and had we indeed heard, she asked, of the numerous losses that the people of the colony had recently suffered? It was a strange thing, she remarked, how five or six of her peers, only slightly older than herself, had been lost within a few weeks of each other: a whole generation of settlers gone. It struck me then, and seemed almost a premonition of what might happen to us too in a few years: the loss of five or six tantamount to losing a whole generation. The whole thing was simple in its inevitability. Recently, however, Bet had been enjoying borrowing books from the mobile library and her daughter had been helping her choose them. One story that she had come across recently was the tale of *Nel Fach y Bwcs* – Little Nell of the Books – and without warning Bet began to relate this tale to us in all its detail. I turned to look at L., and it was evident that she was hanging on every word, but I had some trouble hearing and following the story, and Bet had moved so abruptly from relating her husband's death to talking about the library books and then on to Nel that I don't think I realised until afterwards, when L. explained it to me, that Bet by now was relating a tale from one of those books. So quickly had she been moving from speaking about this and that and the other, jumping from one story to the next and naming many of the town's residents of whom we knew nothing, that this tale about Nel was for me just another one of these stories from this woman's mouth. I was also confused as I couldn't believe, as I heard of event after devastating event in the lives of Nel and her family in the early days of the colony, that this story was factually accurate. The continuous and never-ending suffering was too much – such suffering that could only have been invented as the melodramatic fantasy of some sentimental author.

By now Bet was sailing through the story, and had reached the episode when Nel's father and older brothers were away on a journey far from their home at Llain Las farm, and Nel had been charged with looking after her pregnant mother; if she were to be taken ill, Nel was to ride at once to fetch a Mrs Jones. That is what happened, and that is what she did, but she lost her horse and got lost in the dark as she walked towards Mrs Jones's house. Such fear that came over her. It wasn't until dawn broke that she was able to return to the farm, and there was her mother sleeping soundly and her father weeping at her bedside. And Bet there telling us, 'But oh! – her mother was dead!' and the tears by now filling her eyes. I realised that Bet hadn't been reciting the story after all, but rather seeing it all happen in front of her eyes, and then relating it to us as though from her own experience, and all the grief of the numerous losses that had befallen her over the previous weeks bearing down on her and finding its way out through this tale about one of the first girls of the plain, and she herself at that moment once again a little girl.

Late on the previous afternoon we had walked up to that hill where the cemetery stood. Yes, I had seen Tegai (direct descendant of one of the original leaders of the colony, curator of the settlers' museum, presenter of the local weekly Welsh-language radio show and general stalwart and presiding spirit of the Welsh community) on television tens of times, had heard her voice and learned about her, had even sensed her canonisation and beatification amongst some. But she had died less than a fortnight before our arrival, and we had thought what a shame it was to have missed her – again as though we had some right to see her and to meet her. Now here we were, on some kind of pilgrimage, come to see where Tegai had been laid to rest. But there was no headstone yet, no name, dates, a stanza of remembrance, no flowers either, all the paraphernalia of grief. We even had to ask the groundsman with his flea-ridden dog whether we had the right place. The only thing there was a gap between two graves, between a father and a brother, in fact, and nothing but a slab of cement and some tarp that had been laid to cover it flapping in the wind.

Both of us wondered whether it was because of this that the whole town had been quiet, almost refusing to reveal its wonders and failing to yield to us its history, because it was inextricably tied up with Tegai herself, a place that was locked up in her head and in her memory and therefore unreachable beneath that slab of cement. All the tea houses hadn't been closed because it was low season: they were closed from grief, and from loss of memory.

I don't believe that either of us ever felt more grief after someone whom we had never met in our lives. Her absence could be felt wherever we went, broad and dusty and empty like the plain.

By the time we bade farewell to Bet and stepped out of the shop, it was completely dark, and the street had begun to grow quiet. We both realised the time: we had missed the bus to

Trelew, and with it our chance to meet Siwan for dinner. How quickly midnight crept up on you here, the afternoons lost to sleep and no-one eating anything before ten at night. There was no means of getting in touch with her either: we were at the WiFi's mercy and Siop Bara, which had the best connection in town, was long closed. There was nothing for it but to buy a pack of Twistos and a couple of bottles of cold Quilmes from the kiosk on the corner, and to head back to Plas y Coed to devour them. Never mind: the following night we would see Siwan, Anabel, Nesta and a whole host of others. We would enjoy their company immensely, and then the plain awaited us, the long journey by bus and the sudden braking as we traversed patches of snow preventing us from sleeping, and neither of us able to see its immensity, instead waking up to darkness and fog and the whole sky closing in on Esquel and Trevelin, until the clouds escaped some days later, where Gorsedd y Cwmwl was waiting for us, all covered in snow.

MERCY

FROM *BAD IDEAS\CHEMICALS* BY LLOYD MARKHAM

I am struggling to choose between three long-term career goals –
killing myself, killing my dad, or killing the both of us ...

Louie Jones, lying on his bed, eyes on his laptop, holds down the
backspace key to obliterate the truth. Part of him wants to leave
it in, if just to see his Careers, Lifestyles & Attitudes coordinator's
face when she reads it. But this would only cause trouble. He
mustn't cause trouble. You have to tell them what they want to
hear. This is the purpose of these exercises. Envision, Articulate
& Realise Training. That's what they call them. Because
'Busywork & Bullying' would make them feel bad.

Louie grimaces. Somehow a part of him still doesn't want his
coordinator to feel bad. She's only doing her job after all.

He lets out a long, deep breath and starts over on his
Actualisation Confessional:

I am struggling to make compromises between my long-term ambitions
and my short-term needs. I have to work on my poor attitude. I have to
understand that my poor attitude is why I have failed to find adequate
employment ...

Better. Though he will probably need to swap out 'ambition'
with 'aspiration'. Ambition is something for people with means
and contacts and appreciating assets. Aspiration is more
appropriate, 'realistic' his CLA Coordinator would say for a
young man of his class. Though she wouldn't say 'class' – that
was too charged. She would say 'background'. For someone of
his 'background' having ambitions was unrealistic – a bad idea.

'Ambition' suggests something forceful. Better he lays claim to aspiration – a word which rolls off the tongue in a weary gasp.

I am struggling to make compromises between breathing and ...

Louie holds backspace again, destroys the black text, and rolls over onto his side – away from the laptop screen. It is eight in the morning. Soon he will have to climb downstairs and open up his father's failing shop. Louie works in this crap-hole ten hours a day but still has to claim income and underemployment support because his dad hasn't come downstairs in over a month and the angry letters from the bank are stacking up and the stock is beginning to spoil and Social Services folded their arms and will not do anything about anything about anything –

Louie feels like someone has stabbed fingers into his temples and is rooting around in his skull, scraping behind his eyes and nose.

He stands up and opens the curtains.

Rain.

Perfect, he thinks. Let it rain. May it never cease. Tip the entire ocean upon us and let the whole town sink into the sea like the stubborn, soggy log of shit that it is.

His phone buzzes. Message from the CLA:

Placement Notification. Mercy Clinic. 21:00.

He doesn't reply. Isn't necessary. Attendance is mandatory but the CLA will be thrilled if he misses the text and doesn't pitch. They can hit him with a sanction then and he will be off their books for a year at least.

Louie is only nineteen years old but he feels like a cold, sweaty corpse. His brown hair sticks to his forehead and a blue glimmer bruise throbs as it heals in the gutter of his left eye –

the result of another futile one-sided shouting match with his mad father three weeks prior.

Louie remembers going to Social Services after that incident. The taste of blood in his mouth. His heart full of grim hope that surely this time they would do something. How that hope so quickly crumbled as they found yet more technicalities that prevented intervention and passed him along to another sub department. He can't recall which one. Department of Excuses perhaps? Either way, it was halfway through filling the fifth form – a purple one – that something deep within him gave up and he went home, his face numb but thankfully no longer bleeding.

The last three years, since his mother had enough and left, have aged Louie a thousand-fold. He feels like someone else's cursed painting – as if, in the night, some Dorian-esque twat had slipped into his room and stolen his youth away.

Whenever Louie is given a placement at the Mercy Clinic for Assisted Dying it always strikes him how much it looks like a warehouse. The only hint that the green-grey block does not contain office supplies, but dead and dying human bodies is the fraying poster by the door which depicts a man knelt by an elderly woman in bed. Beneath these figures a slogan in blocky art deco font reads:

THE GREATEST DUTY OF THE YOUNG IS TO HELP THE OLD PASS ON

It is an old advertisement from when Mercy first cropped up – around the time the government privatised the NHS euthanasia services and relaxed the regulations around palliative care, mental health treatment, and assisted dying. Mercy's unique selling point is the idea that young people on benefits should provide comfort and assistance to the more elderly who had decided to pass on but who had no relatives or friends to support them. This has the added bonus of allowing Mercy to cut nurses and rely on the CLA to provide them with a heavy rotation of temps and one-off placements.

Louie steps through the door. It closes behind him suddenly and silently as if in a hurry to move him along. Inside is a windowless reception with off-white walls and brown carpeting full of gum, grime and the occasional squashed roach.

'Can I help you?' asks the receptionist.

'Um. I'm here to do a placement.'

'Name?'

'Louie Jones.'

'Hmmm.' The receptionist puts down her knitting needles and scowls over a register. She is a very short woman with a crown of grey hair that spins upwards like the points on a star. She ticks a box and draws in a long breath, the hairs under her nostrils wobbling like insect feelers. 'Go through to the prep room and get your uniform from Kyle.'

'Thank you.'

'You know your 'placement' used to be someone's job.' The woman spits out the word 'placement' as if it were a bit of rotten fruit, and resumes her knitting.

Louie nods and continues down the hallway to the prep room. Stepping inside, it is much the same as before – a long windowless room with lime walls and no furniture. At its far end is a counter not unlike the sort you'd see in a post office, only the glass screen is grimy, almost opaque, and circular like a submarine window. Beyond, Louie can just about make out Kyle. In the hazy glass he appears as a thin ginger moustache pasted onto a pallid oval smudge.

'Hello. I need a uniform?'

'Oh. Sure. Here you go.' Kyle slides him a blue outfit from under the screen. It can almost pass for a nurse's uniform if you don't pay close attention.

'Um, this isn't my size.'

'Sorry. New policy. One size fits all.'

'Okay.'

'Do I recognise you from somewhere?'

'The CLA have placed me here before.'

'Oh. Guess that makes sense. You remember the drill then?'

'Yeah. Go see Jen in recruitment and then go get changed?'

'Yup. No problem then.'

The smudge behind the counter falls quiet.

Clutching the crumpled uniform to his chest, Louie leaves the prep room and rounds the corner. There, at the end of the hallway, are two rooms and some stairs leading upward. One of the rooms is a staff toilet. The other is Jen's office.

He knocks on the door. 'Come in,' says a tiny voice.

Louie enters the room. It hasn't changed. Sparse yet somehow messy. A single desk on top of which a bulky grey desktop PC, a printer, and stacks of printouts, are crammed, looking like they might spill on to the floor at the slightest disturbance. A wastepaper bin overflowing with crumpled sheets, tissues and sweet packets. In the corner, a dusty model skeleton faces away as if ashamed. And, at the back of the room, towering over the desk, is a long, black cabinet.

'Oh, hello, Louie. Another placement with us?'

He takes a moment to spot Jen amidst the detritus, idly jabbing an empty syringe into an injection training model over and over again. Jen is very short and often sits so still that she blends into the scenery. Her hair runs all the way to her backside. Louie thinks she looks a bit like Cousin It or something out of an old Jim Henson production. Then he thinks that he is cruel for thinking that. Then he thinks that that kind of repression – the constant second guessing and chastising of negative thoughts – is exactly why he has been a doormat his entire life. Then he thinks that that sort of comment is exactly the sort of thing his father would say when he'd had a bit too much to drink. Then he thinks again about whether he should shoot himself or his dad or –

'Hello? Earth to Louie.'

'Oh. Yes. Sorry, Jen. Away with the fairies.'

'Well, don't spend too much time with them,' she says, smiling dryly, standing up. 'Anyway, let me get you what you need.' She opens the cupboard doors. Then, standing tiptoe on her office chair, reaches for a silver zip-lock bag on the top shelf.

Jen has taken off her shoes and socks. Seeing the bare arch of her foot sends an odd twinge of desire through Louie. As he feels an erection coming on, he wonders what the hell is wrong with him.

'Here's what you need.' Jen hands him the zip-lock bag. 'Your client is on the second floor – room 205B.' Louie nods and darts next door to the bathroom.

He exhales and feels his heart rate steady and, eventually, his erection wilts.

The staff bathroom of the Mercy Clinic is wastefully large. Inside, Louie always feels like a trick of perspective is being played on his eyes, as if he is peering into a funhouse reflection. He quickly unwraps and puts on his uniform. Automatically he goes to check himself in the mirror only to remember that there isn't one. He washes his hands and face in the sink and steps out into the hallway – the silver zip-lock tucked under his arm. Then he heads up the stairs to the second floor, holding on to the railing as he does, feeling flecks of paint peel off in his palms like dried glue.

At the top, Louie finds himself at the end of a long corridor lined with numbered doors. He inspects the first one. 201A. The next, 202A. And so on. He walks down the hall and counts – 205 ... 208A ... 215A ... Just how long does he have to go until he reaches the Bs? The longer he spends in the Mercy Clinic the more he feels unsettled by it. What is with the lack of furnishings and decoration? Would it really break the budget to put up a picture? And what is it with this thick gooey carpet? The most unnerving thing, however, is the absence of any human noise. Surely there should be speaking, whispering, crying, laughing. At the very least breathing?

205B.

Louie stands for a moment, hand resting on the door handle, trying to compose himself, to summon up a smile.

Smile.

Yes.

He should at least do that.

Then he steps through into a little room. A bleak little room with a bare desk, a bed and a large window that offers only a grey view of a concrete wall. Maybe if you stick your head out and crane it up or down, left or right, you might be able to see the sky, the ground, the road, but that is a moot point because the window doesn't open out or in and is barred with iron so that no one can jump out to their non-state-approved deaths.

'Grim evening out, isn't it?'

Louie turns to see his client sat in the far corner of the room, arms cradled around her knees.

'I couldn't bear to look at it,' she continues chipperly. 'And this seems to be the only part of the room I can't see it.' She lets out a nervous laugh. The woman is younger than the other clients Louie has assisted – surely no more than sixty. She is white-haired, whisper-thin, dressed in a long polka-dot dress, and has an anchor tattooed on her right shoulder.

'Well, should we get started then?' she says, standing up then sitting on the corner of the bed, facing away from the window.

Louie sits next to her. Up close he can see that there are scars all along her wrists. He begins to wonder. Why the polka-dot dress? It looks new. Did she pick it out especially for this occasion? Why the anchor tattoo? Is it a drunken teenage-dare-turned-heirloom? What is her background? What led her to this place?

As he opens the zip-lock bag and pulls out the syringe, Louie simultaneously feels two irreconcilable desires to at once know everything about this woman and yet also know nothing, to be wiped clean and left blank like a spotless white sheet.

'As an employee of Mercy,' Louie begins, 'I am obligated to remind you at this moment of your rights ...' And so on. Without pause he emits a bureaucratic chant to ward off bad fortune, lawsuits, etc, etc. After ten minutes he reaches his legally ordained anticlimax – '... if you would like to proceed please confirm one last time. If you have any doubts then we at Mercy would urge you to reconsider, Madam.'

She forces a smile. 'Yes, please go ahead, boy.'

'Can I take that as a confirmation, Madam?'

She sighs. 'Yes.'

Louie holds up the syringe, lightly presses the plunger, and inspects closely a tiny drop of clear fluid oozing from the tip. It is working. At the sight of the needle, the woman quickly looks away.

'Alright,' he says. 'I will begin.'

She nods, looking at her feet.

He holds on to her arm and sticks the needle in.

She flinches.

He slowly pushes down on the plunger.

She winces. Then, as the last milligram of poison enters her veins, her face un-tenses. She looks up at Louie. Her eyes are clear blue and Louie cannot imagine how he must look in them. Is he a cold, unpleasant comprehensive school cherub? A disinterested devil? Some teenage summer job ferryman?

She opens her mouth to say something.

'I ...'

And that's it. Her blue eyes roll upward as if to follow her spirit's ascent. Her body goes limp and slumps toward the floor. Louie quickly catches, steadies it. He is surprised how heavy it is, given how slight she appeared. Or maybe this is normal? Maybe human bodies are heavier than he'd thought? It is so easy to forget, when you see them in motion, how much effort goes into making them move, how much strength is needed to carry them. A person might go their whole life only ever managing to carry one – their own. A person might go their whole life and not even manage that.

Louie is still holding on to his client's arm.

He has been holding on to her arm for a while now.

Maybe fifteen minutes.

Sitting next to her empty body as gravity tries to pull it downwards.

The woman's arm is cold.

His hand is cold.

He wonders which went cold first, which had frozen the other.

Standing up, he lays the body on the bed as neatly as he can.

Then he stands up and walks back into the hallway.

In the staff bathroom, he scrubs his face in the sink with hot water, feeling his adolescent skin scabs peeling off in his fingernails, feeling his adolescent needle-prick chin hair sliding under his fingernails, but Louie doesn't remember walking downstairs or turning on the tap.

Louie thinks about his client: was she really given a proper psychological evaluation? The Mercy Clinic, and all of the companies who work in assisted dying, are required to do thorough background checks and examinations of all persons requesting an end. But rumours persist that regulation is lax, requirements are not rigidly or consistently enforced.

Louie thinks about her last words.

Did he hear them right? Maybe what she'd actually said was not 'I' but 'I've ...'

Maybe what she was going to say was, 'I've changed my mind.'

There is a sudden, sharp pain in his shoulder. He probably pulled a muscle when he darted to catch her body.

Despite his sore shoulder and feelings of emptiness, it isn't as bad as his first placement with Mercy. That had involved an old man who, as the needle went into his arm, put his hand down into his trousers and began trying to tug one out. He didn't succeed. The poison finished before him.

I've changed my mind.

Louie wonders why he has come here? What's the point? He's already decided to end things. Perhaps he'd thought he might encounter something miraculous here, something that would reinvigorate him, or at least frighten him off his present path. Instead he feels even more convinced that he is making the right decision.

I've changed my mind.

*

'So ...' says Jen, 'fancy a smoke now?'

Louie shakes his head.

'Suit yourself. Where'd I put my pipe?'

She turns her naked back on Louie and rummages in a bedside drawer. Thirty minutes before in the passenger seat of her battered car, that back had filled him with fire. Now it is just a back. Pallid. Thin skin with blue veins showing through. A 5p-sized bump of red acne just below the neck. The back of a short woman in her early thirties illuminated by a slightly-dimmed light.

'Hmm, I think I left it in the car. Oh well. Want a drink?'

'Yeah. I guess. Thanks.'

Jen gets out of the bed, slips into some slippers, and walks to the adjacent kitchen. There is no wall between the two rooms, in fact all the rooms in Jen's flat (except the bathroom) are combined into one big space that feels stitched together and awkward. Beige carpeting that abruptly gives way to chequered tiles. Mismatched wallpaper. Exposed masonry. It is as if some previous owner had once had aspirations of joining all these rooms together, cohesively, but had only got as far as knocking down the walls before giving up.

As Jen steps into the slightly brighter kitchen, there is a shimmer along her thigh as the light catches some fluid clinging to her leg hairs. Cum or sweat? Cum and sweat? It is hard to say.

'Carlsberg okay?'

'Yup.'

'Good. Because it's all I got.' Jen brings over two cans and sits down next to him on the bed.

'So, Louie,' she says, cracking open her can and handing the other to him. 'Are you a virgin?'

Louie gives her a confused look.

'I mean were you a virgin? Before tonight?'

Louie nods.

'Thought as much.'

'Why?' Louie says, fiddling roughly with the tab on his can before finally pulling it open. 'Was I crap or something?'

'Not really. You just sort of gave off that vibe. You were alright ... Sorry, that was damning with faint praise. I'm not the best person to talk to about these things. My relationship with sex is a bit odd.'

'How so?'

'Well ...' Jen sucks up a mouthful of lager and seems to consider her words. 'I suppose it's a bit like how some people are with junk food. No actually not so much junk food as bland food – like rice crackers or something. It's not exactly nutritional, you're not even sure if you enjoy the taste, but when the opportunity to have one pops up ... well you don't even think about it, you just sort of compulsively eat them.'

'So what you're saying is that I'm a virgin rice cracker you took a gamble on?'

'I think you're making fun of me and I don't like it.' Jen goes quiet for a moment, appears to ruminate on something. She strokes her hand along Louie's thigh, a sensation he finds ticklish. At a glance Jen looks girlish but her hands tell a different story. They are coarse, slightly wrinkled, veiny, a little cool. They remind Louie of another hand.

Suddenly, appearing to reach some kind of conclusion in her head, Jen stands up. 'Anyway, this was nice but we should probably not make this a thing, Louie. I mean you're like what – seventeen or something?'

'Nineteen.'

'Oh. Either way I'm still probably old enough to be your mum. And at any rate it wouldn't look good to my company – me sleeping with some kid sent to us on a placement. You'll keep this to yourself, will you?'

'Yes,' he replies.

'You will? I'll be in shit if you started gobbing off about this.'

'I promise I won't tell,' he says. 'I ...' Internally he finishes the sentence – '... will be dead tomorrow anyway.'

'Lovely.' Jen smiles, finishing the last of her lager and crushing the can. 'No hard feelings I hope? I'll get you an Uber.'

Jen picks up her mobile from the bedside table and turns away from him.

From behind, at this angle, all Louie can see of her are her two ivory-white calves sticking out from beneath a waterfall of damp black hair. She looks in the dim light like one of those ghost women from Japanese folklore that Louie has seen in films – Yuuray? Wuurey? Yurei?

Jen drops her scrunched up lager can. Still talking to the taxi driver, she crouches down on the floor to pick it up. As she does this her legs vanish beneath her dark waterfall hair. And all Louie can see, all that is left of her, is that mass of black. She becomes a black hole in the carpet, shrinking downwards, as if she might disappear.

*

'Rough day, man?' asks the taxi driver, ten minutes into the journey.

Louie opens his mouth to answer but nothing comes out. His mouth hangs gaping for a moment then shuts.

'That bad?' says the driver, his expression shadowed by a broad-beaked baseball cap, a red and white thing with the word 'Player' emblazoned in gold. Louie wonders how he can see from under there.

'You smell of pussy,' the man continues. 'Can't have been that bad an evening if you come home smelling of pussy.'

Louie gives him a stern look.

'Hey. Don't be weird about it. I'm just yanking your chain.' He extends a hairy finger and pokes a bauble hanging from the rearview mirror, a playing card with a naked woman on it and some words beneath that Louie can't read in the dark. 'This here's what you need. All you need in life is pussy, weed, and cash. Got that?'

Louie stares for a moment at the drab bit of cardboard depicting a woman – no, only the idea of a woman – and thinks for a brief second that maybe the driver has suggested something profound. Then a smell wafts up from below.

'Sorry. That was me,' says the driver. 'Anyway, we're nearly there. Just around this corner, isn't it? I tell you, I've been living in this shithole for ages and I still can barely find my way around these rabbit-warren streets. Why don't you Brits try building places for people?'

'I have no idea. I'm not from around here.'

'Yeah. Heard that one. No one ever is.'

The car halts outside the Jones' shop. Louie reaches into his wallet and hands the driver £20.

'It's all sorted, man. You never taken an Uber before?'

'No. Yeah, but this is for you. Take it.'

'That's quite the tip. You sure you don't – '

Louie steps out of the car before the man can finish. He is tired of talking to people. It's exhausting. The repetitious anti-climactic cycle of it. The moment just before the other person talks when anticipation is highest. The expectation. The hope that they might say something different and surprising. The sinking disappointment when they don't. And then the hollow, aching disappointment when you don't either.

As Louie turns the key in the lock and opens the door to the shop, he wonders if humans are no different than animals barking the same calls to each other over and over until extinction. He steps inside and breathes in the air of the shop – dusty boxes and rotting stock. Then he goes upstairs to have a shower. He goes to the shower nozzle, angles it away from his body, and cranks the tap. He sits down on the floor and lets the warm spray blast to the side of him, remaining mostly cool and dry, being hit only indirectly by small droplets.

Louie has been doing this since he was six. Done right, he'd found that it would cause pleasant tingles to shiver along the surface of his skin making his hairs stand on end as if electrified. As a child he would sit in the corner of the shower with the shampoo and conditioner bottles. He would pretend that the shower was a tremendous downpour and that he was a homeless person huddled under a roof which barely sheltered him. The shampoo and conditioner were his fellow homeless friends. Louie invented back stories and personalities for them. Together they would huddle for warmth and tell tales to each other around an imaginary bin with a fire in it. Eventually, when the time came for Louie to actually engage with the business of washing, he would pretend that he had to leave, that the roof wasn't big enough to shelter all of them, that he had to sacrifice himself for the good of the group. Then he would walk out into the rain. The shampoo and conditioner would cry – don't go. But he would dissolve before them like dirt in water.

Now, with his mother gone, his father nearly dead from drink, the family business falling to pieces around his isolated, hopelessly-out-of-its-depth nineteen-year-old head, Louie finds that childhood make-believe game strangely prescient. Maybe even then he was wishing he could die in a way that would make everything right.

Ten minutes pass. No pleasant sensation comes. Maybe he isn't doing the trick right.

Oh well, no matter. He splashes a bit of water on himself,

turns off the shower and reaches for his towel. Then he realises he's forgotten to bring a change of clothes.

Fuck it, he thinks. No matter. No matter. It doesn't matter. Not where I'm going, going, going, gone, gone, go ...

Louie realises he is down the hallway now. Naked. Dick swaying in the stale store air.

He sees his hand knocking on the door to his father's room. The last time he'd done this he'd got a smack for his trouble. 'You still alive in there, cunt?' he shouts.

Louie shoves open the door and is assaulted by the smell of excrement and booze. All over the floor, from the doorway to the foot of his father's bed, are vodka bottles, lager cans, wine bottles – some empty, some half-full, some filled with piss. He hears a whisper from beneath soiled sheets.

'Lou?'

'So you are still alive, I take it?'

'Lou, come here.'

Louie tiptoes around the glasses, but it is hard to make out everything in the gloom and it isn't long before he knocks over a pint glass full of vomit. 'Fuck,' he mutters.

'Closer,' says his father, 'I want to have a look at you.'

'Why? Are you going to finally come downstairs?'

'Just come closer.'

Louie edges a little closer. Suddenly a hand reaches out from under the blankets. Louie flinches, thinking his father might hit him again. But when he sees his withered hand – his frail, shaking hand too weak to even form a fist – he feels stupid for even thinking that.

'Ha,' says his dad, 'pull my finger.'

Louie looks at him, confused.

'Come on now. Don't leave me hanging.'

Louie grabs his father's finger. It feels like a twig that might snap at the slightest exertion.

'I remember,' his dad rasps, 'when your little finger could barely wrap round mine. It was so small.'

Louie can't see his father's face but can sense him smiling somewhere in the filth-covered blankets.

'I promise,' the old man says, 'I promise I will come down tomorrow. Tell your mother not to worry. This will be the last storm of mine.'

The same, Louie thinks. The same grunts and calls, over and over, until you just want it all to stop. He closes his eyes. He can't bear to look at him anymore. He stumbles back over the bottles to the doorway.

'I love you, son.'

Louie wants more than anything to turn around and say, 'I know. That's why it hurts.' Instead he just says 'I ...' and his mouth hangs open for a painful minute.

He goes downstairs to the shop floor. The dusty tiles are cool beneath his bare feet. He strides over to a window and cracks it open, breathes in fresh oxygen, feels it curve and flow around his naked body. Of course, it only seems fresh comparatively. Intellectually Louie knows that this close to the roads every mouthful of air is filled with tiny poisonous fragments. But regardless, something deep within, something instinctual, buried in the nerve endings and neurons of his spine, wants to believe the air is fresh. That he has a choice. That he is making a decision.

He begins to laugh.

Climbing on top of the store counter, like he'd done as a child, like he'd got yelled at for doing by his dad, the young man reaches up towards the rifle on the display.

A Birthday Card From the Queen

Clare Azzopardi

Translated By Albert Gatt

He drops a teabag into a glass. Pours boiling water from the blackened kettle. For a few moments he is swaddled in the steam rising from the glass. He closes his eyes and imagines himself dissolving slowly, slowly, slowly, until there is no trace of him left in the kitchen.

He materialises again as the first rays of the sun come in through the door leading to the back yard to graze his cheeks, his lips. Soon his whole face is bathed in light.

Mornings always loom like this. Kelinu feeling that he's fought another hard battle and emerged victorious. Wondering how he manages to vanquish the night every time. Staring at the glass of cold tea. Taking a gulp. Just the one gulp. A gulp of nasty tea.

He makes the tea early in the morning as soon as he wakes up. It's usually just gone three o'clock. He never manages to sleep longer than that. He shuffles from his bed in the living room to the kitchen table and puts on the kettle he filled with water the night before. He doesn't like tea. Especially not on warm summer nights. But still, he makes tea because it reminds him of the Queen. And the army, it reminds him of that too. They took tea in the army as well. He lets the steam rise from the glass, allows it to take hold of him, elevate him, carry him. He has nothing left, Kelinu, but his memories, slowly, slowly, slowly evaporating, and the years that have passed. Lately he's begun to count the years he's got left until his hundredth birthday, when the Queen will be sending him a birthday card.

*

'You can't carry on like this, doing nothing at all, Unc. Can't you even make yourself a sandwich anymore? I'm not the maid, you know. I just come by to see if you need anything, that's all.'

'I make tea, but that's all I'll do.'

'There's no point making tea, seeing as you don't drink it. Unc, are you listening to me? I'm talking to you. Why do you make tea? You don't even like it, do you? So stop making all that tea then. And I keep finding the kettle in the fridge, you're going to ruin that fridge.'

'Helps it to cool down.'

'Helps what cool down?'

'The hot water.'

'In the kettle, you mean?'

'Right.'

'So you put it in the fridge?'

'Cools it down faster.'

'You don't even drink your tea!'

'But I do drink water.'

'You don't need to boil the water and cool it in the fridge. You're damaging it.'

'That's what they taught me.'

'Who?'

'Back when I was in the army.'

'What army?'

'The army. They taught us a lot of things there.'

'Pull the other one, Unc. You barely lasted a year in the army. Stop making up stories.'

'You wouldn't remember, you weren't even born.'

'Kettles go in the fridge, that what they taught you?'

'Oooh the things they taught us in the army. In the army I had my chin against a gun all the time.'

'Right. Course you did.'

'You don't understand these things, Tess.'

'What's to understand? This rot you keep going on about?'

'We were so much better off under the Queen, but you wouldn't understand.'

'I've no time to waste, Unc.'

'And look at us now, everything's gone to the dogs. There's no discipline anymore.'

'And what's the Queen got to do with it?'

'Tess you really don't understand any of it, do you?'

'Well, as long as you do!'

'We were doing so well under the Empire. Everyone did as he was told. And if you didn't, you found yourself in the line of fire. *Fajjar! Fajjar! Fajjar!*'

'I'll *fajjar* you. Couple of swats with a dishcloth is all the fire you'll get.'

*

The fog rising from the glass makes him forget all about his niece, her husband, her children, her children's children. The lenses of his large, heavy specs mist up slowly, slowly, slowly, until even the kitchen he's sitting in dissolves away, the same kitchen he grew up in, the kitchen in which his mother gave birth to him in 1925.

The Queen was born the following year.

*

Every now and then they spot a cockroach in the kitchen and pass the time trying to kill it.

But the kitchen's full of junk and there's plenty of territory for the cockroach to colonise and hide in. Afterwards, they sit at the table and meditate on the mystery of cockroaches, then recite a decade of the rosary and then spot another cockroach or maybe it's the same one but this time, his niece, who's faster on her feet, manages to land a blow with her flipflop and squash it against the floor. And then they stare at it. It's big. It's red. With its wings spread wide open, it looks like a crown.

*

He's got a few photo albums in which he keeps his years in order. Sometimes he opens them one by one to study the memories, squinting at page after page, holding them up close. So many places already that he can't remember anymore, some people he doesn't recognise, and some moments that he could swear he's never lived through.

But there's this special album, more of a scrapbook than an album. A scrapbook where for a long time he collected words from newspapers and magazines. It contains no photos that bring back pleasant memories, or even unpleasant ones, no moments frozen in a flash of light. What he collects in this scrapbook are newspaper cuttings with pictures of the Queen. The Queen descending from an aeroplane, the Queen waving, the Queen in a car, the Queen waving again, the Queen signing a document, the Queen getting into an aeroplane, the Queen who never stops waving. He tries to see whether, over the years, the Queen has always waved with her right hand. And holding the glass in his right hand, he takes a gulp of cold tea.

*

She calls out from the front door. Tells him she's here but won't be staying long because Sonny, her husband, couldn't find a parking space and is waiting for her in the car. It's cruel, the sun, he'll start hollering his head off if she stays too long. She comes in carrying a shopping basket, doesn't even look at him, there's no need. She knows exactly where he is, her uncle.

She lifts plates out of her basket. The first one goes into the microwave. Half a minute is all she gives it. Then she takes it out and carries it over to him. 'Can't you even turn on the telly, Unc?'

'I'm like the Queen ...'

'What?'

'I expect things to be done for me.'

She very nearly grabs the plate and chucks it at his head. 'Always this nonsense, Unc. I'm your niece and you're not the Queen and you'd better remember that if I decide not to come round anymore, you'll be left here to rot in a chair all alone.' She slams the plate down on the table. He doesn't flinch. Just straightens his napkin slightly. Picks up the pepper pot and sprinkles a little. Picks up his fork and tells her he used to be in the army and she has no idea what it's like to be in the army.

She does not reply.

'We fought for the Queen. We didn't have our chins in the trough you know, we held them against the guns.'

If it weren't for her, he'd be a fossil by now, just part of the furniture.

'We endured hunger and poverty.'

'Course he did, poor man, dying of hunger he is.

'But now I'm on the Queen's pension.'

'What d'you get it for? That's what I'd like to know.'

'Because I used to be in the army, Tess, what else? The things you say sometimes.'

'What did you do today?'

'Nothing.'

'You could've turned on the telly.'

'I read the paper for a while. And the world's going to the dogs, I'm telling you.'

'Really?'

'All these Muslims! If we don't close our doors, they'll go on a rampage. There'll be another war against them.'

'Stop talking nonsense, Unc.'

'Don't you read the papers then? Britain's closed its doors already. America as well. No more Muslims. Don't you hear about it, everything that's happening? We'll be back under the Queen's rule again soon and then we'll be fine.'

'Uncle, you need to start helping yourself 'cause I'm not going to be around forever.'

'They'll kick them all out.'

'Who, Unc?'

'The Muslims of course! Britain's leaving the Union and they're going to kick out anyone who's not British. And we should do the same. And no more of these Africans all over the place.'

'What's this got to do with us, Unc? Or with Africans?'

'Africans. Muslims. Don't you know anything, you? They should stay in their own country. Why don't they stay in their own country? Ruined the country, they have. Shame.'

'Which country are you talking about?'

'Britain.'

'And how do you know all this?'

'The papers, obviously. I'm with the Queen, Tess, that's who pays my pension. She signs my cheque and I'm staying loyal ... to her.'

Rather than answer, she takes his plate, slides the other one in front of him and thinks of Sonny in the car cursing the Queen. She quickly checks whether there's anything else he needs, puts the kettle on and while it's boiling, opens the fridge and makes a note of what needs buying. Tessie pours hot water into his glass, the teabag's in it already, and carries it over to him in a swirl of steam. For a moment, she tries to catch the look on his face, but everything becomes hazy and foggy and she doesn't even see him grab a chicken leg in his right hand.

*

At noon on the dot, he's seated at the table. He spreads a clean napkin across his lap. Puts his elbows on top of the table, clasps his hands together and rests his chin on them. He waits for her to bring his food. But Tessie doesn't turn up before one. So why sit at table so early, Kelinu? He doesn't budge. Doesn't move a muscle. Waiting for her, for his niece. When she arrives, she's in a hurry. Why's she always in a hurry? It'll be gone one o'clock, ten past one, sometimes a quarter past, even. He's always on time. Because he's known discipline, he has. He was properly trained, back when he was in the army and Malta was under the British. He's never forgotten what the British taught him.

*

Steam rises from the glass like artillery smoke. It makes him forget the heat in the kitchen, his niece and the words falling like dust from between her jagged, rotten teeth, and all he can remember now is the only woman he ever loved. He loved her when she danced, when she laughed, when she stitched beautiful dresses for their dances, loved her as she sang, as she teased, as she slept as if wrapped in a dream.

When the tea has cooled he pours it into the sink. He puts a lot of washing-up liquid in the glass and lets the foam rise and rise, then he rinses the glass and rinses away Maria's face, the white dress gliding across the carpet of a humble church and the hard years that followed. Maria lying in the throes of her illness, heavy as the rain clouds dimming the light in the room. Nothing remained of Maria's pear-shaped body, nothing but foam.

*

83

Sometimes they play cards. He tries to collect all the queens, she the aces. When they get bored, his niece puts the kettle on. They wait for it to boil. They listen as slowly, slowly, the whistle gets shriller. As if this was a challenge, neither of them wanting to be the one to get up and turn it off. Finally, his niece gets to her feet. She takes the kettle off, puts two teabags in the glasses. Passes him one. Sits down opposite him. Her gaze turns into a queen's gaze and Kelinu's is lost in the haze of hundreds of water droplets.

*

Once upon a time, there was a man who began to forget things on purpose. He forgot the woman who had given birth to him, he forgot that he was a widower, he forgot he had once been a soldier, he forgot he was taken ill and had to stop fighting and forgot many other things besides. He forgot all about the referendum on integration with the United Kingdom, forgot that Malta had gained independence and even that it had become a republic. At night he dreamt that he stood on the frontlines of battlefields in bloody wars and was first among those awarded medals of honour by the Queen. By day he dreamt that Malta had become a part of Britain and that the lovely Queen was our mother too. Who needs the Virgin Mary when we've got the Queen?

*

During one of the many years that he's got under his belt, he decided to keep all the junk mail he received. He studied it closely, picture by picture, checked to see which prices had gone down, what was new, what had changed, what was on offer. He folded the sheets of paper exactly as they had been when he'd received them and then stacked them up. He measured the stacks with a ruler and once a stack was thirty centimetres high, he tied a piece of string around it and fastened it with a bow. In one year he had filled up a room. His niece screeched louder than a siren because this hovel he lived in was hardly a maze of rooms and he'd have to give it up sooner or later, this room in which he'd crammed his regiments of sleeping leaflets.

'I've built an army.' That's what he said.

'Never mind the army, Unc.'

'Now when they attack ...'

'Who's going to attack? The hounds of hell?'

'You ought to know that the enemy always strikes when you least expect it. As for me, I'm always ready and waiting.'

'Start getting ready for the grave, Unc, never mind the enemy.'

*

Tessie brings him candlesticks from the parish church to clean the wax off them.

'Should keep you busy for a bit, Unc,' she says, 'and you'll be doing something for the parish, at least. How're you going to face your maker otherwise?'

Every bit of wax he removes reveals another piece of his face in the candlestick's surface.

When he's done he collects all the fragments of wax in a plastic bag, fastens it with a knot and stows it away next to the other bags of wax. 'What'll we do with this now, Tess? With all this wax?'

'No idea. But it passes the time, doesn't it?'

'But I've no need for it here.'

'I'll ask the sacristan to come pick it up and melt it down for your sins. All right?'

'I suppose I could keep these bags, Tess, we could start

making candles, I could make a hundred of them, what do you say? Would you buy me some cord for the wicks?'

*

Would the Queen send him a card when he turned a hundred, he wondered.

'Oh bugger off, Unc, would you.'

'You know she sends one to everyone.'

'Everyone who?'

'Everyone who turns a hundred.'

'You won't be a hundred for another eight years.'

'Eight years aren't so many when you've lived through ninety-two of them, don't you think?'

'Even so, where'd you get the idea that she sends them birthday cards?'

'It was in the paper. Apparently it costs her a lot of money to send cards to all those people.'

'All those people? Which people?'

'People who've turned a hundred.'

'How many's that then, how many are living to a hundred?'

'Oooh, if only you knew.'

He gets to his feet to fetch his scrapbook. His niece rinses the dinner plates and glasses. She prepares some stewed apple in a glass bowl. Kelinu turns to the page where he's pasted the article about the birthday cards. He shows it to her. His niece skims through it quickly. Then she bursts out laughing. Says it's not the Maltese they're talking about, it's the Brits. The Queen only sends birthday cards to British citizens. 'We've nothing to do with Britain, Unc.'

'Don't be silly. You don't understand. I don't know why I bother telling you these things.'

'Because you've no one else except me, Unc. That's why

you bother.'

'But hang on a minute, isn't it the Queen who sends me my pension?'

'Yes, but that doesn't mean she'll be sending you a birthday card when you get to be a hundred.'

'If she signs my cheque every month, she'll be sending me a birthday card as well.'

*

There's this man who cherry-picks the events he prefers not to forget. His wedding to Maria, the doctor's daughter, the day of his twin sister's funeral, the day he serenaded the Queen beneath her balcony ... it was like a dream when the Princess – she was still a princess then – came out on her balcony in Villa Gwardamanga where she was staying at the time. He and his friends – they might all be dead by now, he's not sure – had decided to stand beneath her balcony and sing her the folk song about boats coming and going in the harbour, dadadaaadadadadaaaa ... the captain standing at the helm. She'd thrown them a five-pound note.

*

He opens the hot tap and stares into the bathroom mirror until it's completely misted over. He doesn't like to stand under the shower, he's afraid. Instead, he takes a washcloth, soaks it, wrings it and wipes himself down as he sings, 'Rule Britannia, Britannia rule the waves ... Rule Britannia, Britannia rule the waves ...'

He served the Queen and has no regrets. Now that the Queen and Merkel are at loggerheads, he'd like to write to her to say she was right all along because Britain's for the British and for no one else, or maybe it's for the Maltese too, after all the

Maltese are just like the British, they are. It's not fair that we get bundled together with the Africans or that they think we're Arabs; we were a colony of the British and we were not like the other countries. We were treated like kings and queens because Malta was always a good naval base for the British. And that's how it will be once more, once war breaks out against the Muslims. He's steaming when he comes out of the bathroom. Then he spots a fly and a dogfight ensues until it's dead.

His niece, how many times has he told his niece that we're not like the others? We're different because we're an island and the British taught us discipline. They taught us how to make tea and pudding. His niece isn't always in the mood to chat. She hands him a flyswatter and tells him to kill the flies in the kitchen because she can't take his nagging anymore. One time, he killed seventeen flies within a quarter of an hour and she said, 'Go figure, it was worth something after all, that army of yours.'

*

Saturday nights, while Sonny's at Kucnaru's bar, his niece is in less of a hurry and after she prepares his food and has a bite herself, they stare at the images on the telly. Sometimes Kelinu wants to hear about Maria. Sometimes he wants to hear about Nina, Maria's friend, who started making his dinners after Maria died. Sometimes, his niece tells him stories about this woman who used to make dresses out of the parachutes that fell near her house. That's what Tessie'd heard anyhow. And when no more parachutes fell, she began to make dresses out of curtain fabric, including one she made for the Queen, which she wore to a samba dance at the Hotel Phoenicia.

*

In eight years' time, when the empire will once again have spread halfway across the globe, maybe even further, when everyone's being taught some discipline again, Kelinu will be getting his birthday card from the Queen. When he looks at the envelope and notices it's not the usual pension cheque, he'll prop it against the vase of dried flowers that stands in the middle of the table. Then he'll sit on his chair and wait for his niece to bring his food on a plate, take the plate away, serve him a second course, take that away and finally serve him a bowl of stewed apples. After she's gone, Kelinu will wait for night to mount its attack and bury him under layers of sleep.

Then he'll wake up. It'll have just gone three or maybe, maybe that day he might even wake up a little earlier. He'll trudge to the kitchen to put the kettle on, which he'll already have filled with water. Beside it will stand a glass with a Twinings teabag. He'll put the kettle on and as soon as it starts to boil, will pour the water, then a bit of milk. Taking the glass, he'll go and sit at the table. He'll open the envelope leaning against the vase, see the card inside, pull the glass towards him and let the steam engulf him forever.

And should the night not dissolve into a day of burning sunlight, it will not matter.

The Boulevard

Alys Conran

'I, Ferran, am the not official consulate on the boulevard!' he said as he showed me into his workshop on that first day, 'Here is my home!'

His workshop occupies an entire basement flat. Printing, laminating and embossing machines stand heavy all around the walls. As we entered, he switched them on. They whirred and mashed in preparation.

'Here I have much work to do,' he said excitedly 'People I am to process. People who will be *adaptats*, changed!'

And I asked him 'How did you start with this identification racket?'

And he answered, 'With myself.'

He got to work. At the back of the basement is a whitened wall, where I stood that day, serious, to have my photograph taken. I stare out of the polaroid photograph, half myself and half another, made-up, hiding in the porous city where unpapered people slink like foxes.

'*Agafa això*,' he told me, *here take this*, handing me a piece of stretched plastic, '*agafa fort*' *while I press it all together*.

The print of my thumb stood black against the little card, a scrawling signature underneath it, which I had quickly invented. The thumb in the print had the contours of a hill. My print. A hillfort in the middle of the sea.

See, there are many ways you can be born into the writhing city. People come from all directions, and by all means. You can, for example, come fresh off the boat and along the lines, between the people, up the streets, invisible as the rats of the city. Said, Ferran's latest recruit, who is probably asleep under a sleeping bag in that workshop now, came like this. If you're lucky, like me or Said, then Ferran catches up with you, prints you a life on his whirring machines, even gets you a job.

If you get in on one of Carlos' schemes you're not so lucky. No. Like 'Cristina', one of the new Nigerian girls with the almond eyes, who prostitues herself along the dark alleys of El Raval, or like Marianna, the old lady who limps up the boulevard, bent like a curled leaf, with her little pot of pennies, or the dull-eyed roma girls who sell magazines and beg with their sleeping babies on their arms only to have Carlos or another motherfucker like him make meat of their dreams and take most of their pennies for his empire of neon out-of-town brothels and for the billowing circumference of his waist.

I was lucky, with Ferran, who now pressed the machine down onto the card and cut the plastic carefully. We couldn't breathe at all until it was all finished, this alchemy. I held it under the light. The watermark, the metal colour symbol of empire and decay. It was perfect, identical to a million others. *Extranjero* it said: Foreigner, but benign, allowed, bona fide, legal, permitted, *con papeles*.

And then he carefully prepared my papers, pasted them together, watermarked and stamped them until they were perfect, until they were perfectly false. I looked at my face, and my name, typed in neatly on this little card, took a big breath, a bay filling with the sea, and prepared to make my own fresh start in the dying city.

On the metro, later that day, people stared at Ferran, who had the remainder of various colours of stage make-up around his hairline and under his eyes. Ferran started at least three conversations before we got to our stop, simply by offering various fictional reasons for the paint:

'*¡Que estic podrint!*' he announced to a group of doubtful teenagers, 'I'm rotting, the green is mould. Ay! Ay! Ay! God knows what will become of me! I've been covered with anti-aging paint and they've only left this part here untouched, this part is five hundred years old!'

The stories grew and morphed: he was a gipsy, was from Antarctica, the Indian Subcontinent, a village a few miles away and the North Pole. He made fireworks for a living, worked in a factory making bombs, was a famous surgeon, a more famous astronomer, a queen of the circus, a king of the mafia, he owned seventy-five budgerigars, a palace of gold, three shops in L'Eixample, a harem, or slept rough every night in his own tent in Collserola.

Somewhere between it all Ferran came through. A mystery, but just as he was. He filled himself out with an indescribable verity, so that by the time we got off the red line, the whole carriage waved us off.

'*Adéu! Adéu! Adiós!* Gooood byeeeee!' he boomed as we left the carriage. And I was warmed by him, just as everyone else was.

When, a short walk later along the city's alleywayed veins, we arrived at the correct door and knocked, we had to wait an age in the street, which smelt of old fruit and piss.

We waited.

'She isn't there?' I said, eventually.

Ferran who had been standing for an age, nose to the door, tut tutted and remained waiting.

Señora Tapies, when she finally arrived at the door to open it with difficulty, was stooped and tiny, grey hair knotted onto her head, black shoes, a black skirt, a black brocaded blouse, and fierce grey eyes which, once she had accepted Ferran's two kisses, now turned to me. She reached a hand to mine, pulled it and beckoned with the other one for me to bend to kiss her cheek. As I was about to straighten up again, she held my shoulders.

'*Deixem veure els ulls*,' she said, looking into them.

My eyes, are blue.

'Ah,' she said, then smiled at Ferran. '*Sirena*,' she pronounced, nodding, and led me inside by the hand.

The stairwell was exquisitely tiled, each tile made and painted by hand. In the tiles were many citiscapes and gardens, a medieval cloister, a modern skyscraper, towerblocks, a promenade by the sea, churches, cathedrals, graveyards, a courtyard, a market. All these, and so many faces, so many people, dressed in the clothes of so many times, gathered their colours in the tiles as the *señora* led me upstairs. She walked slowly, taking an age over every step, and I followed, with Ferran behind.

As we walked the stairs, slowly, slowly, time seemed to stretch and bend around us. Ferran spoke all the while, in stories that stretched and bent too, so that the way up the stairwell became a pilgrimage or a dance as I ran my hands over one tile and then the other and he told the story of Barcelona as it appeared and disappeared in the tiles.

He told of the Roman ruins which showed their guts like a new sea bed whenever a new foundation was put in the old town, told of how the mediterranean sea itself defined and fed the city with its *marisc* and *gambas* and *bacallá*, its *armadas*, its colombus, its colonies and returns, tells of the old and abandoned Jewish districts with their silenced and unanswered prayers, tells of the old hatreds of *els moros*, who have always come, and who continue to come now, cousins still waiting to be acknowledged.

In a quiet, angry voice, Ferran tells of Franco. Of his bloodthirst, his firing squads. Of the fear of soldiers who hid in the habits of nuns. Of the unremarked and unremedied abuse of gipsies and Jews, the ears cut, the mouths slit. And of how Catalan speech became clandestine and bubbled beneath the surface of the city, its water table slowly rising until it burst forth, chattering and wild into the city's schools and universities and the *Generalitat*.

He tells of the new neighbourhoods, of Andalucians and South Americans setting their backs into the work of unfurling new districts and *pobles* which click one room after another into place in the city, as the outlying districts grow and the city spreads in a steady half-throttle, flowering in towers of tiny apartments. He tells of the young European students who came on EU exchanges from Germany and Austria and France and Scotland, with confused hopes of learning Spanish here, only to find that the long, pedantic lectures were now in Catalan, and to learn those unsilenced words instead as they made love to the locals on the fresh spring nights, their bodies alive with the touch of syllables like *xocolata, petons, foscor*.

Finally he tells of how, where the city's heart once was, technicolour tourists now swarm like locusts, blotting out all sense of city-centredness, so that this morphous new Barcelona, as it sleeps at night, patchworked in its many rooms, begins to fall apart, and can't quite remember how it once dreamt all together of independence, as a freewheeling flight into the open air.

By the time we'd climbed that stairwell, and I'd run my hand along those tiles, one by one, like a long, slow filmreel to the slow merry-go-round soundtrack of Ferran's voice, I'd arrived. I'd arrived in this precise moment in time, in an attic flat in the back quarter of El Raval, and at a quarter to ten on a Tuesday morning shortly after the latest clandestine referendum on *La Independencia*, when the city had voted, again, *Sí*. And then muttered, *we think so*, in Spanish under its breath.

Before her doorway, there were several uncoloured tiles, like the boxes of an unsolved crossword or an unchecked ballot.

Her apartment, its windows wide to the sky and to the sounds of the muttering, rearing city, was choc-a-bloc with relics and trinkets, it ebbed and flowed with smells of food and with the traces of thoughts that had just escaped through the open windows. The smells shifted moment by moment, as if there was some concoction of memories on the boil, or firing slowly in the oven.

'*Posa't aquí*,' Señora Tapies said as she stood me in the middle of the lounge, on the rug between two old armchairs, and began to measure my waist, my hips and the length of my legs. I became a silhouette, reduced to the edges of me, my dimensions. She didn't make a note of the measurements, but her eyes, as she committed them to memory, were muted and precise.

This work of quantifying done, she motioned for me to sit on one of the armchairs, and went through to the bedroom next door. From time to time I could hear her rustling around. There was the sound of cutting fabric, of the *señora* humming a tune.

Moments, or minutes, or hours later she came through with it. Already alive.

I lifted it, instinctively went to put it on. Its colours danced as it moved with every change of air, the wired shape of it stubborn against the rustle and sway of the chiffon, silk, satin, the materials of it layered and set in segments. If you had asked me what the colours were, I couldn't have told you. It was like Señora Tapies' grey eyes. You could have sworn there was every colour there hiding, avoiding its name. Just grey, but also a rainbow, or a kaleidoscope.

The tail, as I put it around my legs, was more alive than I was.

Ferran stared at me hard, pulled a long cigarette of sour black tobacco to his mouth, inhaled, exhaled, and pronounced: 'Mermaid.'

She nodded. '*Agafa-la un mirall, fes-la una roca, y només fa falta el maquillatge,*' she said to Ferran, who stood beside me, waiting patiently for instruction. She reeled off the costume and props that the mermaid needed, describing in barrelling Catalan, which he translated haltingly into our shared bad Spanish and English, the sticky makeup that'd ripple from around my eyes, the bikini to be placed around me, the papier-mâché rock, the beauty spot to be pushed on just here, and how the tail would, later, become me.

Ferran laughed. He got up, strode round the little table to me, and gave my arm a punch, '*Venga! Somriu! Smile!*'

The *señora* got me to undress, pulling at my clothes without any kind of ceremony, then tied on the little glittered bikini before I had a chance to worry at this quick bareness. At her orders, Ferran grabbed a table, draped it with a sheet: a makeshift rock, searched her bedroom and found a little mirror, smudged with long use, and shoved it into my hand with a quick smile. They motioned for me to sit, looked at me, nodded. Then they laughed.

The *señora* came close, a musty scent, of memories and liquor.

'Mmm,' she said, eyes scanning my face. Behind her Ferran still sat, serious, chin in hand, waiting.

A flurry of powders and paints, a sense of being rewritten, melted down and remade, of her flat becoming a kind of chrysalis.

When she finally stood back, the mermaid sat glittering in my little mirror, her blue eyes shining beneath the rings of make-up, the lips pearly pink, the beauty spot a necessary extra on this portrait of a siren, a seductive touch to get the coins tinkling. Pieces of my face stared back from the mirror, segments of the girl I was, and then another thing, these new expressions and nuances and lines, someone else's, a different look in her eye. Someone I don't quite know, I can't quite control. Her.

'*Ara!*' said Ferran, '*Somriu!*'

And, answering the command, slowly, slowly, I watched as the mermaid's made-up face in the mirror, surrounded by this lounge of old trinkets, in a strange city, a strange country, cracked slowly into a smile.

I clambered quickly out of the tail, like getting out of cold water.

Señora Tapies was watching from the doorway and came over to pat my shoulder, take it from me, and load it into its unwieldy black bag for the first time. It was a body in its body bag. I carried it, heavy and aching with weight, as we walked through the slanted afternoon light toward the boulevard, and my first shift, and the sun, Ferran giving me careful, precise to-a-T instructions for how to play Her.

On the long bonanza of the boulevard, horns honked, people pushed, tourists moved along in droves. We made our way down to my spot, which was to be beside the tourist booth, where big stupid Alfi sells little models of Gaudi's masterpieces.

Ferran nodded to me, nodded also to Jorge, in the spot next door, who was dressed as the devil, and left me for his own spot further up. What follows, follows again and again. I don't know how many days, how many months, years?

I take off my jacket, spray glitter on my shoulders, fix a gem in my belly's button, strip my lower half down to just the hotpants she wears under the costume.

Then I open the bag, and take her out.

Her tail springs out, opening like an orchid onto the boulevard. Under the sun, it's aquamarine, no, violet, there's green too, and the petrol swirls of a fishskin sheen. Its chiffon and satin and sequines writhe. It is, always, always, more alive than I am.

I grapple with it, with the shimmering fabric, with the wired shape of it, which has to be wrestled, calmed. Her tail seems to go beserk in the sunshine.

I have it now, and, obedient at least for the moment, it sits at my feet. I am opening the waist of it with firm hands, with my nails. It is only a costume. It is only a costume.

I step my bare legs in, wriggle the coloured fabrics up around my waist, pull the underwire of it into the right shape, the tail shape, elegant and curling slightly. I fasten it around my hips. The tail is my tail now, it sits around my legs, like a skirt with no way out. The end of it lies around my feet on the ground and I know it will slowly coil around me until I disappear. I am tempted to check that I can still see them: my own legs moving underneath under the semi-translucent skin of it.

I can. And besides there is the slit, in the front, where I can step my feet out, and gather the rest of the tail up in my arms, should I want to run. I *can* step out of it. I can take off the tail whenever I want, take Her off. I remind myself of this, and try to breathe.

I stand, she stands, motionless under the sun. A mermaid in the dry city. Her make-up will slowly crack like earth in drought.

I'm not the only one. There are others. We are mermaids, cowboys, tin men. We are goblins and sumo wrestlers. Up and down the boulevard we stand, striking our poses for small change. We wear clothes made of papier-mâché, chiffon, silk, satin, cotton, cardboard. False features are printed in food colouring on our faces - pimples and beards expertly inserted. Our slow-motion dances greet the coppers, thrown at intervals into our waiting hats, pots, boxes. Our hats lie like open hands on the hot paving stones. The hands say c'mon. C'mon say the hands. Mostly the hats are almost empty.

Standing's an art, and also a sport; the kinks in my muscles grow sore, my bones settle their raw joints into each other. The enemy here is gravity. The enemy here is the boulevard. The boulevard pulls my skull into my shoulders into my back into my hips into my knees and down through my ankles into my heels and down again into cold stone. I hold the pose, each fidget a lost penny. I've learnt to hold it pretty well.

It grows, as I stand, the hunger to be watched. If not my stillness is thrown into terrible relief by the people moving past. On my prickling out-of-focus skin I can feel the air rippling with them as they go by. And I feel stuck then, rooted to this spot. When I am unwatched the edges of me begin to fade, and I'm just standing still. I am alone under my costume, waiting for my spectators, for an audience to gather round me with snatchy holiday eyes and pockets ready to empty.

So, a kaleidoscope of blinking eyes. The eyes belong, mainly, to British tourists. Pam and Barry, or Nigel and Helen, or Kelly and John, or to the kids, or to the 'not a kid anymore' kids, whose brows knot unimpressed, or to a drunken hen party, giggling in frills and angel wings, or to some football lads, who look like footballs and who blink at us vacantly, and burp beer into the hot air as they come, staggering up the boulevard, drunk since last night and horny with the strangeness of sunshine. They swagger, laughing too loud, wearing Mexican sombreros, because sombreros they think, are Spanish, and this, they think, is Spain.

The lads stagger up the boulevard toward me now, toward the mermaid: her bikini, her bare midriff, her bare shoulders, her bare leg hinting through the split in her tail. Sitting still, my tail curling at my feet, I throw a little beckoning wink at him, the tallest of them, chequered shirt and gelled hair. I poke my knee further through the split.

'Check this one out,' he says to his friends. Focusing on my knee, he stumbles toward me. 'Give us a dance, darlin!'

They all stop, waiting, mouths slightly open, stupid. I stand. Everything here costs money.

The penny drops:

'You've got to put money in the pot,' mutters the tall guy to the others.

'Oh yeah …' they say, 'oh yeah …' and start checking pockets.

'Nah, fifty's too much, twenty-five, that's it, that'll do fine,'

Having swept round for coppers, he walks over. He stands quite close for a second, smiling up at me, his eyes trickling slowly down.

'Right then, love,' he says, 'do yer stuff,' and bends to drop his coin in the pot at my feet. On his way as he bends he just touches my leg where it shows through the split. His hand is slightly sweaty, hot even against my hot bare skin, and trembling just a bit at the dare of it all. The lads chuckle. 'Dirty bastard, Scott,' one says, laughs. I don't flinch until the coin's safely in the pot. It lands with a dull little clunk. Coppers probably. Probably sterling. Their queen on the brown coin. Still.

As he stands again, there is his pleased-with-himself-face, merging with the faces of the others like him I've known, here on the boulevard and also, *before*, on the dark nights of home coming apart, nights heavy with the smell of shelling and the muffled sound of loved children crying, when a young female body bought you time, and cost you dearly too (the smell of cigarettes on the soldier's bad breath, the weight of his body as he held me down, the sound of the others, laughing).

I reach out quick, give him a stinging swipe across the cheek. I deliver it with a smile, but it's just hard enough to be beyond playfulness, and has enough anger in it to leave his skin red and smarting, and for his friends to laugh at him not at me. I wish I had a ring. Or sharp nails.

But still, a coin is a coin, and I work like clockwork. So, with a flourish, I begin my routine. The mermaid smiles and waves, flicking her sequined tail, sticking her sequined breasts out at the group, winking at them. Hips bucking to the side, she laughs, a laugh coquettish and almost real, then daintily checks her reflection in a little shell studded mirror she always has in her hand. It's funny to see my own blue eyes in the mirror – unblinking in my tanned face, framed against the blue sky.

I freeze there, standing, looking up and to the left at my eyes in the mirror, slightly pouting, my left hip thrown out to the side, and one hand on that hip. I wait again. If I'm lucky, the small change will flow a little easier now.

This time I'm not lucky. Although he keeps his distance, some of the others come closer, start taking photos, grinning and pointing at the mermaid for the camera. The mermaid will be shared then? Later from their phones, shared and liked and commented upon and made into another story again? They go round behind her, take photos of her again from behind, make rude gestures at her for the photos, giggling dirty and low. I don't ask them for money for the pictures. I don't want to have to speak to them at all. It's easier if they think of the mermaid as someone unspeakable, unspeakable to. It's not so humiliating, for me and for them, if they think this body is so intrinsically foreign that none of their langauge is intelligible to her at all, and she doesn't speak the language of their obscene gestures either.

I let it all play out around me, make myself a backdrop. I stand still against the buffeting laughter sounding like seagulls in the air.

They begin to move away. He gives me a cursory spank as he leaves, his hand still stinging even through the papier-mâché, and the others laughing, louder, more confidently this time. I don't move.

Their unspent spare change still clasped in sweaty hands, better spent on beer and sangria, they wander off into the flowing boulevard, red t-shirts fading. Their sombreros and cackles move slowly away up the boulevard, toward Jorge, the devil.

Jorge is red-painted all over. He stands in his spot a little further up, past the souvenir booth with its small replicas of *La Sagrada Familia* and *La Santa Maria del Mar*, which Ferran has interspersed with models of less desireable buildings, such as the tower blocks of La Mina.

I watch the devil through the corner of one eye as those lads gather around him, put pennies in the box, laugh. The devil is stark nude except for a little bit of red cardboard he holds over his groin. The cardboard's shaped like a forked tongue and, when the lads drop the change in his box, and as there are no children around right now, and none of the police stationed in the side streets since the attack last week are watching, he pulls the cardboard away and blows a livid kiss.

They take photos of his naked groin for a laugh. But there's not much funny. Jorge is emaciated now, his ribs give the devil a nightmarish look, make him pitiful, fallen. Statues, they fall down see? After a while. Jorge's box is full already. So I guess he'll be getting his fix tonight.

I keep an eye on the red shirts as they move on, tripping and swaying and tustle-fighting toward the final statue: Ferran. I find myself dropping the pose, standing on tiptoe, craning my neck to see what Ferran will do to them.

For Ferran all it takes is standing still. In the next spot up, he stands, gathering a sense of mass about him, of weight. In terms of earnings he's apparently the least successful of all the statues. In fact, there's no hat for coins at his feet at all. It's uncertain even what kind of a statue he is trying to be here on the boulevard; the clothes are really not a proper costume at all.

He has carefully removed all his makeup, and stands unpainted, dressed only in his own face and a poor looking suit, some tattered shoes, work shoes which have walked too many miles and are set to crumble. Two of his shirt buttons are missing and there's a rip in one shoulder of his old jacket. In his right hand he carries a small, battered suitcase, in his stilled eyes carries the heavy look of someone on the move, although in fact he's uncannily still, and even the tear which has begun to fall from his left eye is hanging, unfalling against his cheek. He looks dog tired. He looks empty. Ferran stands. As the lads pass him there are no smart alec comments, no gestures, no words and no pictures. The lads become subdued and small as they pass, their laughter spiralling lost circles and dying as they are drawn by the dark gravity that he has. They fall silent, and look away, look down. Sobriety beats down on them with the sun. As they walk away from him, they find themselves feeling its ache. The ache of our lost and receeding home.

GLITCH

OISÍN FAGAN

I have this dream that's always interrupted. Usually Khadija, my tag, facetimes me to get off my hole and do a tap, but every now and again she touches my shoulder to wake me, and sometimes I pretend I'm not awake so she touches me again. Then, for hours after I've woken I can still feel the dream inside me, the stars imprinted on the back of my eyes like my whole life has been one big glitch.

This time she wakes me up by whistling at me.

Fill up your bag, you moneyless bitch, she says.

Three of the drones have just glitched off the map, and Khadija, her override game always on point, is on it pronto. She's had their codes since a minute and sequesters them during blackouts to drop grams from great heights.

The bags, shaped like helicopter seeds from sycamore trees, parachute down real soft. One packet lands on target. She clacks her grill, makes a kissing sound with her lips. On the big screen, I can see a fiend with yellow, sunken cheeks smiling. The bag caught between his fingers, he waves at SlayQueen as she ascends. The fiend gets smaller, disappears, but now SlayQueen's POV holds all of Galway in her lens. A cartoon city in a cartoon country.

The gentlest rain, Khadija says, is always welcome.

You'll get yourself done, I say.

Like all young men with decent hand-eye, instead of coding, I went to war when I left school. They kept me in a basement in a retrofitted factory in Ballymahon. At first I'd play games on my phone that killed Islamic nationalists and communists, but most of the time I was just getting my little drone to go across deserts to burn off oil supplies or poison water wells, removing vital terroristic infrastructure, hunting down child soldiers and the like, but then I got promoted and was made a gatekeeper. In this role, I worked on a private contract through the EU, tasked with guarding the coastline of Galway to make sure only the right kind of pharma got in, but recently we'd been handed down a directive that banned us from shooting migrants, though we were still tasked with destroying their property in such a way as would prevent them getting to shore, so, as per request, I'd puncture their life rafts with the sharp end of my drone, which I had christened Tupac, and sink them.

Shit is making me depressed though. Depressed and anxious. Even offline, I'm glitching. Awake, imprints from Tupac's POV burn my dome. I keep seeing drowning children in double vision. Sometimes I can't breathe and I think I'm going to die. Khadija says its screen fatigue, but maybe I'm just jittery. Too much coffee and VR blurs even the hardest perception.

The app we use animates our drone's POV so the migrants we drown look like cartoons. This way we don't get too attached. The sounds are still real, though, and they're even scarier coming out of the perfect black circle of a cartoon mouth, but you can just mute all this when it starts to get too intense. Khadija says that realness means not becoming the screen and that if your body starts to get involved in the screen you're fucked.

I'm Khadija's seventh tag in three years. All her previous ones burnt out.

Why do you hate making money so much? Khadija asks me.

Her diamond grill glimmers in the light of the screen, and her eyes are hidden behind her goggles, so I take a moment to reflect on that big thing she's got in her shorts. Khadija is that good kind of fat, though I swear to God there's no bad kind of fat, and she's wearing these tight shorts, that spray-on kind that you have to top up every few hours.

As my tag, she shadows Tupac for five hours and then we switch and I shadow SlayQueen for another five hours. After, we get a three hour break for screen fatigue and RSI, and then we repeat the shift pattern, and get a day off. No holidays. No summer. Just every second day off. Forever. Till we die.

I get with her whenever we're on break. I know she's just bored, but I don't care. I allow myself to get attached. Riding is the most invigorating way to minimise holistic screen burn, especially if you focus on the rhythmical movements of that jelly, and Khadija is blessed with that jelly. The ultimate coping mechanism for any ailment is ample pussy. Always has been, and my journey to maturity has involved no shift in perception, just a deepening appreciation of thickness. Khadija being my tag has allowed my anxiety to blend into this fetish and now I am totally dependent on her presence. When she's not around me I begin asking questions that don't need to be asked, questions that if they were answered could fuck up my whole life.

I know you're creeping, she says, 'cause you always go quiet and stop breathing. You're the thirstiest cunt I ever met.

Now all of a sudden I'm not allowed to look because I won't risk being blackballed? I say. That's going a bit too far now.

I send her a little praying hands emoticon, so she knows I'm still grateful for her offer.

Did this motherfucker forget I was a boss bitch? she replies. You're sorely mistaken if you think the definition of a boss bitch implies said boss bitch getting caught.

Too much risk, I say.

You don't even know risk, she says, with your fairy tales

about blackballing. This'll get you disappeared forever is all, and nobody's playing back that shit. You disappear yourself between the glitches and your family isn't even told.

Then stop doing it.

Get paid, or stop whinging, she says. Stroppy little bitch.

Khadija's from Blanchardstown, so she is the most hip hop person I know. I'm hyper-Americanised too, but she really one-ups me on this.

My ears are buzzing, she says. Something's incoming.

A DM comes in from mam. It says I've to come home and give my sister her shots. I put her on hold.

Are you sure we're still in the glitch if I'm here getting messages? I ask Khadija.

She checks the signal and then tuts at me, annoyed.

Leave this to me, yeah? she says.

On the screen, SlayQueen is weaving through a populous and ramshackle tent city on the outskirts of cartoon Galway. I see that it's raining there, and I put mam on speaker message, still staring at the screen.

Why can't you do it, mam?

There is a lot of breathing on the line and then some groaning like she's been stabbed.

Too high.

You're messing, yeah? I'm in work.

I won't lie to you, she says. I'm stuck to the floor. Now you can say it's all in my head, but that won't undo me being stuck to the floor in any shape or form.

I unhook myself and put Tupac on standby. He is floating somewhere over the Atlantic ocean in the night time sky. I imagine him, still in the wind, the moon above him. I can monitor him from my phone, so there's no real need for me to ever be physically in work, but the gaffer says a centralised security presence is crucial for morale, that it gives an MNC a conceivable sense of itself, whatever that means. Still, I run my absence by the boss man. He's always online, and is so responsive that Khadija thinks he's a bot.

Ibañez? This better be good, the gaffer says. I'm in Beijing.

Conference? I ask.

Why would I need to physically go to a conference, you tool? he sighs. I'm at my daughter's piano recital.

That's nice.

Well, it's pretty bad, but when it gets too hard I reassure myself by remembering that, at the end of the day, she's probably not my daughter. What is it?

Can I go home for an hour? There's a glitch now, so I can't work or I'd have to manually compile the stats, which is illegal, I say to him.

Thank you, retard, for your concern over whether or not I, who spends well-recompensed summers in the Valley writing your regulations, knew it was illegal.

Look, I say.

Look what?

There's a family emergency.

The gaffer always keeps me waiting. He'll give me what I want, but only once he feels that I've suffered enough.

You know what would be a family emergency? he says. If you got yourself fired.

Can I go, though? I'll only be a minute.

Why are you firing yourself, Ibañez?

Please.

Bring your phone with you and monitor it. Thirty minutes max, and tack it on to the end of the shift.

He hangs up before I can thank him. I slouch back in my chair, and sigh.

Well, that was fairly intense, I say, taking a look at Khadija's enormous arse to de-stress for a moment.

I'm telling you he's a bot, Khadija says. I told you I pirated a programme last year that sounded exactly like him. You could even get the accent add-on. I mean, they even had a Mullingar accent option. Like, what the fuck? Who'd even want that? No way is he real. And you know how I know he's not real? she says.

How?

He's just the right amount of dickhead. Most dickheads are too much dickheads so they are actually cunts, and other dickheads have redeeming features, so they're just twats. Based on user input, he's like what an algorithm would say was the optimum amount of dickhead for a dickhead to be.

It is true that I've never seen him in the flesh.

Surely, I ask, they'd download a sound boss to make us loyal?

HR probably said a nice one didn't match our psychological profiles, she says. Personally, I feel very motivated by what a dickhead he is.

It doesn't even matter. A boss is a boss is a boss, I say. I've to go home for a bit. I'll be back shortly.

Nobody on this planet cares where you go, honey, she says. And I know you're looking at the goods again.

It's just you're so –, I trail off, because there really are no words.

I know, she replies, almost sadly. The goods are good.

Me and Khadija have a complicated relationship. She kind of ruined my sister's life. My sister, Aoife, had a messy break-up because her boyfriend, who I always hated because he was a guard, had shifted Khadija absolutely out of it in the hopes she'd go down on him because she has that whole vibrating tongue piercing thing going on.

Before Aoife broke up with her boyfriend, she had had a good life, mainly on Instagram. She had photoshopped herself to another level of fineness and had more than 500,000 very thirsty followers. Every week she'd get over a thousand DMs for the meet.

I am the photoshop queen, and I do step on these Insta-peasants like bitches, she used to say every few hours, staring happily at the modem at a blow up of her own imaginary enormous arse within tight Adidas in imaginary tropical places.

Her captions were succinct, motivational, and always on point. *Vice* once even wrote an article on her 'expressive, personalised aesthetic, one that provokes nostalgia for, not exactly something that ever has existed, but rather something that has to have existed'. I never knew what that meant, but I do know that in bars lads would come up to me, shake my hand and buy me pints.

When Aoife's boyfriend got with Khadija my sister lost a load of weight, dyed her hair green, changed her name from Aoife to Aaliyah, got a tongue piercing, transitioned her way through seven different genders in quick succession, and when none of this made her happy she saved up a load of money and used it to fuck up her face with permanent contouring.

She looks like a slasher film now, and whenever I do say anything at all she accuses me of perpetuating normative patriarchal rape culture and cis-desire. I don't know what this means either, since I've never raped anyone and the only culture I really like is hip hop, but it is wrong to be mean to people so I never even mention that she is the absolute spit of the clown from that Stephen King clown film.

After the contouring, she seemed to be getting better and her self-care programme seemed to be complete, but then her ex, jelly of her constant presence on the Gram, WhatsApped his garda-crew with one of the home videos they had made together.

In the short video he shared my sister had transformed herself in blackface for him, on his request, and gone down on him after he had cuffed her to a heater and used his standard issue baton as a dildo. It was normal kinky, but obviously it got itself up online. All rivers lead to the sea, and all home videos lead to the cloud, which I thought I had made clear to her – as was my sacred duty as her older brother, but the call of the lens is too strong in young ones, and soon the leakage viralled fairly hard.

The whole sex tape thing only lasted a week because it was a fairly grainy video, but thanks to the blackface she turned into a meme that lasted for at least a month, and, to be fair, the meme was one of the better ones. Even mam found it funny, and she doesn't usually find online stuff funny at all.

But then rakes of neckbeard bitches started leaving comments on her Instagram because her ex was black, detailing the different ways they'd gang-rape her and how they'd snip at her labia with scissors, and how they'd wear her skin on their faces for cucking her own kind, and they'd just go on and on about how they'd fill her vagina with different sharp implements and different kinds of insects. Shortly afterwards the Tumblr bitches got at her. Now neckbeard bitches move on to new prey, but a Tumblr bitch never forgets. They compared her blackface to all sorts of genocide, and said that this flaunting of privilege had to be punished, and they organised a petition to ban her from Instagram. This petition, propelled by a few celebrity endorsement, eventually reached a million signatures, and it was very hard on Aoife/Aaliyah, who would have always self-identified as a fluid, albeit imagistic and moon-based, Tumblr bitch. She tried apologising for the suffering she had caused, but then they wanted her to apologise for loads of other things as well, like she really meant it, and she ended up apologising eight or nine separate times, but every time she did it got worse.

Meanwhile I was going crazy over all this, because she was my little sister and she is really sound and funny no matter what a bunch of retards say. So I thought about planning a drone strike on some of the neckbeards' houses, and I even hacked some of the commenters' IP addresses and triangulated them to their addresses, but I knew Tupac's sensors would shut down past the city limits, and I'd lose my job, if not worse, and then Aaliyah and mam would be well and truly fucked. When I gave up this idea, I tried to purchase a hunting knife online to shank her ex with, but even this delivery was intercepted before it reached me, which was probably for the best, given he was a guard and all.

Everything was all so pointless, and my anger had nowhere to go except inside myself, so I told Aoife/Aaliyah about my thwarted plans, thinking they'd make her feel loved, and she just said:

That's a pretty typical crisis of displaced masculinity you have going on there, bro.

And I suppose she was right, because I was just being selfish with all my spazzing out. At the time she was at her wrists a good bit, and I suppose I wasn't really helping her out much by planning intricate drone strikes.

It all came to an end the day she shut down her Instagram and stopped moving. That morning mam stayed sober for a few hours so she could have the chats with her.

Now I know a thing or two about trying to take your own life, mam said to her, and I can testify that weak bitches commit suicide, but strong bitches stay in the house. Here you can dose up on Valium, have a drink and a smoke. No bother. It's kind of low-energy pleasure all the time. And I recommend it because this self-harming has to stop, and so quick on the heels of your attention-seeking anorexia. If you're looking for attention, suicide's not the ticket. Either you do a good suicide and you're gone-gone, or you do a failed suicide, and that's just like failing at failing, which is really pathetic. No one actually cares about cries for help. Look at me. Do you not think I haven't been crying for help my whole life?

You're coming on a bit strong, mam, Aoife/Aaliyah said.

Whatever. Some faggot blue shirt broke your heart and abused you. Never heard that one before. Fuck are you doing giving any man anything on you, anyway?

Aoife/Aaliyah looked away, beginning to cry, but her contouring was so pronounced the tears formed little pools under her eyes, never dripping down.

You don't understand, she said. I still love him.

You do in your hole. No daughter of mine is falling in love with a guard. You made a racist sex tape and became a meme, mam said, growing exasperated. Big deal. You fucked up, now take your spanking. It's happened to far better women.

She pushed an unlit blunt into Ali/Aaliyah's face.

Get faded, mam said. Nothing else is going to happen. We're not those people.

Aoife/Aaliyah pushed away the blunt.

I'm not a crusty, mam, she said. That's not me. I amn't those people.

So she hooked herself up to her VR instead and has been there ever since. Her avatar is Australian aboriginal and she lives in a desert, where all she can do is walk around and trade things with other avatars. We don't have the money to update her too much so she only has an emotional palette of three emoticons, kind of like her contoured face, but I'm sure she's happy with how few feelings she has given what she's been through.

I don't know too much about her life though, because I am too tired after work, and she doesn't really talk much anymore, anyway, even when the regs force her offline. Mam and me just change her bedpan and hook up her nourishment IVs every now and again.

There are corners of the internet, she says every time she's about to log in, where no one knows you have a racist sex tape.

Let's go out after work, I say to Khadija before I leave. Few shrooms, look at the sunrise. Like a proper date, kind of, for once.

I have two bfs already, she says, swerving SlayQueen down through a car park, adroitly dropping grams on a circle of homeless lads gathered round a bonfire, so I already have enough bitches in my life. I do like you though, Tiernán, but I just keep offering you boss opportunities, and you just keep licking hole.

Well, why can't I just be the nice stable, boring one, I say, and you can be the boss?

You are a little cutie, she says, flashing her grill at me again. Sometimes I just want to bite your cheeks off. But seriously, not interested. All caps. Respect the boundaries I set. It's too embarrassing for you, like. Like, I'm genuinely mortified on your behalf.

Well, can we still at least have sex all the time? I ask.

Of course, she says. Why would you even ask me that?

I am convinced that whatever rake of fetishes me and Aoife/ Aaliyah have are down to mam being so strange. Mam is under the impression that she's black, but she's not. She's just Latin, but she's always talking about how she could pass for white, as though it were some kind of achievement.

When I was younger she had me and Aoife/Aaliyah

114

convinced we were black also, and whenever I'd disobey her as a child she'd start crying and accuse me of acting light-skinned or say something like: I see the Celtic purity of the household must be maintained at all costs. It took me years to realise I was white, and I still can't fully explain how the discovery of my whiteness felt, because I didn't really have anything to compare it to.

I'm not sure why mam thinks she's black, but it could have had something to do with being a foreigner in Westmeath, or it could be over the politics she used to have. She had been a good woman in her youth, but now she's just a full-on degenerate. She's from an enormous slum city outside Bogotá, and had been fired from every job she ever had on some communist, anti-imperialist shit. She used to get into a job, stir up a storm and have all the workers going mental for a while, and then the undercovers would try to kill her and she'd have to move country. When her whole cell had been finally liquidated she came to Ireland and that broke her more than all of her friends being killed by the CIA.

I do understand why she's lost the plot, though. You can't lose your whole life and watch everything you believe in get killed and stay the same. You can't lose forever and keep the same beliefs. So eventually she put down the big books she used to read and started talking about globalists, Jews, Freemasons, the deep state, vaccines, the New World Order and chemtrails. The thing, though, was that half the shite she said was smarter than anything I'd ever heard in my whole life, far better than anything any posh one could come up with, and the other half was more retarded than anything that has ever existed since the beginning of the universe.

You don't need knowledge or learning, she'd always say to me whenever she was fully hammered. The only thing you've ever got to remember is that if you're any good, they kill you. The only reason I'm alive is because I was slightly shit and no one ever really liked me enough to make me a leader, or consider me a real threat. Mediocrity is an encouraged blessing, and if you're exceptional but don't buy into them, you're gone-gone.

My real problem with mam, though, wasn't how mental she was, but that her newfound beliefs meant she went from doing all that communist stuff, which meant she had to get a job to engage workers, to spending all day listening to podcasts, sitting on discussion forums, drinking beer, getting lush, growing old and being hopeless, her mind disintegrating in the imaginary shadows it projected onto everything.

I cycle home in the rain and when I get in the house mam is sprawled out across the couch, all fucked up and moaning.

You've been at my mushrooms, haven't you? I say

She doesn't answer.

I cannot believe this.

Leave her alone, Aoife/Aaliyah says from her station. Don't wreck her trip. You're always wrecking our trips.

Wrecking them with reality more like, I say. Sick of this shit.

Would you ever stop your incessant whinging, mam says out of her fog.

Who is it pays the rent? I say. Who is it pays for the steroids, and the updates? Who is it pays for all the food and the potions ye guzzle on? All ye fucking peasants should be calling me daddy. Do I get no respect?

Whatever, Aoife/Aaliyah says. Like mam says, you can talk the talk but your daddy is the EU.

She reverses her wheelchair to the side so she looks even cooler when the burn sets in.

You're on some dosage of propaganda, I say.

There's some anti-inflammatory in the bathroom if you want to treat that third-degree, she says, and it's true that she does look very cool with her profile to the side.

My sister has not moved from her VR station for nine months, and her muscles have degenerated and her bones have become brittle. She's on a heavy programme of steroids, but these will never be enough to reverse the muscle atrophy if she doesn't move. Four months ago, after a lot of useless coaxing, I unplugged her and forced her to take a walk around the kitchen. She got a panic attack and fainted. When she woke up, the panic attack began again, and that one lasted for two days.

Once I've given Aoife/Aaliyah her shots, I bathe her.

Why don't you just find a nice boy in your game that you can ride? I say. Wouldn't that be nice?

T, she says, you know I love you, but you're holistically retarded.

Yeah, whatever, I say, sponging her hair. I'm not well, so I can't think properly. I keep seeing things. I need a break.

I put on her neck brace.

You poor creature, she tuts. Do you not think there's a few things I wouldn't rather be doing at the age of twenty than getting sponge baths from my holistically retarded big brother?

Fair enough.

I carry her onto the toilet and let her do her business.

How's Khadija? she says, as I'm blow drying her hair. Will you ever bring her home for a visit? Or are you too embarrassed by us?

Lol, I say. I wish it was that simple. But yes, you also do embarrass me.

Maybe if you were less of a pussy she'd be attracted to you.

Does that really work?

Nah, she says. It's just based on what kind of bacteria is in your body and if your pheromones match up. All the other things they say about love are just there to sell product. If you don't have it, you don't have it. And don't be worrying about this Khadija one too much, anyway. There isn't much you can get up to in the world that you haven't wanked to on the screen already.

Damn, girl.

You have me, though. Amn't I enough for you? she says, and then she laughs in my face.

She's full of darkness, this child. I dress her and carry her back to her station.

You know you're not the only one who's seeing things, she says, as I'm putting her goggles on. I get glitches too, but mine are backwards. I get imprints of my real life when I'm online, like my real life is the dream.

I look down at her for a moment. The contouring makes her look like she's suffering from a permanent nightmare. Whatever fear was inside her is now her face. This face is new and will stay new forever, while the rest of her degenerates. Her neck and arms have become so tiny and wrinkled that she looks like a doll made of flesh, one of those ones that have their heads half the size of their body. One day she will disappear and her face will be all that's left.

I love you, I say.

Hook me up, macho man, she says.

Khadija also has a fucked up family. Her little sister, Aminat, falls asleep all the time, and she can't concentrate on anything. She's only five and she's already got scars on her face that she'll have to get surgery to remove. There is a constant swelling on her forehead that never goes down from where she bashes her head against the wall whenever she gets a pain in her stomach. Khadija brought her into work one day and I played with her for a while. The child wouldn't stop laughing at how stupid I was and I think Khadija liked that and that's why she puts up with me as much as she does.

Nobody knows what's wrong with Aminat. Half this country is sick and the other half is left taking care of them. Some people say it was brought on by the lead pipes. Some people say it's the food. Some say it's the vaccines. Some say that when the permafrost melted it released airborne diseases that had been trapped in the ice for billions of years. The tendency to sickness is slightly more prevalent in mixed-race children like Aminat, which mam has an absolute field day over. I used to think it was always this way, but mam says it wasn't.

Get people sick and you control them, she said once. You'd do anything for a family member that's sick.

You don't, I said.

Lol, she said. You can't help anyone because you don't even own your own self, so they can do whatever the fuck they want with you.

Don't pretend you know who you are, I said. And you know there's one thing you've never let on? You've never told me who they are, the ones that do all this.

Laugh at me all you like, she replied. You'll be the same as me one day.

And I suppose I will. She fucked me up enough. Khadija's a bit like me too, though. She's also the only earner in her family. But, unlike me, she doesn't ever talk about her family. It's like they're too real to talk about.

Mam's asleep on the couch, twitching, having her own private nightmare. I don't want to talk to her, but she looks cold so I go to the hot press and get a blanket and throw it over her. She turns on her side.

You know they sterilised every single Mapuche woman that went through the public health service for twenty years, she says to me, her eyes still closed.

I wish they fucking sterilised you, I say. Besides, you told me that five hundred times already.

Ease up, comrade, she says, sitting up and blinking slowly. You've gone very cruel since you started that new job.

Sick of carrying you is all. You're healthy, but you may as well be dead.

She picks up a half-finished bottle of beer from the floor and swirls it around, bringing up its froth.

There's a coding job going in Athlone, you know, I say. It's only temp work. You wouldn't have to commit to it for too long.

I'm not working for that scum, she says, taking a sip of her beer.

Her teeth are grey. You can almost see through them. The glass of the bottle clinks off one of her incisors. I can't even look at her anymore without feeling disgust.

Suit yourself, I say.

When I was young I wanted to be just like her, and I think this made her happy somehow, in some way I can't understand. Then, when I was nine or ten, something in her went, but I don't remember what it was that she lost, so now there's no way into her.

You used to be cool, I say.

No, I wasn't, she says. I just used tell you bullshit stories and you were stupid enough to believe them.

I was a child.

Still are.

She takes another sip of beer.

See you tomorrow night, yeah? I say.

She doesn't answer me. I put on my coat and leave.

When I get back to work we're out of the glitch and Khadija's not in her booth anymore. I don't think anything of it, because maybe she had to go back to Aminat, but after two hours I put Tupac on standby and facetime the gaffer.

I need a subtag. The wrist's going.

You ratting on your tag now? the gaffer says.

I switch screens, but he doesn't have his cam on, so I can't see his face. The screen in front of me is black.

Just hook me up with someone in the other plant, I say. She'll be back in a bit.

No, he says. She won't.

When's she back?

The third drone came back online before hers did.

So?

She's gone, he says.

Gone?

Gone-gone, he says. We need to have some integrity for this whole thing to work.

Tupac's sensor goes off. A colony of seagulls are circling him, challenging him. I rise him above them to assert his dominance. This high up, through his POV, I can see a life raft emerge from the darkness of the night. It is a faint blur, a small spot amongst the big waves. I zoom in on the faces of the migrants, and then I glitch and the screen becomes real and all their faces are full of a terrifying clarity, their mouths are snarling with the cold and their eyes are bloodshot from the salt on the wind.

Are you even fucking real? I ask the gaffer. I want to know who you are.

There is silence for a moment. Then the radar beeps, locking in on the raft, charting Tupac's trajectory towards it. I blink behind my goggles and the screen is a cartoon again.

I don't respect you enough to prove my humanity to you, he eventually says.

Sometimes I have this dream where I'm swimming in the ocean at night, and I can't see land anymore. The waves are big and rolling, but they move so slowly that it seems like they're trying to protect me. They wash over my head, calming me. My body is numb with the cold and I know that I'll drown soon, but I don't care because I'm free. I am just floating on my back, looking at the stars, and they feel very far away. The waves carry me further and further into nowhere. The ocean is empty. There are no fish, no life. There is nothing. I am drifting, alone. Everything seems to have no end, and I'm just waiting to die, and I'm happy.

This dream will go on forever.

The next day I am in work the gaffer facetimes me. He is using a voice mapper that refits stock from the recorded conversations me and Khadija have had, so whenever he speaks it is in Khadija's voice.

Whenever you fall asleep I'm going to wake you with this voice, he says.

He does this to taunt me, but I thank him.

THE BOOK OF NEW WORDS

ELUNED GRAMICH

At the airport, Mareike doesn't look back at her parents. She's anxious to get on after all the planning and dreaming and leave-taking. No farewell lunch, not really, apart from a sandwich Vati foists on her in the car. Mutti kisses her goodbye again and again.

Pass auf dich auf. Take care *kleine*, she says.

No one cries. Only later that day, on skype, Vati describes how he took over the wheel so that her mother could sit in the back and stare out of the window; he describes how strange it was to lay the dinner table for two instead of three, the quiet before bed. Mareike bites her lip. She doesn't like these sad stories from her family. It spoils things. After all, she is in England.

Uncle Sepp and his English wife, Jane, greet her at arrivals. They're wearing mostly beige. Uncle Sepp squeezes her hand and her aunt gives her a packet of crisps.

Are they supposed to be like that? Mareike asks when she tries one, lips smarting from the vinegar.

What, don't you like them?

Oh I do. Very much. Thank you.

Their house is small and welded onto several other houses and Mareike thinks, oh *gott*, how will I live being so near to other people? But then there is a garden. A slip of perfectly stratified and flowered earth with a swing that she and her aunt sit on, rocking gently through the afternoon, the sound of English chat drifting over the fence.

It is genteel. She thinks: Opa would have liked it. She can picture him bending over the fuschias, watering hose in hand, humming to himself.

Dinner is at five-thirty. Lunch at twelve. She learns that bread must be put in a toaster before it can be eaten. Meat must be accompanied by pickled condiments. Biscuits are not cookies and are to be dunked in tea at two hour intervals. The answer to *do you want a biscuit?* is yes. Always yes. Tea, yes. Seconds, yes. The food is bad but isn't that just, she thinks, the quintessential English experience?

Even in those first, tender days she learns so much. It's an adventure, hearing the funny way English people actually use the classroom words. If her aunt wants something, she says *I fancy*, which Mareike doesn't understand until Jane says it enough times for the word to make sense.

In her new pocket vocabulary book, she writes:

I fancy a hobnob = I desire a chocolate biscuit.

Uncle Sepp rarely talks: he prefers reading and tussling with the piano in the front room (he hasn't got as far as actual melodies yet). Retirement is full of activities he'd wished for earlier in life. Mareike spends her first days in their terraced house (*terraced = stucktogether*) being inducted into the weekly shop, compost bins, the system of used/non-used bathroom towels etc. They never had children for reasons Mareike cannot understand and is forbidden to ask about.

For her book:

pull your socks up = sit straight and/or do something sensible like ironing

treat yourself = sit on sofa and watch reality television while eating biscuit

The school – the reason she is here - does not disappoint. It's as grand as the pictures online: the squat cousin of a gothic cathedral, with spires and animal sculptures and weeping saints along the eaves. An enormous arched gate juts out of it like a fighter's chin. The lawn is not to be touched. (The sign *keepoffthegrass* excites her. So English!) There are many buildings – blocks, they are called – housing this or that subject. Some are made of brick, others glass or stone, so that it feels more like a town, with its separate districts and communities, than any school she has known.

This is where you'll be, says the teacher giving the tour. Year seven.

He gestures at a concrete wing, which glowers like a north German flak tower: thick-walled, suffocating.

Shall we go in? he asks.

She nods. She is, suddenly, a little afraid. But her fears are dispelled as soon as they enter the classroom.

This, he says, is yours.

All is forgiven. Her own desk! One she can open up, hide things in. She pictures her textbooks all in a row, her pencil case fitting snugly in the corner, the notebooks she plans to adorn with stickers and cartoons. She runs her hand along the surface while the teacher-guide talks on and on.

For the school, she must take a test.

For the school, she must wear a uniform.

For the school, she must get a bus every morning at seven forty eight am.

Also, she must label every personal possession with her full name: Mareike Dünschede.

She listens obediently. Yes, she thinks. Yes! Finally something is happening.

You see: it's boring in Gifhorn where she comes from. Backward. In the winter, there's nothing to do. In the summer, the Dünschedes while away their weekends at endless barbecues in neighbours' gardens. Vati prods the meat while Mutti boasts lightly about her only daughter.

Her mother spent four weeks in Brighton when she was sixteen. Since then, she takes milk in her Friesian black tea; sleeps on a Union Jack pillowcase; orders shortbread on Amazon. The English, she claims, are the friendliest people in the world. They're not straight-laced and boring like the people in Gifhorn. Mutti also mentioned that there would be black people at the school. *Multi-kulti,* she said. You can learn something, Mareike. Make friends with people from other backgrounds. In Gifhorn there is no one interesting. Everyone in Gifhorn comes from Gifhorn.

But Mutti, it seems, was wrong. There are no black people at this school, neither are there children from other backgrounds. In fact, there are only very few children who are not white and English. There are very few girls, too. Five girls to twenty boys in a class. The prospectus promised something quite different.

It used to be a boys' boarding school, the tour-guide-teacher explains. They changed the policy last year.

That's nice of them, says Mareike.

Girls or boys, for the school, they are all customers. An education here does not come cheap. It is Opa's money that pays for her flight, the fees, her hockey stick, the lot. He died last winter (pneumonia) and it was his wish that Mareike go to England, because everyone must speak English. Her Opa did not have the knack with languages, only going so far as learning a few words of Russian when it was needed on the eastern front.

Sometimes, when she is cycling to Aldi, say, or her swimming club, she sees him, leaning against a tree or sitting at the S-Bahn:

skinny, bespectacled, bald, watching the world go by.

*

The first day of term. It's the happiest, most frightening day of her life so far. On this day they must sit behind their desks and wait for the teachers to come in, one by one, and write their name on the board, which they are obliged to copy onto the cover of their exercise books in neat. She is thrilled by the initial *Mr* – demure, sophisticated. No longer the cumbersome *Herr* for her! The teachers are mostly men: young, old, fat, thin. The register is called. The geography teacher with a wart on his chin has left his reading glasses in the staff room. *No matter, no matter,* he says, like out of a black and white film, and perseveres, holding the list close to his face.

Charles, he calls.

Here, Sir.

Derek, he calls.

Here, Sir.

Oscar, he calls.

Here, Sir.

Marcus, he says.

No one answers.

Marcus.

Again, no one.

Marcus? Isn't there anyone here by the name of Marcus?

The sniggering begins near the front, then creeps to the back where she sits.

Oh, right, she thinks. He means me.

She is forced to correct him. Her voice is very, very quiet. She has never heard her voice like this before. It's hardly coming out of her mouth at all. The teacher must lean over his desk to make out her words. The teacher with the wart is apologetic but not, in the end, overly bothered by his mistake. He regards them as miniature adults; believes it doesn't matter, a mispronunciation here and there. He doesn't understand the damage he has inflicted. What Mareike must live with now.

Marcus! What are you doing hanging around inside at break don't you have any friends, *Marcus,*

give me your rubber

give me your pencil case, *Marcus,* what's with your bag, why's it so massive, why're you so massive, *Marcus*

hit the ball if you can, fucking hell, try to *catch* the ball, *Marcus*

are you dyslexic, can you actually talk normally, *Marcus,* only I can't understand a word you're saying?

On the second day, the Chinese boy next to her has advice:

You should change your name, he says.

To what?

Something easier. Your name is too long.

He is serious; speaks to her conspiratorially, like he's cheating on a test. You see: he himself has changed his name Qiang Li to John. It's worked out well; in fact, she hasn't heard a single person make fun of him yet.

Isn't Mareike already short enough for a name?

Do you think? Mary's good. Why not go for Mary?

Well, she says. Alright.

A Welsh girl gets wind of it and comes over to her when she's pretending to play netball but really standing at the edge of the court, avoiding everyone.

They can't say my name either, the Welsh girl confides.

Why? What's yours?

Llinos, she says. It's a ll sound.

A *ll* sound.

No, says the Welsh girl sadly. Not quite.

Soon, she has all the teachers calling her Mary. They are relieved; they need not bother remembering that other, thorny name. The teachers first, then her classmates, and suddenly there she is: a Mary. A real one. They are calling her Mary and she is turning her head to Mary and running after Marys: it's fine. She likes it. She fancies people are more welcoming now, letting her join in, directing questions at her. Apart from those who still insist on -

Marcus, can you even hear me up there

Marcus, what are you eating, did they put drugs in your baby feed?

Marcus, what's, like, wrong with your voice, can you even speak English?

All that. That carries on in the background. But it's not as bad as some people get it. There's another girl, not tall like her but broad. The boys say she's fat and the girls say she has nits. So. There's always someone worse off, isn't there?

It *would* be nice if she were more normal in size, say five foot four, that's a good number, and also if she wasn't quite so incomprehensible to others. At break time, she tries to start a conversation with a not-so-popular girl with funny teeth. Mareike ends up pouring her heart out by accident - vomiting it up, more like, that's why they call it home*sickness*, because it comes out of you when you least want it to - she goes on about Gifhorn, Fanta mixed with coke, school finishing at one pm, playgrounds with properly functioning see-saws. At the end of her speech the girl looks faintly embarrassed, says nothing, because she hasn't understood a single word Mareike has said.

She writes in her book:

I must remember to speak slowly.

I must replicate the speech of my classmates as perfectly as possible.

I must forget the insufficient pseudo-English of my primary school.

A boy shouts Minging Mary at her at the bus stop. She looks it up in the library but it's not in the dictionary, so she Googles it on John's phone.

Oh, she says, wishing she hadn't.

Still. She adds it to the book of new words.

*

Twelve thirty and Mareike/Mary is sitting alone in the canteen. There were girls from her class next to her a moment ago only now they have finished their food and are gone.

Oops, she thinks. Failed again.

There's something wrong with her, but she can't put her finger on it. She can't do it; can't quite read other people. What do the girls mean when they say *maybe*? I will see you *maybe*. I will add you on Facebook *maybe*. Why do they sometimes chat to her and yet, at other times, act as if she doesn't exist? Why does a smile from them sometimes smart like a cut? There are meanings underneath the meanings she has written for herself in the book of new words. What does it mean, for example, when they say *I'm starving* but then don't eat anything? What does it mean when they say *I'll definitely be there* and then don't turn up?

She speaks their language and yet at the same time she cannot speak it.

Opa is sitting at her table. He's wearing his gardening clothes, a pair of brown overalls and a sun hat. He looks round the hall, taking in the nineteenth century pomp.

Very impressive, he says. Do you eat lunch here every day?

Yep.

By yourself?

This was your idea, she says, annoyed. Sending me here. Your fault.

It's good for you. It'll make you stronger, you'll see.

Will it?

Personally, I always preferred eating alone. You can digest your food better when you don't have to talk.

She lays down her fork, says: I miss you.

So I heard.

Can you stay here for a bit?

I would, he sighs, if I didn't have flower borders that need tidying.

But you'll be back soon?

He peers at her through his old-fashioned aviators. I expect so, he says.

She takes the tray to the window and thanks the dinner lady who snatches it away, muttering, *what a waste*.

She looks back, but there's no one left at the table.

serving hatch = a hole in the wall for half-eaten lunch

losing your marbles = talking to your ninety-year-old grandfather who is dead

Secretly, she's counting down the days until Christmas and, at the same time, pretending not to be counting down. Because now that she's arrived in the place she'd always wanted to be, she can't admit that it's not what she'd hoped for. When asked how things are during the weekly Skype call, Mareike/Mary says everything is nice. The people are nice; the teachers are nice; her aunt and uncle are nice; the weather is, well, so-so. She assigns herself friends; that is, people who could be her friends, theoretically.

We're proud of you, her parents say. For being so brave.

November. The not-so-popular friend she's made, Olivia – plump, braces as big as ten-pee coins – appears before her at break, wearing a red pin and eating chocolate.

What's that? Mareike/Mary asks.

Club bar, she says.

No, what you're wearing. That badge thing.

Poppy.

Oh right. (Another entry for her book).

Don't you know what a poppy is?

Course I do, she says. Can I have some?

Get your own, Olivia says, licking the wrapper.

At the tuck shop (soon to be discontinued for health reasons), she spots more of these red badges. It doesn't matter to her at the time: she hardly notices it as she hands over the change for a pack of citrus polos she'll suck on all through double chemistry, but she'll look back at this moment later, at this proliferation of red badges popping out of unwashed school jumpers and teachers' lapels, and wonder how blind she'd been, how comfortably ignorant.

Friday. Assembly. They're marched into the Great Hall (it's called that because it's massive and there are black beams criss-crossing the ceiling and a throne and a big old bible). The deputy head makes a speech, then the headmaster makes a speech and then, naturally, the head of history makes a speech. He's quite nice, the history teacher, she likes him, his pleasing, unthreatening sleeveless jumpers, his timid smile that comes and goes as if reserved just for her. He gets up on the lectern in his suit and tie and poppy and they must all be quiet. Quiet because of history. Quiet because of barbed wire. Mud. Poets. Young men. Generations. Quiet because a man was crucified on a Norman shed wall. Quiet because of the blinding terror of it.

People died on both sides, he says. Well, of course? She thinks nervously. Of course they did? Why point it out?

Afterwards there's singing. (She doesn't know the tune; does her best to mime). She fails to make out the words in the unified drone.

> *rage shall not really them*
> *nor the hairs haunt them*
> *we will november them*

A boy from the upper sixth plays a golden trumpet. His eyes glide across the sea of students before resting on her.

Her heart stops.

He looks away.

The red badges flash. Her face burns with shame: she does not have a red badge. What must this beautiful boy think of her? She must buy one. She must get one straight away, or is it too late?

Mary/Mareike goes to the toilets and sits on the seat and puts her head glumly in her hands but doesn't cry in the end; she's not a weeper. The desire to sob leaves and a worse feeling takes its place. She carries it around with her like sharp stones, like the links of Olivia's metal braces, rubbing and cutting away where no one can see.

For the book: *mustard gas, pal's battalions, last post, shell-shocked.*

She remembers Vati saying – don't mention his name, just say 'H' if you must. But she never needed to say H instead of Hitler at home. In England, though, she hears his name every day – on the news, in the papers, in songs. Also, the word 'nazi' which she only ever heard on the TV in Germany, but here, it seems, you can just throw it around anywhere, at anyone.

English people are unafraid.

There are two rules about the nazi thing. The first is obvious: she is German and therefore a nazi. The second is more complicated. She can't say she's not a nazi, because this means she has no sense of humour. And she has no sense of humour because she is a nazi. So: that's the second rule.

It's the boys who call her 'nazi', but she doesn't hate them for it. She knows they're in pain, these boys, sees their desperation to be near to power. Yet power is out of reach for them, spindly, knock-kneed and spotty as they are. She fears the serious questions more, the arrogant wheedlers who take the time to sit with her in class, forming a semi-circle around her desk, demanding, *Tell us a joke.* And then, when she does, they look at her stonily and say: *that wasn't funny.*

Why did you choose to call yourself Mary? they ask. Are you embarrassed?

Yes, she thinks. No, she says.

Why not Mareike?

I don't know.

You've got to get a backbone, they say.

I had one, she thinks. But you broke it.

It doesn't stop there. The history teacher gives them an assignment for the Christmas holidays: they must ask their grandparents what they did in the war. She goes home to Sepp and Jane. At dinner, she watches her uncle spoon clear soup into his mouth and chew the rind of a baguette and cough when he eats too fast and all the time she says nothing, asks him nothing. She cannot, cannot bring herself to ask about the war, because what if, what if the answer wasn't the right – what then?

Everything will be better in Gifhorn. Everything will fall into place, she thinks, but it is not to be. On Holy Evening, after they have dutifully gone to the church down the road to sing *leise rieselt der schnee*, and after her parents have opened the white wine and turned the heating up and settled down on the sofa in front of the TV where they are showing *Home Alone*, they ask:

Mareike, can you understand it, every word?

She nods.

Vati shakes his head in disbelief: well, well, well, Mareike, look at you! You've grown. You're an adult now. That school has done wonders.

And she hears herself agreeing, hears herself tell them about the Great Hall, the Latin songs, the black teaching robes. When she talks to Auntie Jane in English on the phone, her Mutti is near tears.

How you've come on, she says, kissing her.

This girl, Mary, has astounded them.

Mary is a good and eager student and so, again, she attempts the history assignment. She rifles through Opa's things, the boxes in the spare room her father hasn't yet cleared away. Old photographs, some of which she's seen before at one time or another. Here is Opa beside the tram station in Königsberg; here he is with his university classmates; here he is in his army uniform at twenty-one. Not in the familiar grey of the Wehrmacht, but in darker colours. Didn't she already know that from somewhere? From long ago, didn't Vati mention, or Opa himself explain ... ? Her hands are trembling. She puts it away. There is nothing you can do with stuff like that. Vati says it belongs in an archive.

She kicks the box under the spare bed.

What is all this? she asks him. Is this what you left me?

Winter. Mary stops speaking for an entire day. The day Olivia is ill. The only time she opens her mouth is to apologise for accidentally nudging someone's foot. Olivia is ill for a second day. The history teacher holds her back after history class.

I notice you're very quiet today, Mary. Is everything alright?

In a moment of madness, she considers answering in German, but it passes, thank God.

He continues: You can tell me, you know, if there's something upsetting you?

She wishes there were so she could tell him – a dying relative, a buried pet, but it's nothing like that, whatever it is.

Remember life isn't all work and no games. Treat yourself. Go easy, he says.

treat yourself = sit in front of the television and eat biscuits
go easy = smile, relax, pretend the world is on your side

He pities her. Good. This means she will not have to do the assignment. She made it up anyway: her grandfather was not a soldier, she lied, but a farm boy – too young for the war. Her grandmother was a housewife. They experienced nothing but the standard privations of war: noisy nights, difficulty getting hold of leather goods, that sort of thing. She wishes she could write, like Olivia, my grandfather was in the RAF. But there we are.

Opa is waiting for her by the school gates, wrapped up in a raincoat.

I want you to know I didn't say anything. I didn't tell them the truth.

Opa says: Planted the tulips yesterday. About fifty bulbs.

Opa, listen. I saw the pictures.

What pictures?

You know.

Everyone has pictures, he says. They had to take them so there'd be something left of us if we died. A keepsake for the mantelpiece.

Were you proud? You looked proud.

I was and then I wasn't. You don't stay the same, you know. Gradually, the person you were fades away and the person you are takes its place. It happens again and again until you're too tired to change. The soil, as it were, is exhausted.

I'm exhausted, she says.

Oh dear, he says. I'm afraid you've got a long way to go.

Spring. Things should be looking up: there's the unpeeling of scarves, the tucking of gloves into pockets. A season of mild light, rainjackets, new words. *Gelbe Narzisse?* Daffodil. *Maiglöckchen?* Lily of the valley. The little book is full; her aunt buys her a new one. It is also the first time she sees a fox – a wild one – creeping under the garden swing. She tells no one, only watches it slinking about in its dirty red fur.

For her new book:

foxglove = a finger hat flower, white, purple
a stone cold fox = a glamorous woman who feels nothing
cunning as a fox, sly as a fox, crazy as a fox, trot the foxtrot

Yes, things should be looking up.

And yet. The wind here, she feels, is too strong. It chases away the clouds and rushes in new ones. The weather changes from one hour to the next, and she loses patience with it. She wants it to stay put. Everything ought to stay put. Olivia should stay put. Why is she talking to those girls, the stuffy blonde ones, the girls who don't understand her accent, who say that she sounds like a cross between Schwarzenegger and a BBC presenter?

Have you got a packed lunch? Liv asks one day.

No.

Next time, bring a packed lunch so we can sit outside with the others.

So. That's what Mary must do. Sacrifice a hot dinner for Auntie Jane's rye bread and Emmenthal door-stoppers. The sliced tomatoes bleed into the bread. No sweets or dunking breadsticks or pre-packaged cheeses for her. Her lunch comes squished in foil; the others have theirs in dinky Japanese boxes.

Olivia makes excuses for Mary's lilting mixture of Englishes.

You get used to it, she confides to her new friends. She's quite nice really.

Mary grimaces. Quite Nice Really. Tomato juice has dripped onto her shirt. A seed's got stuck between her teeth and she has to use a pencil to get rid of it, leaving a stain on her incisor.

Is that all you've got? asks Clara whose mother lets her dye her hair.

Mary looks down at the ball of soggy bread waiting to be digested. She gets up and chucks it in the bin.

I'm on a diet, she announces.

dieting = what you do when you're no longer acceptable to yourself

The girls nod appreciatively. Finally, something they understand.

The girls have a sleepover at Olivia's. No reason, only it's Saturday and that's what they do now. Her bedroom is large and covetously private, tucked away in the roof where they can't be reached by siblings or grown-ups. They lounge around on the bed and talk about everyone they know, giving them marks out of ten.

Olivia declares: For John, three marks.

Three? He's alright, isn't he? Mary says.

He smells gross.

Does he?

Like gone-off something.

But then they all do, don't they? Boys, Clara says.

Whenever they're near, the older boys, she can't see straight. Can't see their faces for their bodies. Chests thrown out, scary, commanding, like real adult men, stalking the playground in their suits, bantering with teachers like they're equals, their eyes sweeping over girls' legs, smelling of coffee, hairspray, sweat. They seem more real than the boys who jump on her desk in the morning, the twelve-year olds who get hysterical over a dead wasp on a windowsill.

Occasionally – more than occasionally – she thinks of the beautiful boy who played the trumpet. She thinks of him and doesn't know what to do with her thoughts. She can't see herself kissing him or touching him, so she just recreates his face, his expression after he'd played those few sombre notes, his downcast eyes, the shape of his mouth and nose. Painstakingly, she recreates him in her mind and then, if she sees him in the corridors or the canteen, her body jolts back into a dream, she forgets where she is, who she is, she trembles and then, when he goes, she begins the work of recreating him again.

That night, Opa appears next to her in his nightshirt, glasses off.

So are you in love now, little Mareike?

No! she says.

With that trumpet boy?

Shut up!

He laughs: don't you think he's a bit old for you?

Leave me alone! She pulls the sleeping bag over her head.

Summer. There's Mary with her troop under the trees in the single corner of green. The girls pick buttercups while the boys throw grass. Llinos has her head on Clara's ribs. Clara has her head on Olivia's stomach. Olivia has hers on Mary's thigh. Mary sits cross legged, back straight, wary.

Soon school will be over and she will be on a plane back home. The month of August opens up like an eternity, the rest of her life, insurmountable. It comes to her suddenly: the realisation that she will never be here again, never be with these girls again as they are now. The impossibility of having things stay put. Stay still, for God's sake, why can't it just stay still. Why must she go now when she's finally made it? Why must she have these thoughts now when she's happy?

She will lose Olivia because Olivia will spend her summer with Clara and Llinos and the others. She will lose the school because her English will rust and buckle underneath her German accent. She will lose Sepp and Jane because they will grow old, day by day, and will die, and she will eventually also die. And so will Olivia. And she might one day have to stand at her friend's graveside and read her name on the stone.

She breathes. And thinks: one less breath to breathe.

What's wrong?

Mary feels the vibration of her Liv's voice on her thigh.

Nothing. Don't want to go home.

Don't worry. Back before you know it, she says.

They lose her suitcase at the airport. The officials make out as if it's her fault: are you sure you checked in at the right desk? Did you put a label on it?

Mutti is there: she sorts it out.

At home, Mary faces a wardrobe full of clothes from a year ago. Too small now. Ugly, too, the bright primary school colours, the childish obsession with glitter. She wants black and grey. She wants baggy jeans and hoodies with logos she bought in the outlet with Liv. She wants, though she doesn't admit this, to be back in her school uniform.

I need a uniform for everyday. One that conceals me, one that stitches me to the rest of the world, one that stops me from asking questions every morning when I stand in front of the mirror.

She pulls her shorts back on, goes to the spare room and

shuts the door. The box is where she left it. She gets the old pictures out and stares at them for a while.

Opa has her back to her, looking out onto the garden, sun hat dangling around his neck.

There aren't as many swallows this year, he tells her. The cold winter did for them.

She waves the photographs at him: Do you need these?

No, I don't think so. Not at the moment.

I was thinking of sending them to a museum.

What about the official documents, the identity passes?

Them too. All of it.

You don't want them?

No. I'd rather forget about it if it's alright with you. I'd rather, you know, think about the future and all that. No offence.

None taken.

Opa pushes his hat over his ears. I'd better go, he says.

Will you still come and visit me now and then?

If you want, he says.

She folds the documents into an envelope and closes the box. From downstairs her mother calls: Mareike. *Mareike*. Where have you got to?

The way her mother pronounces her name sounds strange to her now. *Ma-rei-ke*. She collapses onto the bed and closes her eyes and says, I'm here, *Mutti. Ich bin hier.*

COURTYARD SMELLS

KARMELE JAIO

TRANSLATED BY KRISTIN ADDIS

The apartment complex was called Olarizu Gardens. It was on the south side of the city. Through the living room window you could see the mountains, and the kitchen balcony looked over a sort of private park. There was a garden there, some small trees, and a playground for children: swings, a red slide, and two wooden horses rocking back and forth on springs. A newly planted hedge covered the white fence that separated the private area from the outside.

It's all just like in the model, Leire thought happily on the day they moved in, looking at the white fence peeking through the hedge, and the playground.

Two years earlier, looking at the model of the apartment at the agency, Leire had been delighted with the private playground:

'We'll be able to watch them playing from the window,' she said to her husband, smiling and tilting her head slightly to one side, just as she had in her wedding picture.

She was pregnant at the time and Jon was two and in the end, having the children's playground right in the complex tipped the balance in favour of the most expensive of their options. Leire used the children again and again in her arguments to convince Txomin. She told him that when she saw the model, she felt butterflies in her stomach.

'I felt butterflies in my stomach, Txomin.'

And Txomin knew that when Leire saw something and started talking about those butterflies, she would not rest until she had what she wanted. So he didn't put up much resistance. There was little he could do in the face of the butterflies. Besides, they were in a good position to swing it, after all. Leire had a steady job as a librarian at the city library, and Txomin also earned a decent wage in insurance. They did not have much extra money, but one way or another, they'd be able to cover the mortgage.

'It's a bit more expensive, but … They'll have little friends right there, without even leaving home. And it's perfectly safe, no one from outside can get in …'

It was important to Leire that her children should make friends since she and Txomin had very little social life, their own relationships with friends having chilled long ago. When the weekend came, their son had no one to play with. Not because there were no children in the neighbourhood where they had lived until then, because with increasing numbers of immigrants, there were more children than ever there. But Leire wanted a different sort of friend for her children. Their own isolation did not worry her much; a good book was all Leire needed to get through the weekend, and Txomin was quite capable of spending the entire weekend lying on the sofa watching television, barely even blinking. She wanted her children to develop relationships, though not just any kind, but the kind they deserved.

In the new building they would have the chance to make friends, thought Leire. It would be easy with only twelve families in the complex and a private park besides. But more than that, and in addition to the feeling of protection that the white fence gave her, what attracted Leire from the first was something else: the park at the apartment complex had nothing to do with the courtyard that she had known as a child. For the courtyard at the new house was not so much a courtyard as a beautiful garden.

No clothes would hang to dry there, amid the smell of frying food like in her parent's courtyard; nowhere would there hang the clothes of factory workers, nor the large underpants of older women; never would the shrill whistle of a moving clothesline be heard, since most of the neighbours used a clothes dryer; from those windows no women in housecoats would lean out, nor men in white muscle shirts, yawning or smoking black cigarettes. It was clean, free of noises and smells. As perfect as a model.

'It's a little more expensive, but the neighbours won't be just anybody …'

And she was right. In the new apartment there were no neighbours named Omar, or Abdul, or Irasema, as there had been in her previous neighbourhood. Not even a Josefina or a Desiderio, like at her mother's house.

When Leire was little, her mother often left her at their neighbour's house when she had to run errands. Maria Angeles' terrace took up a good portion of the courtyard and Leire played there with little Miriam, amid the smell of laundry detergent and stew. But Leire always thought that she did not belong there, that she deserved better than a courtyard like that one, that she stood apart from the world of Maria Angeles' apron and slippers. And she did play with Miriam, but in the way that famous artists play with third world children they visit. Knowing that they can leave at any moment. Feeling that they do not belong there.

I am not from here.

Her mother often went to the window to talk with Maria Angeles when she was hanging out the clothes in the courtyard. They talked about recipes, or about the price of tomatoes at the market. Other times her mother went down to the courtyard saying that she had dropped a sock, and the two whispered together in Maria Angeles' doorway. Maria Angeles was very fat, and she was always making croquettes – Leire must have eaten hundreds of Maria Angeles' croquettes there in her courtyard – and she always carried something in her apron pockets: keys or clothespegs … She always said goodbye to Leire by pinching her cheeks gently, and Leire could still recall the smell of garlic on her rough hands. She also remembered Maria Angeles' house slippers, plush slippers that had once been pink. She remembered seeing Maria Angeles in street clothes and proper shoes only once, the day when Maria Angeles showed up on the doorstep with a tray of pastries to celebrate her daughter's First Communion. With her make-up on and her lips so red, she looked like a man dressed as a woman.

When her daughter grew up and left home, Maria Angeles went back to Galicia, to her parents' hometown, and a family of Romanians moved into their house. Everything had changed in the last few years in Leire's mother's neighbourhood. Only old people and immigrants still lived there now.

The new apartment was nothing like that one. Most of the neighbours in the complex had children. Leire sometimes thought that maybe all of them chose the complex because of the playground. Almost all were around forty and looked like civil servants. Almost all had two cars: a larger one that they kept in the garage and that in most cases was used by the men, and another smaller one that they parked outside, for the women. Both the men and the women worked outside the home and most of the neighbours ate lunch out, including the children, who had their lunch at school. So there were no smells of beans or fried fish at midday.

And Leire felt comfortable. She had always had issues with food smells. Even when she was a teenager, when she went home from school for lunch, she would take off her street clothes and cover her hair with a scarf so that she wouldn't return to class smelling of fried food or cauliflower. Just as some immigrants try to hide their origins, she tried to hide the smell of her house, of her courtyard, of her neighbourhood, as if her classmates would be able to see the reflection of Maria Angeles' courtyard in that odor. Or worse, as if they would be able to see it in Maria Angeles herself, dressed in her street clothes to celebrate her daughter's First Communion.

When they first moved into the apartment, Leire had had their third child two months before, and had a year of maternity leave. From the very beginning, she enjoyed the midday silence of the complex. With her five-year-old at school and her two-year-old in daycare, she often looked at the swings and the slide in the private garden while she breastfed the baby. It was still March then, but she dreamed that her children would enjoy the playground once the weather got better, playing with little blond children who smelled of cologne. It made her happy inside to think that her children would spend their childhood in the place where they belonged and with the friends they deserved. They would never have to be ashamed of anything.

Then she met Maria, who lived on the third floor. When Leire and Txomin first moved in, Maria was pregnant and, since her doctors considered her pregnancy to be high risk because of her age and because of previous miscarriages, she was put on maternity leave in her sixth month. She already had a five-year-old and after this child, had made many fruitless attempts to get pregnant again. Now, finally, she was.

At midday, then, when the complex was almost empty and once the weather was nicer, the two women often ran into each other in the garden. There were two benches there, and at first they each sat on one, Maria almost always with a book, and Leire with the baby in her arms or pushing the stroller back and forth so the baby would sleep. But little by little they began to make friends.

Maria was a professor at the university and taught 20th-century literature, and Leire was fascinated as soon as she found out. The passion she had always felt for books had led her to study library and information science. And when she was studying to become a librarian, Leire always felt that, while all the other students were learning to classify books in order to get a job in a library, her own aspirations were greater because of her love of literature. Even as a student, she was not like the rest; her studies were artistic, intellectual. It was difficult for her to enjoy literature without having a well-ordered library. Sitting with Maria in the private garden, Leire finally began to feel that she was in her proper place, talking with a woman of her own class.

At first they talked shyly about the weather, then about their children, and finally they began to talk about Proust, about Chekhov, about the review of a poetry book they had read in the Saturday supplement of the newspaper. Few people would have been able to guess just by looking at them what heights of conversation were reached by the pregnant woman and the breastfeeding one. They did not often discuss their children's diapers, or complain about how little they had slept, and this filled Leire with pride. In the afternoons, when the children came home from school, they talked about the novels of Mercé Rodoreda while they were taking sandwiches and bottles of juice out of their bags for snacks, or Ramon Saizarbitoria, whom Maria had read in Spanish since she did not know Basque. They were not like other people. Motherhood had not anesthetized their brains, as it had the brains of so many other women. The private garden defined a subset within the set of the city. An excellent place.

However, the midday silence disappeared suddenly when excavators were moved into the next lot over and began digging a big hole.

'They must be building more apartments,' said Leire to Maria, shading her eyes with her hand to see.

'They're not going to block our afternoon sun, are they?' Maria answered, raising her eyes from her book.

'I don't think they have permission to build tall apartment buildings in this area.'

'Perhaps it's a complex like our own.'

'Perhaps.'

The hole got bigger and bigger with every passing day. Often, when they took the children to the playground in the afternoon, the noise of the machines stopped them talking. Then each would take out the book she carried in her purse and they read in the sun while the children played. During those noisy times, Leire would sometimes look over at Maria out of the corner of her eye. She was truly a special woman. Swollen belly notwithstanding, she was thin and not very tall, but everything she wore looked good on her, despite her pregnancy. Her growing belly made her look more feminine, for there was something androgynous about her, not only because she wore her hair short, but also because of the way she dressed: she often wore a jacket, jeans, and tennis shoes, and when she read, she put on glasses with black plastic frames. She looked like a modern Brooklyn intellectual. Her hands were very large, with veins that stood out. When she spoke, she moved her hands up and down constantly, like an expert in a documentary. Leire imagined piles of books in Maria's house. She often imagined Maria's library. How did she have her books organized? Alphabetically? By genre? By publishing house? Fiction over here, non-fiction there?

She admired Maria.

One day, after three rainy days when she didn't go down to the garden, Leire found Maria sitting on one of the benches, distressed. Her eyes were puffy from crying. Leire didn't dare to ask her anything. By then she was in her eighth month and at first Leire thought that something might have gone wrong with the pregnancy, but that was not what had happened.

'My father died.'

'I'm sorry … really sorry.'

'He was fine. It happened so suddenly. His heart …'

'What about your mother?'

'She's devastated. We're going to bring her here.'

Maria brought her mother to her house. She did not want her to be alone, at least not right at first. When Maria told Leire she was going to bring her mother to her house, Leire imagined a wealthy, elegant woman, tall and slender, a woman who went to the hairdresser every week.

Her name was Adelina and she was a very fat woman with red cheeks. You could see the tiny red veins on her face. White hair, cut in the style worn by nuns. She walked with her legs wide apart. Her legs were covered with varicose veins, and her ankles were almost lost in all that flesh. The day Leire met her, she was wearing a loose-fitting dress in a flower print, one of those dresses that women of a certain age often wear. Leire would later find that all of Adelina's dresses were made from the same pattern. It was a shock to meet her.

From that moment on, Maria started to show up every afternoon with her mother. One fat and one in the final stages of pregnancy and unable to contain their bodies, they waddled rather than walked, rocking from side to side like boats in the harbor. They approached slowly until they sank their weight onto the bench as best they could. When at last they sat, they sighed in unison, and left their legs wide apart. Between Adelina's legs, under her dress, a dark and mysterious cave was created.

Leire was astonished at the mother-daughter relationship and above all at the transformation in Maria. Not only had she changed the way she dressed – she was almost too big to fit anything now and wore long pants that looked more like pyjamas – but also she seemed like a different person in front of her mother, who spoke to her as if she were a child. Even her voice was different when she talked to her mother; she spoke with less certainty. Her mother ordered her around endlessly.

'Take that sweater off the boy, please, he's drowning in sweat.'

'Yes, Grandma.'

She called her mother Grandma.

Grandma.

Since Maria's mother had arrived, their conversations about Cheever, about Mansfield, about literature and genre had ceased. And others took their place: tricks to remove stains, recipes for marmalade, cough remedies for children …

It had been a month since the death of Maria's father, and her mother was still there.

'You have a beautiful courtyard.'

She was comfortable. So comfortable and so much at her ease that she began to wear her house slippers down to the garden. And, even though she did not want to admit it, Leire was unable to hide her desire for that woman to disappear as soon as possible from her sight and from her private garden. She was destroying the image of the model apartment complex that she had dreamed about for so long. She was turning her beautiful garden into a courtyard.

One day Maria's mother took her grandson down to the garden on her own.

'Eight and a half pounds,' she said proudly.

'Congratulations …' Leire almost said *Congratulations, Grandma*, but she bit her tongue.

It must have been a difficult birth and while Maria was recuperating, first in the hospital and then at home, Adelina took her older grandchild down to the garden every afternoon on her own. The two women sat together on the same bench, Adelina taking up three-quarters of it. She brought down bacon sandwiches for her grandson or cut pieces of cheese for him right there on a kitchen towel that she spread over her knees. Compared with those snacks, the processed buns and bottled juices that Leire gave to her children seemed like food for astronauts. Leire often brought down a book, but every time she opened it Adelina would start talking to her, so she soon gave up.

'What the hell are they doing over there?' asked Adelina one day, still sitting, and using the towel to dry the knife with which she had just peeled an orange. 'What a racket!'

'They say it's new apartments, but I don't know for sure.'

'That's the end of your peace and quiet!'

Leire decided that she had to keep her distance from that woman, and that one way to achieve this would be to develop her relationships with the other parents in the garden. Taking advantage of the fact that her older son was about to turn five, she planned to celebrate his birthday in the garden and invite all the neighbours' children.

The day of the birthday party arrived and Leire had everything ready for the celebration. While the baby was napping, she took two folding tables down to the garden, covered them with paper tablecloths, and set out bottles of refreshments and plastic cups and plates. The sandwiches were ready in her apartment, and she had already fried the potatoes for the tortillas, so she had only to add the eggs at the last minute.

It was half past five and time for her to go upstairs to make the omelettes, but she didn't know what to do with baby on her lap. Txomin wouldn't get home until eight and she had to leave the baby with someone.

'I'll look after the kids, don't worry. They can't come to any harm here.'

Adelina made the offer and even though it was hard for her, Leire accepted. It really would help. She left the baby on Adelina's floral lap.

'It'll only take half an hour, I'll be right back.'

Leire ran up to her apartment, tied on her apron, put the pan on the fire, and started beating eggs as fast as she could. She was sweating. Once she tipped the last tortilla onto the plate, she went out onto the kitchen balcony for a bit of fresh air. And there she saw her children, eating nuts that Adelina was cracking with her bare hands. They looked like pigeons gathered around her, waiting for bits of bread. She felt each crack of the nuts in her stomach, and she felt like crying.

She closed her eyes, opened them again, and then realized that they had put up a sign at the building site across the way: 'Luxury chalets: with swimming pool, two garage spaces, and private garden.' She noticed the fence that surrounded the site. It was taller and stronger than the fence at her own complex.

'Not just anybody would be able to buy a place like that… Not just anyone would be able to get in there …' she thought with a sigh.

She went back into the kitchen, picked up a tortilla in each hand, and went out. She had to set one tortilla down on the stairs to be able to close her front door and call the elevator. In the elevator, while the tortillas warmed the palms of her hands, she started to feel a tickle in her stomach. There were the butterflies again.

'Not just anybody would be able to buy a place like that... Not just anyone would be able to get in there ...' she said to the image she saw in the elevator mirror. And, very slowly, a smile came upon her face and she tilted her head to one side, just as she had in her wedding picture.

When the elevator door opened, Leire strode decisively toward the garden, with enthusiasm, with hope, without noticing the smell of frying food she had left in the elevator.

At the Door

Eddie Matthews

He turned the radio volume up:

Blackout in Swansea neighbourhoods happened at half-five when several trees from Brynmill Park fell on power lines. Currently Brynmill, Uplands, and Sketty are without power. Residents in these areas are advised to be cautious due to the rise of looting during blackouts…

Bo's knuckles turned white gripping the steering wheel on his way back from his firm's meeting. The M4 was backed up, and he was stuck behind a teenager's nacho-cheese-coloured Volkswagen whose brake lights flashed like red goldfish. He pressed his back against the seat, fully extending his legs against the floorboards and thought about his wife home alone reading a paperback by candlelight. He called her phone and it went straight to voicemail, but he stayed on the line just to hear the Welsh lilt of her voice in the answering message, one that seemed common to most was not to him – in-person, it was Mecca, and muffled by lint-filled speakers, it was still Jerusalem, for he found in her voice what pilgrims did in those holy places. The recording ended … he dialled … began again … ended … then the sound of his windshield wipers fighting locust rain, radio host echoing in his mind: … *rise of looting* …

He shook his head. *Blackouts usually last for like 45 minutes at the most, power will probably be back when I get there. This is Wales … nothing bad happens in Wales.* He dialled again and again and again, her voice pacifying his mind each time until his phone died. He thought about how they witnessed her innie belly button swell to an outie during her third trimester and remembered her laugh when he said, 'Welcome to the club'. He thought about her favourite orange candle from Tesco. The oval one with three wooden wicks that glowed like honeymoon fire, smelled like pumpkin and cinnamon, comforted the womb, and could last all night or at least til he got home. And she'd be reading one of those lifestyle magazines to pass the time and probably find a tiny cabin with a yellow door in the Swiss Alps to live in and try to convince him to raise their child in a snowy village where they don't speak English or have smartphones and part of him would want to do it just to see her eyes light up. That's who she was. But he knew he'd reference his path to partnership at his firm and the moment would pass. That's who he was.

*

Molly broke a match against the striking surface of the box, then tried another, scraping it a few times until the phosphorus wore off, then got the third match to ignite and transferred the flame to a long-stem candle that she used to light the smaller ones that she placed around the den. Each candle demystified the dark room a little more – Welsh Lovespoons hanging on the wall, *American IV: The Man Comes Around* framed above the bookcase, turquoise rug by the fireplace, hand-me-down baby clothes folded on the sofa. She blew out her candle, feeling the wax that'd cooled down the side and set it on the coffee table, leaning over to touch her toes, and laughing when her fingers dangled inches from the floor. She settled onto the sofa, draping a quilt over her and curling against the armrest. Her phone was dead, and she tossed it on the rug then got up holding one of the candles to peruse her bookcase opposite the sofa.

The light fell across the forty book spines on one shelf dedicated to American novels. Bo hadn't noticed this and she hadn't told him. It featured the classics, Kerouac's *On the Road*, Hemingway's

The Sun Also Rises, among others. One of her girlfriends dropped off some baby clothes the prior week and noticed the shelf lacked a single female author and assumed they were all Bo's books. Molly told her they were her books, then explained how the few men that explore the truth found in one's feelings are regarded as literary geniuses, whereas women routinely sit down for a coffee and find that same truth in an hour. Reading Hemingway write about impotence helped her understand why Bo can tell her the exact blend of IPA his best friend prefers, but can't tell her one insecurity his friend has, even though it's clear from the silence between his words. Her bookmark nestled in *The Adventures of Huckleberry Finn* at the chapter where Huck chooses to go to hell rather than give up his friend, Jim, to a church-going slave-owner. She put her favourite candle with the pumpkin scent she loathed on the armrest and remembered how its low murmur, which she initially mistook for Bo's pacemaker, calmed her that first night after they'd implanted it under his skin.

She flipped a page then heard a tapping at the door, soft, like someone using the side of his hand rather than knuckles. She put the book down and looked through the sheer curtain to see headlights coming down the hill. Bo parked the car and fumbled for the handle of the glove box, opened it, and removed the torch it contained.

'Hey! What are you doing here?'

A man rested, limp-headed, against the back of the door, eyes half-closed and blood leaking near his ribs and mixing with water – the two fluids running as one through the cracks in the floorboards. The man looked up at Bo before him, black hair mopped against his forehead, raincoat torn at the wound. He cut the air with his hands and Bo backed away. The man rolled over then got to his knees, head nearly touching the ground, one hand on his torso, the other searching the floorboards for something and Bo pointed the torch down at his probing hand and saw a broken syringe and yanked his foot back as if were a coiled rattlesnake.

'Get the fuck out of here.'

Molly stood in the open door and Bo looked at her, then stepped past the man, and shut the door behind him, turning the knob and deadbolt lock. He looked at his wife, holding her face in both hands.

'Are you okay? Did he hurt you?' Bo's baritone voice cracking.

'What – what are you talking about?'

'*Shit!* This is why we carry in Arizona.'

'What?'

'There's a guy outside with a broken syringe trying to break in.'

A low sobbing came from the porch, rising with the wind.

'What, right now? Does he need help?'

'It doesn't matter.'

'What are you talking about? What'd he say to you?'

'He is not our concern, okay? Okay? You are my concern. Our child is my concern.'

'Well, he's *my* concern, I'll check on him.'

'Fuck that, no you won't. He's bleeding, You're not going anywhere near him.'

'He's bleeding? Is it bad?'

'I don't know.'

'Bo, he was probably in a car crash or something.'

'There are only two streets to get to this house, one of them is barricaded. I took the other way, there were no car wrecks.'

'This isn't like you. Are you – are you – seriously going to let a man bleed out there?'

'No, I'll wait until power comes back on so that I can charge my phone and call an ambulance.'

'We don't know when that's going to be – don't you have a charger in your car?'

'I got a new phone, the cord doesn't fit.'

The banging on the door began again in sporadic intervals. She stepped toward the door and he put his arms around her, stopping her momentum. She struggled to get free and he lowered her with him slowly to the kitchen floor, his head leaning against the fridge-freezer, hers against him. He kissed her head, burying his lips in her hair that smelled like eucalyptus.

'Why are you holding me?'

'Cologne. Germany. New Year's Eve 2015.'

'This again, Bo?'

'Four-hundred-and-ninety-two rapes in one night.'

'Those weren't *rapes*, they were sexual assaults.'

'Do the semantics really matter?'

'You're a solicitor and you're asking me if the semantics 'really matter'?'

'Four-hundred-and-ninety-two in one night. One thousand Middle-Eastern suspects.'

'What does that have to do with anything?'

'Did you see him?'

'What do you mean?'

'You know what I mean. Explain why he's carrying a syringe.'

'It doesn't matter.'

'Yes it does – look at your hand.'

She looked at the leaking scab on the side of her hand she cut while peeling potatoes the day before.

'If he has AIDS and touches your hand with his blood – '

'AIDS? Really Bo? Are you *listening* to yourself?'

She moved to get up, but he held her closer to him. She could feel his wide fingers on her back and remembered the first time they shared a bed he kissed each of her vertebra that formed the S-shape of her scoliosis-ridden backbone she'd been ashamed of until that moment.

She closed her eyes and breathed in … out …

'Remember how we first met?' she said. 'Your car broke down in the rain.'

In the candlelight, he could see her hand clumping the material of his shirt around his stomach that'd gotten a little rounder, like hers, but he lacked her alibi. The chorus outside swelled like an atonal opera.

'I remember.'

'And you knocked at the door, and I happened to be there house-sitting for a friend that night. That night it was me. And I answered the door.'

'The power wasn't out.'

'You had these blue-blue crow's feet eyes that gave you away. All sixteen stones of you standing there in a red flannel like some lost-in-time lumberjack. And you greeted me as 'madam'.'

'I was new to the UK.'

'You'd watched too much 'Downton Abbey', you had.'

The moan subdued to a whimper; the towel, duct-taped to the bottom of the door to stop water leaking, soaked red.

'And you smiled – dimples so deep they cratered your beard. And those creases on your forehead – saw those the first time, I did.'

Her husband closed his eyes.

'And I knew your heart was good. Don't give me a reason to question that, Bo. Right now, that man outside is you.'

He thought of his sister lying prostrate on a hospital bed in Tuscon, Arizona, nine years ago. Her neck, jaw, torso – red, black, blue – like a satellite image of Mars. He never asked if the intruder did more to her and she never said. The day after they brought her home to their parents' house in Nogales, he bought an AR-15 with the tip money he'd saved bartending a Mexican restaurant and moved back in with his parents to the room next to hers, close enough to hear her night terrors through the wall. She spent every night with an orthodontic head brace to correct her jawline. He drove her to and from uni for the next nine months and every time he thought about the intruder on the way back, he'd have to pull off to the side of the road until the rage passed.

He put his hand on his wife's stomach. It rested there, undulating with her breathing – the rhythm of time. Alpha… Omega. He felt the baby kick and he smiled. The quilt slipped from Molly as she turned to him, showing the blue t-shirt with short sleeves that cut off just below the shoulders he cherished. He saw her brown eyes.

'You won't touch him, okay? If we need to move him at all, I will do it,' Bo said, giving her the torch. He stood with her as she opened the door and shined the torchlight on the man sitting splayed-legged with his back against a rusty patio chair. The man focussed his eyes for a few seconds and saw her standing in the doorway and he scribbled in the air with an imaginary pencil. She walked closer. He winced and she pointed the torch at the blood leaking through his fingers that were pressed undercoat on his skin; the stranger's beard a mass of wiry grey-black hair above the collar of his khaki raincoat and blood-stained shirt.

Bo squatted to his eye-level. 'Listen to me, how did this happen?'

The man pointed to his ears and shook his head.

'Listen to me. Okay? Listen. Do you speak English?'

'We need to take to him to the hospital,' Molly said.

'No, we need him tell us what happened to him first.'

The man pointed again to his ears, shook his head, and

continued scribbling in the air. Molly went into the house, opened a drawer of mail and picked up a used manila envelope and a pen. She put the envelope down on the patio table outside and Bo pulled his sleeves over his hands and hooked his arms under the stranger's armpits, lifting him into the chair by the table. The envelope soaked up the water and tore as the man put the pen to it. She went inside once more, scanning the room until she found a cookbook. She went back to the porch and put it down in front of him with another manila envelope to write on, and he began writing, but the ink didn't come through and she realised he hadn't clicked the pen. She reached for the pen to do this for him and he grabbed her wrist.

'Hey!' Bo said and yanked her arm out of his grasp and pushed her back inside, shutting the door.

'He needs to go to the hospital.'

'What that fuck was that?'

'If someone comes to your door, you help. That's how it is here.'

'He just grabbed you, Molly. He's lucky if I don't beat the shit out of him right now. Did you see the syringe?'

'I think he was just trying to talk to me – '

'Did. You. See. The. Syringe?'

She bit her lip as the wind blew against the house, making the foundation creak.

'This is Swansea, Bo, not Nogales, okay?'

'We don't know this man – he could be dangerous.'

'He could be. And that's okay.'

Her eyebrows curved up in a way he felt must relate the truth of creation, at least in his life. He looked at his carpenter hands, while the sound of his sister's breathing ventilator thrummed his ears, then rubbed his eyes with his fingers and breathed.

'Are you absolutely sure about this?' Bo said.

'I am.'

'Fine. Don't touch him. I'll get him into the car if you hold the door open on the passenger side.'

He turned the deadbolt, the chain and knob-lock as Molly grabbed a few tea towels from the kitchen. The door opened and Bo walked to him, picking him up from the chair and carrying him to the car like a father with a napping son. Spittle dropped from his mouth onto Bo's hand. Molly opened the passenger door of the SUV and Bo grunted as he hoisted him onto the seat, grabbed the tea towels from Molly, then dropped them in the man's lap and shut the door. Molly got in the back and strapped on her seatbelt.

'Bo, you didn't put his seatbelt on.'

He looked back at her, then at the man gasping as he pressed the tea towels against his wound. Bo leaned over and stretched the seatbelt across the man's chest, pinning his hand under it. The car lights blinked on and he reversed onto the road, then drove down to the main street below, putting his indicator on as cars passed in each direction, while the stranger bled on the leather seat and the user manual in the door compartment. The seatbelt kept the towels pressed against his wound and he began signing with both hands, but Bo slapped them down.

'Stop.'

The man tried again but Bo batted them.

'Stop. Stop doing that.'

'He's deaf, can you not see that? He's speaking BSL.'

'It makes me uncomfortable.'

He kept at it and Bo relented. The man's eyes wandered around the car while his hands moved. Bo lowered the setting on the windshield wipers, sped up, and took a right down a side road that hugged a retaining wall, ivy hanging over it like squid entrails. Rocks and felled branches splintered under the tyres.

Molly sat in the backseat looking at the passenger's hands acting from muscle memory.

'Do you remember the last time we were at Heathrow?' Bo said.

'What now?'

Fist waving in a circle, two fingers in each hand tapped together, hands straight stacking on themselves up to the roof of the car;

'In London flying to Phoenix, about to board the plane. We both had to pee and I said I'd watch our bags and wait for you to get back, then you asked the guy nearest us if he'd keep an eye on our stuff while we went.'

'I don't remember that specifically, but it sounds like me.' The car came to an intersection and he put his indicator on and looked back at her.

'Concentrate on the road, Bo, there's a bleeding man in the car.'

He nodded and took a right.

Both hands to his forehead motioning out, a clenched fist, two fingers; Another clenched fist, open hand to head then bouncing before him as if shuffling cups, fists together, cracking; Circle with both hands, index fingers together, then stacking up again;

'What made you think of that?' she said.

'It's just a way you and I are different, I think. I never would've done that in a million years.'

'Why?'

'Why risk it?'

'Risk what?'

'Our luggage getting stolen.'

'To be fair, I asked the nearest bloke to keep an eye out.'

Hands up high then brought down as if removing Tupperware from a shelf, a hand coming from himself, cutting motion on an open palm;

'I know, but you didn't know him.'

'So?'

'So, why would he make sure nothing happened to it?'

'Why wouldn't he?' Molly said.

Hand to mouth, two rubbing together, pinkie out, spreading on an open palm; Pointing in, hand to mouth, two rubbing together, pointing at the windshield with index fingers, then pinkies;

'I think it'd help if you were more like me in this – especially once our baby is born.'

'What are you talking about?'

Hands forming circles away from him, then interlinked fingers; hand wiping away, a pinkie out;

'Protecting what's yours,' he said.

'You think I'm not going to protect our child, do you?'

'I didn't say that. What I mean is… you need to look out for your family above all else. It needs to be your priority, regardless of anyone else, regardless of what happens around you, you have one priority.'

'I'm doing that right now.'

Hand cupping the head, moving out, fists together then out; thumbs shimmering up an invisible ladder, a single fist out, hands open, fingers spinning like a film reel;

'You sure?'

She winced.

Tapping knuckles together.

They drove along the bay and she looked out the window at Mumbles, lights dotting the skyline to the lighthouse like flower petals to a bride; low tide made the beach extend a half-mile into the bay. The SUV slowed and stopped in the hospital car park in front of the main entrance. Molly went to get the A&E nurses and left Bo leaning against the side of the car, looking at his passenger's brown eyes through the windshield. He turned away and paced the sidewalk, rubbing the rain droplets that clung to his thick hair until she emerged from the sliding doors with three nurses. Bo opened the door and the first nurse positioned the gurney as close to the seat as possible while the other two gently unbuckled the man then guided him onto the gurney. The first nurse tried to place an oxygen mask on the man, but he was still signing, so she set it down and signed back to the man who stopped long enough to be fitted with the mask and wrapped with gauze. When they rolled him toward the hospital, he started up again, the same motions repeating like a carousel whose operator kept it spinning long after the night's last ride. Bo helped his wife into the backseat, then got in the car and moved it to a visitor's space in the corner. They sat listening to the rain hit the car roof and he looked at his wife and watched her open the door of the SUV and start walking toward the hospital slower than she was used to. He locked the car and walked with her across the car park, salt on the pavement making their steps crackle, breath turning to mist. He put his raincoat around her and she shrugged it to the ground and he picked it up and said nothing as he wiped the dirt from the sleeves.

The fluorescent-lit waiting room had three open chairs at the end of a row. He sat in the last seat and Molly sat two over. Across from them, a five-year-old boy dangled his feet off the chair, shoes flashing pink and blue with each wave. At the end of the row, a balding man in sweatpants with an oxygen tank and tubes to his nose read about the royal family in *People Magazine*. Bo looked at the carpet, an uninspired tan with black zig-zags crossing it like a heart-rate. He walked over to the coffee machine in the corner and ordered two coffees on the touch screen and waited as the cocoa-coloured streams filled little the paper cups. A woman wearing a hijab played Lego with her son on the floor next to him near the reception counter while he stirred sugar into one of the cups and walked them back to his seat.

'I got this for you.'

'I can't have caffeine, now can I?'

'It's decaf.'

'What's the point of decaf coffee?'

He set his cup down at a side table at the end of the row, walked over to the bin and tossed the other in without a lid and the liquid soaked the bin bag, running in streaks down the sides and pooling at the bottom. He watched her hand make an even circle on her blouse just above where he reasoned the baby's head was.

'What are you thinking about?' he said, sitting back down.

'Why we waited so long to do this.'

'I wanted to earlier, but you were trying to pursue – '

'What?'

'Why we waited so long to have a baby?'

'What? No. I said I was thinking about why we waited so long to bring him here.'

'You didn't say that last part.'

She moved her eyes from an Australia-shaped carpet stain to the mole on her wrist that was usually hidden under a sleeve.

'Having a baby means you have one more person in your life you can't control. You'll be exposed to suffering regardless of what you do.'

He looked at the carpet stain, cracking his knuckles out of habit. She cringed at the sound. 'I don't want to control you, honey, I want to protect you,' he said.

'Yeah but you don't have to sacrifice someone else to do that. We create the world we live in, and I'd rather raise a kid in one where someone opens the door to him when he's bleeding than one that makes him crawl to the hospital.'

The nurse who fitted the oxygen mask on the man came toward them and Molly straightened in her seat, picking up the clipboard with the document she was supposed to fill out.

'You alright?' the nurse said.

'Yes, thank you.'

'I'm sorry, I didn't catch your name,' the nurse said.

'Molly Madison. This is my husband, Bo.'

'Right. The patient is in serious condition. He suffered a haemorrhage and an incision above the pelvis.'

'Did he lose a lot of blood?' Molly said.

'Yes, about two pints, he did.'

'Is he going to be alright?'

'We don't know yet, love, it depends on if his body responds to the blood transfusion.'

The nurse told them that the man's family had been contacted. Molly thanked her and started filling out the form that documented their involvement while Bo walked to the bin and threw the second coffee in, then stood there and made a muddy smear on the linoleum floor with his boot. He remembered the syringe and waited for the nurse to come back out.

'Hiya, I wanted to tell you something about the patient we brought in earlier.'

The nurse looked at him, then at his wife filling out the form.

'You mean Mr. Davidian, do you?'

'Yes – I believe so. I just wanted to let you know that we found a syringe on him and I believe he might be intoxicated, not sure exactly with what, but I thought that would be helpful information.'

'Thank you for informing me about your concern, but he didn't test positive for any drug or alcohol substances.'

'Did he tell you how it happened?' Bo said.

'No. Just his name and the names of his family.'

'So that must have been what he was saying the whole car-ride here. He was going on and on and on but we don't speak BSL – I saw that you did.'

'He gave his name once we were in A&E. When we were transferring him from your vehicle he was reciting the Lord's Prayer.'

Bo shuffled to the entrance and stopped in the middle to look at his mud-caked boots, confusing the door sensor in the process – the glass sliding toward him then back, toward him, back. Molly dropped off the form at reception and stepped passed him, shoulders hunched, her long brown hair dishevelled in the back. Bo's hand dangled off his hip, waiting to be held. She continued through the entrance doors and stepped off the sidewalk to the pavement and he put his hands in his pockets. She walked to the driver's side and told him she'd drive back and he protested, then relented when he saw her eyebrows curve up. The sky cleared as they drove down Mumbles Road beside the sea – beach strewn with shells, stones, driftwood, seaweed, and the rest of nature's purge. Molly drove with her right hand and put the other on the middle console between the seats. She looked in the rear-view mirror and saw her husband's hand trembling on his mouth as he looked at the flats that shared walls along the road, most of them taupe or white, then one blue, one gold. The tide returned to the shore foot-by-foot with each small wave. She patted her hand on the console and he looked at it, then leaned forward and put his open palm under hers and she rubbed his knuckles with her thumb.

SPLIT

DURRE SHAHWAR

Faiza watched the woman on the other side of the double glass doors hammer her fists against them repeatedly. There was a look of panic and desperation in her eyes that you see so often on telly in a documentary or the news but never in real life. It was the kind that comes from having lost home, lost a country, to become a life passed as papers through foreign hands. But the woman had come in late, and without all of those papers, and so had to be sent straight back out. Those were the rules, and rules had to be followed – and not only because of the cameras. The rules were stated clearly on the Life in the UK Test website when you booked the test. They warned that if you didn't have this or that, or if your name didn't match, even if it was just a typo, a single letter missing or if you didn't bring the correct proof of ID or address, or arrived later than ten minutes, you would not be allowed to sit the test you had spent all that time and money preparing for. And the woman had made at least two of those mistakes and well, she really should have read the rules properly.

But now the woman was on the floor, with her insufficient documents in one hand, her fist against the glass, her bags also on the floor next to her and it looked as though she was crying but without any tears. She had travelled two hours to be here – Faiza had overheard the woman tell Shelly when she had come in. But Shelly had said, *yes, yes, I understand but there is nothing we can do so you must leave*. Then she had pressed the green button, opened the doors and in the next second, the woman was out before what was happening could even hit her.

At first, the woman had stood, shocked and still. And then the questions had come: *What do you mean? Why not?* Those ones were the common ones. But Shelly, who now stood on their side of the doors – the side that locked them in and everyone else out – had simply gestured to the woman that she must move away from the doors. *I have explained it not once, but twice. You must leave.* But once out, the woman had started shouting that time was running out for her, that she really needed to sit this test.

Now her hair was slowly becoming dishevelled and her jacket was coming off from one shoulder. It was like watching a very slow and painful movie. Flashbacks of the time when Faiza was in school and her own mother would come home from yet another failed attempt of the same test pulsed through her mind. Her mother would be upset for days, complaining that it was all a government plot designed to keep her and her children out. That the invigilator had failed her on purpose. And now Faiza was that invigilator. And the woman behind the glass doors could have been her mother.

It was days like these that were the hardest. It had been a whole year since graduation, and between the unpaid internships, and her slowly trickling savings, this was the only job she had gotten in an office, which paid at least the living wage.

But this place allowed no time for guilt or empathy. Faiza had learnt early on that guilt came as part of the job and dwelling in it would eat at her and keep her awake entire nights. And despite the fact that sometimes, when she was absolutely sure that she was out of earshot, she would switch to Hindi or Urdu to help a candidate struggling to follow instructions in English, she also kept quiet at other times for the sake of just getting through the day. She knew she could lose her job doing it, but it made her feel at ease, seeing the relief of recognition in another's face.

Lately she found herself thinking about it all more than ever.

About the time that was now unspoken about in her house. Faiza would wonder whether her mother too was referred to in pronouns, made to take off her headscarf, the seams searched thoroughly for wires. Her hair prodded and poked for hidden devices, all under the watchful eyes of CCTV cameras.

Most people she spoke to didn't even know that such a place existed. A place where you had to take a test that asked questions about where Robert Burns was from and when the first Christian communities appeared in Britain. Questions that most of her friends wouldn't even have the answers to. But here in this place, these trivia questions were used to determine the future of people's whole lives.

The Test Centre had gotten busier too in the last few weeks. Each morning, Faiza would look through the bookings to find new names, increased numbers on the list and prepare herself for another gruelling day. They called them candidates at the Centre, but to Faiza, they would often look like her uncle, her aunt, her parents or even her own self if of similar age to her. All with the same anxious concern in their eyes, turning up promptly in front of the soundproof, shatterproof glass doors. They would be carrying their pieces of identity and belonging (or lack of it) in their hands, stamped and signed by various governments and bodies, declaring their various statuses. These were the documents these candidates feared would become invalid in the upcoming years. And so they came here, to jump through hoops to receive new documents, new proofs of their belonging as citizens of this island.

One time, one of her managers from an old Saturday job she had, had shown up to sit the test. Faiza had hidden in her own cubicle for the entire two hours that he had been there. Always reluctant to let anyone down, Faiza had remembered how awkward it had been for her to quit that Saturday job she had hated, and the manager's half-arsed attempt at convincing her to stay during the busy Christmas period. She had remembered how he would mark her lateness, allocate her duties like stacking the rails. And now, suddenly, she had the power to mark his lateness, nose through his documents, decide if he met a certain criteria or not. Yet the thought of it had filled her up with embarrassment for him rather than a sense of delayed satisfaction for herself. Thankfully, the rules also stated that invigilators could not deal with people they knew personally. Which meant that after the formal hellos, Faiza was not to be in the same room as him. But somehow this made her feel like even more difficult, as she wondered if he thought she was avoiding him on purpose.

'Please move away from the doors. You are blocking the way for other people.'

Usually one to enforce the strict, KEEP NOISE LOW, policy, Shelly was now shouting at the woman through the double-glazing. There was no doubt that the candidates sitting their tests this very minute in the room just behind them would have been able to hear her loud and clear. Faiza half-welcomed the complaints that might be filed should any of them fail their tests and blame it on the disruption.

'I'm going to have to go out there,' Shelly turned to Faiza and her other two colleagues, who too had now come out of their cubicles. None of them uttered a word but silently watched Shelly prance around her desk, hooking her keys in one pocket, swinging her lanyard around her neck before walking up to the door. Then after a moment's hesitation, she walked back to the desk to grab the walkie talkie that was to be used only in emergencies. Like most struggling managers, Shelly's response to difficult situations was to enforce strict authority. Faiza had seen it all too often.

Finally, in a big stride of determination, Shelly stamped her hand aggressively on the green button to release the door before lunging for it with the other hand and swinging it open. For a few seconds, sounds of crying filled up the room before being cut off again by the clanging of the doors after Shelly. Faiza bit the inside of her mouth.

'Look, you need to move away or I'm going to have to call security. You can't sit the test and that is final.'

'Why though?'

'You were late. You did not have all your documents. And your timeslot has passed now. You need to go home, rebook it, and come back another day.'

'No, I can't go home. I will be in trouble.'

'I'm afraid there's nothing we can do.'

'No ... please. I can't go home. I will be in trouble,' and with that she reluctantly lifted the bottom half of her shirt to show a purple bruise the size of a baby's palm blending into her skin around the edges, before dropping its corner immediately. It was so quick that Faiza almost wondered if she imagined it.

'I'm sorry. There is nothing we can do.'

'Just let me sit. Even if I fail – I can just sit it. Please.'

'You need to leave or I will have to call security. That's final.' As she said this, Shelly swiped her lanyard and stepped back in.

'I'm going to give it another 15 minutes and then I will call security,' she announced.

'Should we maybe also call someone else? Like, report it to a women's charity?'

'No, that's not our job. That's a personal matter and we can't interfere with that.' Faiza bit the inside of her mouth again.

'Plus, that might get her in more trouble. Maybe he'll just send her back. Who knows? But under no circumstance can we get involved. That's against the Home Office rules.'

Faiza nodded and turned back to her cubicle. After a moment, the banging picked up again, until it became a background rhythm to their work.

'I'm going to call security. She's banging her head on the door.'

Faiza nodded again without looking up from her papers. Instead, she focused on issuing the candidate in front of her with his result, before asking them to be seated in the waiting area while they dealt with 'a situation'. She did this for the next three people in line.

When she poked her head out again, she saw two policemen, and a medic, slowly prising the woman away from the doors. Other candidates who had turned up for their test in the meanwhile, stood back outside the doors and watched. One tried to gather up her belongings helpfully and pass them on to her to no response. Instead, one of the policemen took the papers and thanked them. Meanwhile, the medic spoke quietly to the woman on the floor who seemed to be staring off into a distance, far beyond the inside of the testing centre.

Faiza thinks about the woman the entire way home. She wonders if she got home, where it was, who gave her that purple mark? Did she have more? Could she be in danger? Whether the paramedics called the closest kin to come and collect her from the A&E or the van – wherever did they take her? What was her name? *It's always the African women who are the most aggressive.* Shelly's voice rang in her head. She finds her hand shaking with anger as she puts the key in through the front door of her flat. She thinks about it as she eats her food, perched in front of her laptop, Googling up local women's aid and domestic violence charities. She writes their names and numbers down. From her bag, she pulls out a yellow sticky note she had snuck out of the centre after Shelly had told her to write the incident report for that day that was to be passed on to the Home Office. Then she rings a number.

'Hi, I'm calling about a woman that may have been brought in earlier. It must have been around half four.'

Faiza gives the name.

'Are you sure? How about maybe spelling with a ie rather than a y? ... No it wasn't an accident, there was an incident, it was at the Test Centre at the college? I was there ... No I'm not related, I just wanted to know if there was anyone brought in from there at that time ... She had a plain blue shirt on. And trousers. Can you not look through the records ... ? Look I just need to know if a woman was brought in at that time. I was there when it happened. I'm just checking that she was okay ... Yes I understand it's confidential, but I work where the incident happened ... No, I'm not manager ... It's just that she could be in danger and I want to help ... Yes, I understand that the A&E can help too. I just –'

Faiza hangs up the phone and drops it on the table. *There's just too many of them coming here.* Words casually uttered by ex-boyfriends who had been unaware of Faiza's own history rang through her head.

That night, she dreams of running through endless white corridors, trying every door for a way out, while CCTV cameras watched her at every turn. She hears clanging of gates behind her and her mother's voice somewhere lost among them. She knows that she will find her behind any of these doors if she just keeps looking, but Faiza wakes up before she ever finds her mother.

No Harm From Them

Zoran Pilić

Translated by Tomislav Kuzmanović

I need no sorrow getting its grip on me, not now, I think, and it's already too late. I fall into the trap of my own mind, which recognises the favorable conditions and materialises on its own into a demon that has no problem finding the shortest path to my heart and then opens the first few wounds with its sharp claws.

I snap out of it and grab my black bag with four poorly sawn white lines, which, even a fool could tell, show that it's an Adidas knockoff; it too has somehow withdrawn into itself, broken in two as if there's nothing valuable in it nor could there ever be. Yet the bag is not to blame, but the misery, hundreds and hundreds of years of pain and misery that keep depositing in our blood, from one generation to another, like oil under dead layers of soil, under skeletons of mammoths, of princes and of paupers, under the skeletons of *Gastarbeiter* in Germany.

I walk slowly on black asphalt, between thick, yellow lines, I follow the same path that countless columns of my quiet countrymen followed as if, each and every one of them, going to the scaffolds and not into a completely different, better life. And when somewhere up there, through the ancient domes of Hauptbahnof, my first dawn in the foreign land is slowly breaking, my father comes to my mind. Is it possible, Father, could it be, that all this was destined for us a long time ago?

The world has changed, it no longer looks like itself, but we, well, we're still running away from something: from misery and wars, from small, overcrowded countries, towns and villages, where everyone knows everyone else, we're running away to a place where a man can hide from others and from himself, we're running away from injustice and despair, but not only from that, we're running away from our friends and from our foes, from the dead and from the living, from thievery, we're running away from hatred as much as from love, from insomnia, debts, revenge, knives and concentration camps, from stinking bars where we spend our every God given day and night drinking coffee by the gallons so our blood too must have gone black, and if you at least run away from all that coffee, you'll get a feeling that you've done something with your life, we're running away from indifference, from the madness that's so contagious in our midst and it emanates left and right, except that its rays are invisible, we're also running away, it seems to me sometimes, because it is in our blood to run.

You, Father, grew up in the world without colours. You say it isn't so, but even I remember that the first colours appeared in the early seventies, maybe back in 1974 when Katalinski, in Frankfurt, scored a goal against the Spaniards, before that people lived in a black-and-white world. I'm sure it was better than it is now, in colour. I remember it well, the sun was glisteningly white, the river transparent or, come winter, as murky as a plowed field, and the pearl was black and that was its name – *Black Pearl*. It stood on that rickety table, and somewhere to the side or perhaps on the bottom shelf of that slim-legged table, which today, well, reminds me of sad creatures from *Somewhere I Belong*, the video by Linkin Park, we kept a heavy wooden box with a switch. The stabiliser – that was its name. You turn on the stabiliser and in some ten minutes a black-and-white image appears. A miracle, a miracle of television.

At the time of your youth, the sky was closer to the earth, and the wealthier gentlemen wore sable fur hats, heavy, ribbed gabardine coats, and they kissed the ladies' hands and addressed them with 'madam', or does all that belong to some other time and space?

Germany didn't sit well with me from the very beginning. I'll admit that to you. It didn't, by God it didn't, and as I walk slowly through this giant station, my own steps terrify me. They echo as if I'm in a cathedral, everything is, you know, ominous, and at the same time clean, polished, oiled. And if you happen to find a crumbled scrap of paper or something, there comes a guy with a waste cart, slinks in from somewhere silently as a snake, picks it up in a blink of an eye and moves on, simply disappears. Spotless, all of it, no question about it, but only on the surface. When I look a bit deeper, when I peer into that darkness gaping at the farthest corner, at the place where, if this were a real cathedral, beautifully carved confessionals would stand, it appears before me, I see someone's yellow eyes glaring in the dark, I hear a whisper, as if the leaves or Necromancer's cape is rustling. Ah, no harm from them, I comfort myself, these are all carnivores whose nature is not to heedlessly pounce upon their prey, they wait until it wanders into their cobweb on its own, and this always happens, sooner or later. The strategy of a spider sitting in the dark. Not even the cleaners venture there. That's a country unto itself, a land of ancient hunters, a waiting room between two worlds – that one that's vanishing and this one that's only just showing itself in the distance.

Drunks, swindlers, pickpockets, shoeblacks, hookers and beggars do what they do and they're easy to recognise, but there are others. Those who talk among themselves, or who appear to be waiting for someone, who stare into passengers' faces, get up on their toes, crane their thin, pale necks careful not to miss even the farthest carriages, and who then slink back into their coats and scarfs not hiding the disappointment because that someone hasn't come and they've been waiting for years, but one special day will dawn and at that precise hour – that someone will come and they will be there to meet him. You see, the thought flutters through my mind like a frightened bird, you see that life is unrelentingly passing by these people who are all waiting in vain, you see that they are turning their heads away from the truth; nowhere on this whole earth of ours you can better feel the relentless arrow of time than at places such as this, so vast and sad.

Come on, drop that foolishness, apparitions and empty words. There, now, after I've made this, as people say, the most radical move, perhaps things will really get going for me. So, Father, could this be the meaning of life, to start from scratch, here at the heart of Europe, in the land of milk and honey, get a good German car, perhaps a two or three years old Audi, and then, come summer, head down to that seaside of ours, and what fucking sea it is, as if other countries don't have a sea, they do, all of them do, the Greeks, the French, the Italians, even the Germans have it, except that theirs is cold, good for nothing. I'd love to see the Caribbean once. Visit Jamaica, relax and such. I'm not the worst man in the world, am I? Maybe the sun will shine on me once too.

Sure thing, it crosses my mind, you'll see a lot of sunshine here. I better get one of those sunscreen lotions, with good SPF, so that I don't burn in this German sun of kindness.

I don't want to remember, I want the opposite – if only, Father, I could forget it all, but it takes time, half a life maybe, or maybe less. I finally step out into the open, and it's pitch dark everywhere. Thick Bavarian clouds have run over the dawn, the icy wind is whistling, flinging first drops of rain into my face, and that thin line of light has remained somewhere far, far away in the east.

For the first couple of days it's raining non-stop, first it pours, then slowly it recedes, loses its breath, and finally it turns into a dull, numbing drizzle; it's going to drizzle, just like this, I imagine, when the world comes to its end. On judgment day, the rain is not going to paint rainbows in the sky, it will just quietly sprinkle the earth. Soon after, as all the books say, darkness will descend upon everything.

I found my first refuge in one of the *heims*, homes. In rooms with four, five or more beds, misery shows itself in its full splendour and glory, at that moment you know you're standing one step away from hopelessness and if you don't get yourself out of there as soon as you can, that feeling of infinite doom blinds you, shreds your soul to pieces. If I take for granted that the eyes are the mirror of one's soul, what I saw when I looked deep into the soul of an old man from Greece, some poor wretch sitting at the edge of his neatly tidied bunk with his hands in his lap, was a barren wasteland.

Christos is my name, he said.

We exchanged a couple of words, that broken man, the Jesus taken down from his cross a long time ago, and I. There's a man, I thought, the son of God, who could have thought I'd see him right here in this Munich *heim* so old, so broken. The devils thought of a more horrible punishment than dying an agonizing death: let him live.

Stay away from our people, he said.

Our people, our man, be he a Greek, an Albanian, a Croat, a

Serb, a Bosnian, a Turk, is difficult, as hard as the black soil, so blinded by the castles in the sky that he sees nothing else. This phantom gets a hold of him, the idea that one day he'd go back, and then when he does go back for a couple of days and sees what he has left behind – he runs back into that other life, into the country he will never feel anything for just as it will never feel anything for him, and then again, after a while, he begins dreaming that one and the same dream: I will go back, if only to die back there, if I couldn't live a decent life, here comes the great conclusion, let me at least die like a man.

Stay away from our people. Some work, slaving day in, day out, others want it all and they want it now. Such will lead you into crime, and there, trust me, you are doomed. And that's why I tell you: when you see one of our people on the street, turn around and run because, if nothing else, he will unload his misery, his sorrow and loneliness on you, such are our people, difficult.

The apartment in the *ausländer* district does not feel like home, not at all. It doesn't look like me nor do I do anything to change that. I hear voices of women, children and men through the walls, I hear whispers, cries, screams, moans, on occasion a sharp bark or yelp of a German Shepherd when one younger Turk, his head shaved, takes it out for a walk. One evening I caught him tugging at the dog's leash and screaming something at it. When he kicked it, the devil wouldn't leave me alone.

Don't do that, I said, it's not the animal's fault, and he grabbed the dog by the hide, threw him through the door into the building, and then approached me, poked his bald head at me and yelled: What is your problem, huh, what is your problem, man?

I almost told him something. Something about my problems

and the problems of all of us. But I saw, luckily, that he was so beside himself that he wouldn't be able to understand so I just put my arms in the air and said: It's your dog, brother, do as you please.

That's right, my dog – my problem! My dog – my fucking problem!

He had to repeat it all two or three times as if he himself didn't believe what he was saying.

I hear people through the walls, our people, as Christos said. People I obviously belong to. Sometimes they break into a loud laughter too, they talk to each other, shout, change moods, and all that to escape apathy. Exaggeration is the only thing that keeps a man above the surface: great outpours of happiness, sadness, love, anger or jealousy, affection, hostility or the desire to reach the impossible – that's what makes you alive.

Apathy makes life quietly fade away.

It's spring, Father, but you wouldn't be able to recognise it. Everything happens in just a few days and nights, you don't have enough time to raise your head and the sun is already scorching the earth, even the perfect German asphalt turns into dough, and the air flickers distorting the city's image. Some moving company hired me. Munich and its surroundings: Čabo is driving, Vladimir and I carry furniture, boxes with children's toys and books, sometimes even musical instruments. Pianos, cellos, guitars, drum sets, old synthesisers that look like barbecues, and speakers, big and small, mountains of speakers.

Vladimir, he pronounces his name more like a Russian – Volodimir, he has thin, pale arms and unusually large hands which could, so it seems, move hills if he chose to do so. He grew up in former GDR, he never complains, and the moment you set your eyes on him, you know his life wasn't nice. The

Germans don't do such hard, physical jobs – I'd dare say, more fitting for a rat. Actually, maybe they do, but I, except for Vladimir, never saw one.

Those born here, in Germany, Čabo says, will rather sit and do nothing than dig canals, lug wardrobes, hey brother, you'll never find a Kraut wiping asses at those wards where old folk go to die. We do all that and that's why the Kraut puts up with us, isn't it so, Vladimir, my dear friend, isn't it true?

Vladimir just blows a cloud of smoke, smiles and says: 'It's true …'

While I'm working, I'm calm, those heavy thoughts do not haunt me, and what you said, Father, about idle hands being the devil's workshop, you know – that's true too. Weekends are difficult to bear, a day is a year, and at night, the ghosts of past come back again. Sometimes I sit on my bed, and talk to them.

You know, Pop says in the dead of one of such nights, how horrible it is to die when you're as innocent as I was?

I can only imagine, I reply.

Believe you me, you can't even imagine, there's no greater horror than seeing yourself dead. You're screaming, but no one hears you, you're crying your eyes out, but there are no tears to be found. My friend, why did you kill me, huh?

I didn't recognise you, Pop, you asked me the same question a hundred times over, why don't you leave me be?

Damn you, why didn't you wait a second longer?

I can't go back in time, it's too late now …

And, my friend, how do you live with it on your soul, huh?

It's not easy, how else, you see it for yourself. And even if I wanted to forget – I can't …

You thought I wouldn't find you? Ah, what a fool you are, going to the edge of the world is nothing for me, if need be. Why are you on your own, why don't you find someone? Loneliness makes a man go mad, especially here.

Sometime by mid-July people began leaving the city. The Germans went on their vacation, to the Adriatic or some other seas, Čabo went with his family too. I have to, he said, dip my toes in.

And all of our *Gasterbeiter* jumped into their cars and hit the road. Not all, some don't take vacations, they have their reasons. Vladimir and I stayed behind, we hung about for a couple more days and then they sent us on *Urlaub* too.

Listen, Vladimir tells me, next Sunday come to my place, it's my sister's thirty-fifth birthday, we'll throw something on the grill, have a couple of beers, no excuses, be there.

But, I said, I don't even know the woman. It'll be strange.

Elsa doesn't even want to celebrate, that's why I always fix up a little something for her. So, we're clear, no excuses, you better be there.

If it were anyone else, I'd think of a reason why not to come, but I couldn't say no to the good man Vladimir. He is, Father, just like that Slovenian of yours from Maribor, the one you worked with for all those years and once brought him home. He'll never make your head hurt, a real cure of a man.

I didn't know what to do with myself until Sunday. I got some books in German, I said, why not practice the language a bit, but the thoughts kept running to all sides, you couldn't bring them back to their place, not a chance. One night, the police came too, they were looking for that young Turk – they didn't find him in his apartment. I hadn't seen him for days. His mother took out the German Shepherd, but you could see the woman didn't care about it much, the dog ran here and there, jumped, yelped, wanted to play, roam freely, but she had other things on her mind.

There are days when I try cooking something for myself, but I'm no good in the kitchen, I don't have that feeling. I order takeaway or go to a restaurant, they are all over the place: Italian, Chinese, Greek, Indian, Dalmatian, Bosnian ... I don't know if it were like this back in your day. The city is the same, but the times are different and the people have changed.

As I didn't know anything about Vladimir's sister Elsa, and it's not polite to show up empty-handed at someone's party, I spent the whole Friday afternoon searching for a gift not knowing what I was actually looking for. And as usually happens, my legs took me right into Mr. Keßler's bookstore. I found him there sitting at the large desk, surrounded by heaps upon heaps of books, smoking his cigarette without a filter, polishing his glasses with the edge of his shirt. At first I thought it was strange that a man smoked with so many books around, but something in the old man's posture cancelled the strangeness of the tobacco smoke as if with the very act he wanted to say: Children, I've spent my whole life among the books, and let me tell you, until you throw them into the fire, the smoke is the last thing they're worried about.

'I'd like to look around a bit, if that's okay ...' I said, but the old man waved his hand and interrupted me mid-sentence. 'Have a seat, young man, take those books off that chair, put them on the floor, just put them down there on the floor, that's right, would you like some brandy?'

Without getting up, he pulled a bottle and two glasses out of somewhere and poured the brandy. We said cheers.

'Where are you from, wait, don't tell me ... ex-Yugoslavia?'

'That's right.'

'Which part?'

'Bosnia,' I said and the word dropped to the desk like a coin and clanked strangely, then disappeared in the smoke.

'Eh, Bosnia, Bosnia …' he said and a shadow crossed his face.

We sipped our brandies in silence.

'Are you looking for something for yourself or perhaps for someone else, as a present?'

'It's a present.'

'I see, a present for a lady, if I'm not mistaken?'

'A present for a lady I've never met, a German woman, my friend's sister.'

'Don't say, well, that won't be a problem …' he said, reached somewhere again and pulled out a book with red covers. 'Here it is, *Wegzeichen*, an ideal present, you heard about Andrić and you read him at school, didn't you?'

While I leafed through the pages, the old Keßler silently placed the old Yugoslav edition of *Signs by the Roadside* on the desk. I knew the book well. 'This one's my gift to you, to bring up old memories …'

Vladimir's house on the city's periphery and its surroundings reminded me of village ways and yards in Vojvodina. Sure, there were no raven black stallions, gaggles of geese, haystacks on the horizon, curs barking on long chains, or tall gates protecting the yards from foreign eyes, but there was definitely something there – maybe that zen of the plains, the peace and steadiness of life that keeps its pace regardless of what we do and what evil we inflict upon each other.

On my way there, it crossed my mind that even though Elsa didn't care much about her birthday, I could have brought her a flower instead of the German edition of *Signs by the Roadside*.

Andrić is good, of course, but I feared that it might be a bit rude that I, a Bosnian *gastarbeiter*, brought her a book by a Nobel Prize winner. Ah, when all is said and done, what do I care, it's just something you do, I was not going to rack my brains about it too.

At that very moment, when I first laid my eyes on her, she was sitting at a large table in front of the house, all alone under the parasol, moving her hair from her face, with both hands like when you open the curtains on the window, she glanced at me with those green eyes of hers that, I guess, find everything interesting, eyes that smile even when she is not smiling, and I, what a fool, looked away and just stood there like a child.

'*Alles Gute zum Geburtstag …*' I said and offered her the book but I dared not come any closer, as if there was an abyss between us, and so I had to stretch and mind not to fall into that bottomless pit, which, I thought, perhaps wouldn't be all that bad.

She was pleased, so it seemed, and I was pleased that she was pleased, she also said something, and then invited me to sit down at the table, but as I was still in that strange, foolish state, I just stood there, and so finally she approached me, took my hand and led me across the abyss.

When the next morning, tortured by nightmares, I woke up transformed into myself again, Father, there's no need to lie, it was yet another heavy defeat. Once again the same I from the day before. One day closer to death. As I watched from close by the scenes of a family life, I must have thought for a moment – I could do that too. I could mock all that vanishing, if in no other way, then by imitating other people, doing what they do.

Elsa, who carried her own scars just as everyone else did, had patience with me. At critical moments, when I'd sink under the surface, she wouldn't run away. I told her, once, go, woman, and don't look back. You don't understand, I kept repeating, you don't understand.

'Maybe I don't understand, but I'm here, see.'

On one of those nights, I woke up with a start and she really was lying there, on that narrow bed. I heard voices from the hall. They came again to get the Turk, this time he didn't run away, he surrendered peacefully. Before they took him away, he came to my door.

'Well, neighbour, I'll be going now, don't hold anyhing against me, and take the dog and look after it, please. Sultan is his name.'

'What about your mother?' I asked.

'She's gone, we parted ways.'

The Turk and me exchanged these couple of words in German with a thick Balkan accent. The two officers in their civilian clothes behind his back, and Elsa, who's woken up in the meanwhile, let us take our time. They don't interfere. The three Germans and the German Shepherd, standing between the two of us, wagging its tail are politely waiting for the conversation to come to its end.

'Alright, Sultan, have you got your things?'

As if it really understands what I'm talking about, the dog takes two steps back, sits by the green plastic bag that is standing in the hall and stares at me.

'Here are his treats, his bowls and a couple of toys,' says the Turk.

Early in the fall, Elsa, Sultan and I moved to Theresienstraße, close to her work at Neue Pinakothek. She changes the way I see the world around me. I'm already imagining a time when it will no longer be important where I came from, how I lived and what I believed in. On that day, in the future that I dared not even think of for such a long time, I will come to understand that I don't have to carry that heavy cross. I'll toss it somewhere by the road, let it lie there until weeds grow over it, let it rot, what do I care.

In the evenings, Sultan and I go out for a walk. We meet other people and dogs in the park. Small dogs are nervier than big ones. Sometimes they attack Sultan too, and they bark – you'd think they're mad or something – and the good Sultan just watches them in surprise. He's not the quarreling type. Other times, there's no one there, so the two of us patrol the park on our own.

On one such evening, there's a breeze coming from somewhere, but not a soul in the park. Not a man, not a dog. The whole day that strange feeling of the most ordinary happiness of life has been choking me. It troubles me. Where has this come from, I think, how could such misery befall me of all people, and happiness is a misery and nothing else, because once it's gone, everyone knows that those clouds begin to gather. One part of me would gladly give itself up to it, but from experience I know that that's not good, and so I'm fighting against myself. And it goes like that until the evening and the time when Sultan and I go out for a walk. We come to the green space of ours, I sit down on a bench, light a cigarette and throw the tennis ball in the middle of that large circle delineated by benches, wastebaskets and trees that on the other side turn into a forest. Sultan follows the ball's flight and starts running. And, logically, there's no chance he won't find it, so it's not much of a game. What matters is the sprint, and finding the ball, well that's the least of his problems. On the third throw, I get up, walk almost to the middle of the park, and only then throw the ball and immediately lose sight of it in the dark. Sultan sees me and starts running, and I follow slowly behind. I make out his shadow in the darkness. As I approach the forest, the feeling of happiness abandons me as if it has never existed. The dog sniffles the grass, goes left and right, and then comes back to me.

'And where's the ball, buddy, huh?'

Sultan who already knows both Turkish and German, has no problems understanding our language.

'What are we going to do?'

Sultan doesn't make a sound and watches the darkness spreading from the forest. We're approaching it slowly, I don't feel like it, but we're going anyway. Now we're close. And that's where we stop. I peer into the darkness, but looking at it like that, directly, I see nothing. When I glance at it from the corner of my eye, as if trying to look away, it seems, I see yellow eyes, glowing in the dark.

'No harm from them,' I whisper.

I grab Sultan's collar. There's a bench in front of us, behind it is the forest, and there in the darkness, between two worlds, something is lying. Maybe it's our ball, I can't tell. The dog growls quietly.

FI, YR DINOSAUR

Marcie Layton

I'm never really sure if eisteddfods are about the language, or about the music. 'It's about *The Language*, stupid!' is probably the most common conclusion. Of course, with all the other stuff going on at the same time – the dance, drama, art and crafts – I'd guess eisteddfods say more about Wales, as in the country itself, which makes it a bigger topic than either the language or the music.

I'll always be an outsider at an eisteddfod, having been neither born nor raised in Wales, but I do find them a source of fascination. I often imagine what it must be like, being a child in this country, raised with the comforting regularity of these events: the national eisteddfod every year in Llangollen, and the national and local versions dotted all over the countryside.

I get the impression that some children are totally in it for the competition, the thrill of performance, and the show-bizzy win, win, win of it all. Other children I've talked to seem to love the mud-spattered, caravan-towing excuse to stay up way past their bedtime, while their parents bang on about the Welsh Assembly with a large group of friends, knocking back a pint or two in the process.

I do suspect there have been several crash-and-burn scenarios at these events in terms of performances; I never know if those failures damage children for life, or if they just get over it and move on to the next one with a shrug.

If you're not involved in an eisteddfod, and forget that it's that time of year again, then you will perhaps wonder why your town or village will be devoid of children, teenagers, and caravans for a week or so around Easter and half-term. You will wonder why everybody you meet comes back a week later full of extraordinary amounts of juicy gossip from all over the country, and with baskets and baskets of dirty laundry.

My son was in an eisteddfod. Well, sort of. He was in the first round of pre-lims for one. That hardly counts. He was about as far away from 'seeing the stage' as a penguin is from seeing Texas.

And, he was dressed as a dinosaur.

His primary school was very keen on eisteddfods, and there was much fervour and anticipation about them. Everything, and everyone, was thrown into the pot: *dawnsio gwerin*, crafts, recitation, choirs, art, everything. Someone once advised me to find a craft option that wasn't very popular, like puppetry, and go for it; it was a sure way to get through the first pre-lim. (Mind you, I was given this very same piece of advice about entering the village fair in August: find an obscure vegetable category and go for it.)

I had seen the pre-lims for these events before, and it seemed to me that everybody was being coached to do precisely the same thing, in precisely the same way, and I didn't see how anybody could possibly tell the difference when it came time to adjudicate them.

I was not a sheep. I wanted my son to be different.

He was taking singing lessons at this time, at the tender age of eight, with a wonderful, fun-loving singing teacher who was no stranger to eisteddfods herself. She had told me what song was going to be sung: a chirpy little number about a dinosaur and his little dinosaur antics. We agreed that she would coach him on it instead of the teacher at the primary school.

We had the costume from a long way back; I think it came from the Disney Store. It was a large, full-body creation: green, and scaly, and vaguely, mildly, authentic-looking. We're not talking Barney here, is my point. It had a thick, swishy tail, and a big pot belly, and when your Mum or Dad zipped you into it, you couldn't escape without help. The dinosaur head sat on top of your own head like a crown, and your face peered out roughly where the throat should be. The feet were big padded claws with elasticated straps that hid your shoes, and collected all sorts of bits of rubbish wherever you walked.

Well, I got my little lad into this creation and we began to work on a surprise for the singing teacher. All the other children we'd seen rehearsing this song stood calmly, singing their little hearts out to the FIRE EXIT sign at the back of the school hall. Their eyes popped open unnaturally wide, and they would barely move a muscle, save for the in/out/in/out of their little ribs heaving as they sang.

I got my son to do a few little gestures, to support the lyrics: a little kick here, a little teeth brushing there. At one point, I got him to do a big 'ROAR' that he performed with great gusto. We hid the costume when we got to the music lesson, and, giggling nervously, I asked the teacher to wait briefly while we prepared ourselves 'backstage' in her hall.

Her face was a picture when we came into her front room and she saw the costume. My son looked both delighted and mortified at the same time. The room shuddered with good humour as he stood there, being admired. This was nothing compared to the response when he began to sing. The little kicks and gestures went well. The teeth brushing was cute. When the little roar came out his teacher let out an exclamation that was just delicious! I'm not sure she'd ever seen anything like it, at least, not in her front room.

We all fell about when he'd finished and I thought to myself: I am NOT a SHEEP! Dare to be different!! I asked her what she thought, and reminded her that I'd had no experience of these things. Could we pull it off?

We had some discussion about whether or not it would work. She brought her husband down from the office in their loft conversion, and he also had the marvellous double-whammy reaction – first to the costume, then to the song with its little bit extra.

What a high! I felt cute, I felt clever! I felt daring, and original. My son was getting a bit fidgety in the costume, and I thought perhaps he needed the loo, so he was extracted , like some sort of curious caterpillar, from his padded monstrosity.

Over the coming weeks we worked on this risky new take on traditional Welsh musical form. I was getting rather sick of the song, but on we bashed. His teacher's daughter, a choir conductor in the local church, came over and listened to it, and there was much giggling and fidgeting and bonhomie in the lessons.

Finally, the big day arrived, but there was trouble in Paradise. Someone didn't want to wear the costume. Someone had been watching rehearsals at school, and nobody else was wearing a costume. Someone was worried about looking silly.

The heat was on from my end, as well, because the parents had been asked to 'volunteer' for various jobs during the trials, and I got volunteered for 'Cash Box on the Lunch Queue'. This meant that when all of the competitors, and their parents, and the adjudicators, had their lunch breaks, they would take a tray in an orderly fashion, pick up their food of choice, and hand me their money at end of the queue. I had to make change in the Urdd's little metal cash box.

Now, math is not my strong suit, and my Welsh is even worse, but for some reason (perhaps, because it's about *The Language*, stupid) I felt compelled to wade through these transactions in Welsh. I was dreading it, and left for the village hall muttering '*un, dau, tri, pedwar* ...' in a state of ever-increasing anxiety.

Well, the music pre-lim came first, and it was not a pretty sight. A cold, lino-encrusted classroom had been filled with cold plastic chairs, and a cold, wood-veneered table, and the view to the outside car park was cold and grey.

Warm, comfortable and thick-waisted mums padded about with their warm and comfortable children, murmuring gently in Welsh to each other, and there was a lot of hugging and gentle guiding of performers into their little rooms.

We, however, stood shivering in the cold corridor, and argued, *sotto voce*. My son was tortured. He did NOT want the wear the costume. He tried alternately pleading, and demanding, not to wear the costume.

I ganged up on him with the ammunition that Daddy, and Mummy, and Teacher, and Teacher's husband from the office loft conversion, and Teacher's daughter the conductor from the local choir, all had seen the dinosaur costume and thought it was wonderful . We were not SHEEP. We dared to be different. He WOULD wear the costume.

I actually had a long moment of deep reflection in which I nearly let him off the hook. I nearly said 'no' to the costume. I just didn't want to embarrass him and, you know, totally screw him up for life so that he would run away from home, phone CHILDLINE, and write a *MOMMIE, DEAREST*-type book about me from the comfort and safety of his new foster parents' home. But somehow, personal pride and vanity won out. I think it had something to do with my trying to take on the school, and the system, and the culture, and the country, all at once (not to mention *The Language*, stupid), and just, somehow, do things DIFFERENTLY and BETTER, or maybe just SHAKE THINGS UP A LITTLE.

I really don't know what the hell I was thinking.

Anyway, I stuffed him into the costume, like too many bags in the bin on the night before rubbish collection. We waited in the corridor, and every child who passed by stared, and then grinned, and sniggered at us, and then quickened his pace, as if to race off and tell as many children as possible that there was a dinosaur in the corridor, preparing to sing.

It was our turn. We tiptoed nervously into the room. The adjudicators went deadpan. The other children gaped. My son tried to say his name, whispering in terror from the larynx of the dinosaur. The accompanist was a portrait: not a twitch of a smile.

The music began, and my son inched forward. We could barely hear him. He started to do his little kick but thought better of it, or maybe, he was too busy being mortified to remember to do it. He forgot the words. He stammered. The tail shuffled around the floor morosely, gathering any bits of dust and rubbish that the elasticized feet had left behind.

I tried to get him out of there as quickly as possible afterwards. Did I imagine this, or did we both try to go through the door at the same time, Mummy and dinosaur, competing for space and bumping into each other, and getting ever so slightly stuck on departure?

There was retribution. Big time. Nothing I said helped. It was disaster from start to finish. I was sure he hated me, and the costume, and the song, and singing, and the cold room, and the deadpan adjudicators, and anything else associated with that particular day in Wales.

He went home with Daddy, and I stayed on. I had 'Cash Box on the Lunch Queue'. Oh goody.

I'm not exactly sure how many people got short-changed during that lunch break, but I only hope I erred in favour of the

Urdd. I can't count, in any language. At least I could devote my full attention to the little compartments of change in the cash box, because I was determined not to make eye contact with anyone. I couldn't bear to see the memory of the little dinosaur reflected in their eyes. The slightest hint of a giggle would've pushed me over the edge. I may even have short-changed the adjudicators, I don't know; I didn't look up at anyone, at all, ever.

After about the first transaction I gave up on the *un, dau, tri, pedwar* thing as well, because, honestly, who was I kidding? I wasn't Welsh. I never would be. I was just a foreigner: a very, very foolish English-speaking mother with a tear-stained child in a dinosaur costume.

It all came to a head in the Spar shop, down the aisle where the really cheap sweets were. I don't mean where the big boxes of Celebrations chocolates and the posh-sounding dark chocolate Bourneville bars were stacked. I mean down where the red licorice whips were, the jaw breakers, the oddly coloured gummy things., and the left-over Easter sweets on the cusp of exceeding their sell-by dates.

I was in pain from pent up emotion. My throat ached from supressed unhappiness. I had the mother of all headaches, and of course this is precisely when you remember that you've run out of milk at home, and even though the wisest thing would've been to go home and go to bed, I had to get a pint of milk from the Spar shop.

I sloped down the aisle, hoping not to see anyone, with two big three-litre jugs so I didn't have to go back there for at least a month. Suddenly, from behind the Walkers Big Eats, 'Aunti' Gwyneth said, Hello! How was I? How was the family?

It was all too much. I opened my mouth, and tears came out. They leaked down through the laughter lines around my eyes, and dribbled into my shirt collar. I tried to sound perky, or polite, or, even at this point, like a NORMAL person would've helped, but it was very clear that I was in great distress. I was crying dinosaur tears.

I was crying for myself, and my little boy, and for Wales, and for the po-faced adjudicators, and for all the people who I'd short-changed in the lunch queue. I cried for the fun-loving singing teacher, and her fun-loving family, and for 'Aunti' Gwynedd who had to stand there with her cabbage and her thick-cut marmalade and her Denbighshire Free Press, asking if I was all right.

It's been four years now, since the Year of the Dinosaur. My son used to remind me of the incident on a regular basis, and it never failed to push all of the most important guilty parent buttons in me.

He doesn't mention it quite so much now. I think my penance is nearly over; probably one or two more years and I should be reprieved. We've moved house, and he's got a different singing teacher now. He sings scales with funny vowel sounds, and arias in Italian. I think, perhaps, his dinosaur years are over.

We don't do eisteddfods in our family any more. None of us. We can celebrate the victories of our friends, and commiserate with the losers. We can watch the results on S4C and avoid the caravans, and perhaps even attend one on occasion, weather permitting. But we don't do eisteddfods anymore. It's my way of saying 'thank you', and 'sorry', to Wales.

When Elephants Fight

Eric Ngalle Charles

When I walked into the living room that afternoon, my daughter was in a reflective mood; she would not acknowledge, let alone talk to me. When she did speak, she seemed breathless.

'What is the matter *Ekulekule*[1]?'

She remained quiet, she seemed to have been crying. She removed some tissue from her bag, blew her nose into it, then wiped her eyes. She lifted her head up to look in my direction. My sixteen-year-old daughter reminds me a lot of my mother: her mannerisms, her *mbanyanya*[2], how her dimples move when she speaks, and the fact that my mother and daughter both have a birth mark just under the right eye (as a boy I once mistook my mother's birth mark for a mosquito. Thinking I was being helpful, I reached and pulled it. My mother screamed and slapped me hard, thinking I had done it on purpose).

'Dad, where are you from?' my daughter asked, interrupting my thoughts. The picture of Nelson Mandela on my wall looked at me, as if asking, *yes Eric, where are you from?*

This question had never come up in conversation between my daughter and me, never. She knew I was from Cameroon and she knew I came to Wales as a sixty-seven-year-old Zimbabwean citizen called Oscimile Ajole Thambvani. Many times my daughter has referred to me as a Nigerian, which I allow. I had told her about the scramble for Africa in 1884 and the British colonial rule of Nigeria and Southern Cameroon. My maternal grandfather was a colonial officer based in Nigeria where, so I believed, my mother was born. Whatever the case, it

---

1 tortoise, one of the many nicknames I have for my daughter
2 space between the front upper teeth

was the first time my daughter had asked me such a question.

'Dad, where are you from?' She needed a reassuring response.

'I am from Cameroon, *Ekulekule*, and you know that.' This did not alleviate her worries for she continued:

'Dad, where are you *really-really* from?' Before I could answer, she proceeded, 'Dad, I am in a socio-cultural dilemma.'

I wanted to laugh, as the last bit of her statement caught me off-guard. You see, my daughter loves using big words when she expresses herself (the other day, in a conversation we were having in the kitchen about the Russian Revolution, she said, 'Dad, my friends are talking bosh when it comes to their understanding of the Bolshevik uprising!'). But, seeing how serious she looked, and because she seemed to have been crying, I composed myself and said, 'Pardon?'

'I am in a sociocultural dilemma, Dad.'

'What do you mean, you are in a *sociocultural dilemma*?'

'Well, Dad, the thing is, my mother and my grandparents voted Brexit, but you on the other hand are a migrant from Africa, well, Cameroon, a country in Africa ... more importantly, you are my *father*, and you voted *Remain*. Why should your vote as a migrant determine the fate of a country you were not born in? I don't know how to contribute to the immigration debate which seems to be everywhere at the moment! In Nan's house, you are seen as 'The Good Migrant' – at least you are doing something for yourself, they always say, contributing to the artistic development of our society. They do not have a problem with *you*, it is the *other* migrants they have a problem with, those who claim Child Benefit for their ten children not even in this country!

'Brexit dominates conversations on the bus to and from school, during lunch breaks, at home through Sunday dinners. And Dad, you couldn't have given me a more African name –

Iya Efeti – my teacher, Mr Jones, calls me *Ilya Efetee*!

'On one hand, I love my mother and my grandparents very much; on the other, I love *you*. Sometimes I think I am stuck in some kind of purgatory! It is only now I am beginning to understand the African proverb, *When two elephants fight, it is the grass that suffers*, for Dad, I am suffering! If I'm pro-Brexit, I am accused of xenophobia, but if I'm anti-Brexit, my mother's family doubts my loyalty to my country! It's so disheartening.

'So, please tell me, if my friends should ask about you, your last days in Cameroon, how you ended up in Wales, how you came to be my father, what do I tell them? Today, during dinner in the canteen with Katie and Lucy, Ceri joined us on our table. It was unusual as she's not in our group of friends. She looked deep into my eyes before asking, '*Jolie*, where are you from?' Thinking she was being polite and friendly, I answered, 'I'm from Ely, innit' but then Ceri said, 'I mean, where are you *really* from?''

It had not occurred to me until then just how much the post-Brexit era is affecting my daughter, how anxious she is, and how she now sees herself as the 'grass' that the elephants were busy fighting upon. For the first time in her life, my daughter is worried about the future, *her* future. Not knowing how to respond to her worries, I went into the kitchen and, for the first time in years, made myself a cup of tea (I did not drink it, I have a passionate dislike for tea, as in 1993 whilst waiting for my GCSE results, my mother managed to get me a job as a Tea Harvester in Tole Tea Plantation, Buea, Cameroon. I was sacked after six hours, not being able to master the technique of picking tea whilst adjusting a basket on my back). After a few minutes in the kitchen, I went back to the living room and invited my daughter for a walk along the River Taff to try and lighten her mood.

As we crossed at the traffic lights where Clare Road meets Penarth Road, I tried distracting her by telling her how, as a little boy, growing up in the small village of Soppo Buea in Cameroon, I had learned which flowers had the sweetest of nectar just by following the flight path of the weaver bird. That was how I first came across the sweet juice of the hibiscus flower. My efforts were futile; *Ekulekule* looked apprehensive. She was in a deep reverie, the uncertainties of Brexit, a heavy weight on her young shoulders.

It was one of those extremely rare, extremely hot summer days in Cardiff. A few days earlier, my daughter and I had complained about how cold the weather was but on that day, everyone was on the brink of breaking the law due to their indecent exposure. I was hot, my daughter was hot, and by the time we reached the bridge, we were walking at a snail's pace. I stood under the tree on the Taff Trail and stuck my tongue out (I was reliving a scene from the film, *Madagascar*, where humans had blocked water from reaching the animal reserve and one lone fish lay gasping in a small pool of what was left of the water). I gasped and my daughter broke into a small smile. We could smell the beer aroma from the Brains SA Brewery. I remember when I first came to Wales in the summer of 1999, the same smell greeted me. The smell hasn't changed but on that day it was amplified and with no breeze to blow it away, it simply hung in the air. The sky was perfect blue. Young men and women were sitting under the bridge, half-naked, drinking beer. There was a young man on a chair, casting his net into the river and my daughter and I looked at each other and smiled at our telepathic understanding; we have walked this trail many times and, many times we have seen someone sitting in that same spot trying to catch whatever is lurking in the dark waters of the Taff, but, we have never seen any of them with a single fish. We have looked in this area when the Taff is clear but we have not seen a fish. There are ducks which we stop and feed, huge geese, pigeons everywhere, diving swans, but a fish we have not seen.

As we walked, I asked if she had watched a television series called *Gavin and Stacey*:

'Yes, but I am not a big fan.'

'Did you know, *Gavin and Stacey* is set in Barry Island?'

'Yes Dad,' she answered grumpily, 'Mum and my sister and I have visited Barry Island a couple of times. The sea there is very brown. I'm not sure if it is just brown or dirty. Now we prefer going to Tenby. Last year, Mum drove us to Anglesey. Anglesey is absolutely beautiful Dad, you should visit.'

'You recommend Anglesey then?'

'Yes, Dad.'

'Yesterday, I was watching an episode of *Gavin and Stacey*. In this episode, an old lady was relaxing with her grandchildren on the beach in Barry Island. It was one of those extremely rare, extremely hot days and she could not take the heat any more, so she decided to get an ice-cream, as you do in such weather. She was gone for ages, and when she came back, she sat and grumpily ate her Cornetto. Seeing how withdrawn she had become, one of her daughters asked what had happened. The lady's response was, 'I can't feckin' believe it! I was in the queue for bloody ages! So many bloody foreigners, here in our country, takin' our jobs and our benefits!' and her daughter asked, 'These foreigners, were they Polish, or Romanian, Mum?' to which the lady responded, 'O no, they were from Newport!' My daughter laughed and laughed:

'But Newport is just down the road!' she said, 'how could she call them foreigners?!'

We followed the Taff Embankment in silence and enjoyed the beautiful buildings across the river. From there, I could see the tall skyscraper of Loudoun Square in Butetown. Every time I see that building I am reminded of my time in Pechatniki in Moscow, and the many depressing months I spent running from immigration and student officials at Stavropol State University in southern Russia. How the heck *did* I manage to get myself to Wales, for truly, those were dark days.

My daughter held my hand. In the distance, a young woman was picking up what looked like dog excrement, but instead of putting it into an appropriate bag, she simply chucked it into the River Taff. Perhaps this explains the lack of fish.

We walked on until we got to where the Taff Trail meets the main road, and turned left on the bridge, carrying on towards Mount Stuart Square. We stopped at the Polish shop, *Polski Delicatessen* and bought four lollipops, and I tried to show off my basic understanding of the Polish language to my daughter (actually I have no understanding of Polish, but I speak Russian and know the Russian alphabet). I was explaining to her that *khleb* means bread, *pomodoro* means tomato, *miesam* means meat etc., when I heard 'Eric, Eric, *eta ti?*' As I turned around, I recognised an old client, Misha, for whom I had translated at the Welsh Refugee Council in Cardiff.

'*Misha, kak dela?*' (Misha, how are you?)

'*Ploha, ochen ploha, brat*' (bad, very bad, brother.)

I knew it was going to be a long conversation. If a Russian answers the question of how are you with, *ploha, ochen ploha*, it requires you to listen to how crappy or hellish their situation is. It's usually better to stick to the simple pleasantry of *priviet* then to walk away. But, I had asked for it and Misha was about to unleash Dante's Peak onto my shoulders. When I first met Misha, he told me he was from Syria but he spoke perfect Russian and we bonded. He had had very serious immigration problems. He had first claimed asylum in Bulgaria where his fingerprints had been taken and then, during a lull in the Syrian conflict, returned to Syria to reunite with his family. However, as the war escalated, he had packed his pauper's belongings and followed the flow of migrants crossing Europe into France. Eventually, via the underbelly of a train, he ended up in the UK. The Home Office rejected his asylum claim and began the process of repatriating Misha to Bulgaria. He argued that his human rights were not protected there but his defence meant that he had to report to the Home Office in Cardiff each day at 10.00 a.m.. His family had been killed by a friendly American missile which had fallen on a school in Aleppo (the Americans blamed the Russians, the Russians blamed the Turks and the Turks blamed the Kurds). As we spoke, Misha started crying.

'*Davai, davai bratan, ne plach*' (please, brother, do not cry.)

Eventually, Misha gathered himself, but my daughter had noticed him crying and walked away to wait for me outside the shop.

'What can make an old man cry in the middle of Cardiff Bay, Dad? What language was that?' she asked.

'Russian.'

'Can you teach me, Dad?' *Ekulekule* smiled again.

We went past Bute Street, past the traffic lights and were greeted by the grandiose sight of the Wales Millennium Centre. All along I was thinking of ways to tell my daughter that people leave their homes, their countries for different reasons. Maybe telling a story of animal migration? After all, she understood the complexity of human interaction within the context of George Orwell's *Animal Farm*: 'All animals are equal, but some animals are more equal than others'. With this in mind, I told her the story of the ethnic minority rabbit.

A rabbit had wandered off from his original feeding area, abandoning his friends and family in search of greener pastures. Their land was constantly ravaged by colonial wars, arms trade, droughts and extreme weather. Whilst growing up, the rabbit had given up his traditional beliefs and embraced the bible as the truth – he was an avid reader of the bible and had come across a biblical verse that states that in a time of drought and famine, a group of rabbits crossed deserts and seas until they came across a new land. The sage amongst the rabbits used a stick and made water burst from a rock to quench their thirst, and food fall from the sky to sate their hunger. The rabbit explained his understanding of the verse to the other rabbits but they laughed at him. After weeks of endless pondering and having lost weight, the rabbit decided enough was enough, and simply picked up his rucksack and took off, climbing mountains, crossing seas, seeking new lands, new adventures and a new abode.

After several years in foreign lands, feeding from faraway fields, the rabbit returned to his original clan. Not only was the rabbit unrecognisable, he spoke a funny language with a strange accent. He was greeted as a stranger amongst his own kind, seen as foreign – an outsider and an outcast. The other rabbits laughed and mocked him, they threw stones at him and they shunned him. He was not allowed to join them in their daily routine of gathering nuts and sticks, and building new homes to accommodate their every-increasing families. When it rained he was only allowed to stand on the veranda. He was nicknamed 'Ethnic Minority Rabbit, No Mates' (EMRNM). While all the other rabbits gathered around the fireside and listened as the elders told stories of their adventures, EMRNM could only listen through the window. Sometimes the other rabbits poked his ears for listening too closely, and closed the windows. When they went out to feed in the morning, as the rest of his clan gathered together, EMRNM ate in isolation.

One morning, the sun had risen early and had confused the rabbit clan. They wandered far afield for feeding and came across a new patch of fresh grass which was extra sweet, extra juicy. It seemed as if the migratory swallows had dropped extra nectar onto the grass. The rabbits ate, they rolled around, their bellies got bigger, and bloated – some of them lay on their backs, unable to move. The one rabbit that was supposed to be the lookout was caught up in the feeding frenzy – the taste of the new grass was to die for! With heads down, they ate, but little did they know that they had wandered into another territory, crossed a border, a protectorate governed by huge foxes, an animal equivalent of the Russian Special Forces! One by one, they were gathered up and taken to a police station. Their fate was sealed, they were destined for the slaughterhouse - these foxes were expert butchers. Crowds gathered, cheering, for there was to be a meat feast - one hundred caged rabbits! Each fox was to have enough meat to see it through the harsh winter months. The chief hunter was praised for spotting the stranded rabbits and called into the leader's inner chamber. He was honoured for his tracking skills and decorated with the highest award in the land.

From a distance, EMRNM could hear the sirens and rushed over to see what was causing the commotion. At first, he wanted to run back to the safety of the village for even in the distance, he could see the chief butchers sharpening the blades on the guillotine, sharp enough to glint in the sunlight. But he did not return to the village. When the other rabbits saw EMRNM casually walking toward the crowd, they shouted for him to run for dear life! But instead, EMRNM carried on, calmly. When the fox guards saw him, they rushed in his direction with their assault rifles drawn and ready to shoot. But when they got closer, the foxes dropped their weapons and ran towards EMRNM to greet him! They hugged and kissed, cheek to cheek, like pilgrims, then touched noses and sniffed the back of each other's ears. The captured rabbits did not understand. They shouted and screamed, warned EMRNM that the fate that had befallen them would soon be his. But EMRNM walked past their cage with the fox guards, ignoring their warnings.

'Traitor!' shouted one rabbit.

'You stitched us up!' said another, 'if we ever get out of this cage, we'll kill you!'

Touching paws with the foxes, EMRNM quietly walked straight past *and into the fox leader's inner chambers. After what seemed like an age, during which time, the guards toyed with the caged rabbits, taunting them with the skulls of previous victims, the fox leader emerged, followed by EMRNM, both of them laughing. They were clearly tipsy from palm wine, still chatting loudly and hugging. The chief guard suddenly ordered the release of all of the captured rabbits, and each was handed a bag of sweet nuts and some extra juicy grass. As it turned out, during his time away, EMRNM had met and lived amongst the foxes, learning their language and their ways, even their stiff upper lipped satire and sense of humour. His friendship with the foxes had saved his clan from the guillotine.*

My daughter had been listening intently to the story, gripped by the adventures of the ethnic minority rabbit, but now she laughed, and laughed again as she realised that the lollipops had melted away. We crossed the road and got some ice-creams – Cornettos, but there was no queue and the shop owner was from Italy, not Newport.

'So you see, *Ekulekule*, people leave their homes for many different reasons. I for one never thought I would come here, to Wales. My mother could not afford to send me abroad with her wage of twenty pounds a month. But I remember so very well the day my life changed, the day I came face to face with the devil and lost my faith, to eventually become a victim of human trafficking to Russia and to end up in Wales as a sixty-seven-year-old Zimbabwean.'

It was a Saturday. My nephew, Lyonga and I had been fishing in the small streams of Mosre Water, a short walk from my mother's house. Fishing in Mosre Water is a rite of passage. All the villagers have at one time fished in these waters. No matter how hot the weather is, Mosre Water remains cold.

We had been fishing for tadpoles and crabs. Mosre was serene and extremely cold and it seemed that the cold water had impacted on the metabolisms of the tadpoles and crabs as they were sluggish and could not get away. It was easy pickings – every stone we lifted had a small, scared-looking crab underneath for whom the day was marked. The tadpoles were no different. We used tiny baskets or just our hands and caught bucket-loads that day. There was no happier time in my life than that spent in the open with Lyonga. I love Lyonga. We are connected spiritually by a cord which has never been severed.

It had rained a little, and rain water had collected in some bricks by the side of my father's house. This became a temporary fishpond for our catch, but some of the tadpoles and crabs we wrapped in banana leaves after marinating with salt and pepper. My great aunt, Aunt Eposi was in the kitchen cooking maize in palm nut soup and she took the banana leaves and placed them into the hot charcoal. Lyonga and I went outside and played tabala, hopscotch.

'Elickie *yaaay ja eeeh*' (Eric, come). Aunty Eposi loved calling me 'Elickie' instead of Eric.

Lyonga and I sat at the front of my late father's house and ate our delicious catch of the day. Every crunch of the crab was met by the extra sweet, soft tadpole melting into our tongues – divine! We licked our fingers, ignoring the attentions of the jealous weaver bird that had nested in Mr Enongene's eucalyptus tree. Little did we know that the weaver bird was a wise old bird; it had discovered our improvised fishpond and had smuggled most of our tadpoles and crabs back to fatten its own family.

Suddenly, there was a kick, a loud bang on the door. It was Mr Jacob, my uncle. He walked past us brusquely, without his usual smile. His face was red in anger and I thought he must not have seen Lyonga and me. Mr Jacob loved me. He was a wonderful gardener and I worked in his tomato plantation. I climbed the mango and guava trees behind his house and all of his daughters were sisters to me.

Mr Jacob went straight into the kitchen and spoke with Aunty Eposi.

'Lyonga, Lyonga, *janu kasri, kasri.*'(Lyonga, hurry up and come here).

I didn't think much of it. I thought maybe Lyonga was in trouble, serious trouble. I waited five, ten, maybe twenty minutes for Lyonga to come back out. There were no loud cries, no shouting, so I knew for a fact that no one had died. In the village, if someone dies, you will hear tears, wailings from far and beyond. Then I heard the front door being locked. I stood up, took a deep breath, and tried to open the door. It wouldn't open, so I knocked and waited. Aunty Eposi opened the door slowly, her eyes as red as if she'd spent the afternoon blowing fire, the smoke going into her eyes. She then spoke these words, in Bakweri, words that have haunted me since. Most nights, I hear her voice, her voice, the harbinger of danger, the bearer of terrible news:

'Eric,' she said, instead of her usual Elickie, 'you are no longer welcome in this compound. You are not allowed to play with Lyonga. You are no longer a member of this family. If you ever set foot in here again, you will see what I will do to you. I will kill you.'

I tried to force my way into the kitchen to see what Lyonga was doing. He had his head on his knees and seemed to be crying. Mr Jacob's eyes were blood red and he looked at me as a lion would at its wounded prey. I saw danger in his eyes and his anger seemed to have polished his face of every wrinkle. That was the last time I saw Lyonga, the last smile we shared. It was the last time I spoke to my father's family.

I looked at my daughter. Her eyes were wide as she listened. It was as if every inch of her body wanted me to continue, so I did.

Haggard, broken, I walked towards my mother's house, my knees hardly able to carry my body. I couldn't breathe. Even the small bridge leading to our house seemed to be experiencing some kind of tremor and was shaking underneath me. I saw Moki Monyama shaving Peter's head. Aunty Frida was just returning home from Saturday market in Great Soppo, chastising Moki Monyama for not giving Njoh and Karine a bath. Moki would later tell me that I walked like someone who had seen a ghost, in a trance, for normally I would stop and chat. Aloga and Martin were trying to steal apples from Aunty Enanga's compound, Mephisto (aka Victor) carried a bucket of water on his head. On the hill, Mola Teke and Etongo were sharing the latest gossip from the village.

'Mama, Mama, what is the matter?' I asked, but my mother remained silent. I could tell she had been crying.

'Mama, Mama, tell me!'

My mother tried speaking but instead she only cried. She removed her once-white handkerchief from her pocket, blew her nose into it, folded it and put it back in her pocket. She tried to speak again, but was breathless, gasping. She handed me a letter.

From the Justice of the peace Mr Chief Justice Epouli
Re: The Will of late Mr Oscar Ngalle Charles

Dear Mr Eric Ngalle Charles,

Your father's Will is being contested by his family. Their argument is that late Mr Oscar Ngalle Charles had no son and therefore you are not entitled to the inheritance left in his Will. You are hereby summoned to attend the court if you are to challenge the claim made by your father's family.

Yours truly.
Chief Justice Epouli,
Family Court, Buea,
South West Province, Republic of Cameroon.

My mother was forced to hand me over to a Juju Man, a witchcraft practitioner because of the threat to my young life from my father's family. There followed a long and distressing legal battle and the first chapter of a very difficult time in my life.

On the final day of the court case, Chief Justice Epouli thanked both families and every witness and he spoke at length about the evidence heard. He began his summation of the case by addressing my mother.

'Miss Sarah Efeti Kange. The boy seated next to you – is he truly the son of the late Mr Oscar Ngalle Charles?'

'Yes, your honour. Ngalle is my son. Ngalle is the only child of Mola Ngalle.' My mother removed the once-white handkerchief from her handbag and wiped her tears. The same question was asked of all of my other witnesses. They all answered, yes. They all referred to my father as late. Only my mother spoke of him as if he were still alive.

It was now the turn of my father's relatives, first my Aunty Eposi, my father's aunty.

'Miss Eposi. The boy seated to your left, Eric Ngalle Charles – do you know him?'

She removed her glasses, blew into them and wiped them with her handkerchief. She then looked right into my eyes, straight through me, and turned to Chief Justice Epouli and said:

'No, your honour, I do not know this boy. I had never seen him until this court case.'

'So, Ngalle Eric Charles, the boy seated to the left of you, is not the son of late Oscar Ngalle Charles?'

'No,' Aunty Eposi looked at me, then looked at the judge, 'No, he is not.'

My father's sister answered the same. All of the witnesses brought by my father's family answered the same to Chief Justice Epouli's questions: 'No, he is not the son of the late Mr Oscar Ngalle Charles.' Each time they answered and disowned me, I felt I had been stabbed under my breast bone.

Then it was the turn of my adopted sister, Katherine, Lyonga's mother. She was the child my father had chosen, the sister I had grown up to love and cherish unconditionally. I could cope with the betrayal from my father's family, but I knew Katherine could not betray me. She loved me too much and I loved her. Her children were my brothers – Lyonga, Molua, Charlie – nothing could separate us.

'Katherine L.D. The boy seated to your left, Eric Ngalle Charles, do you know him? Is he the son of your adopted father, the late Mr Oscar Ngalle Charles?'

I had never felt so scared. I quaked, I panicked. The venom of a black mamba had filled my fangs – I could bite and kill! Sister Katherine did not look in my direction. She bowed down her head, silently folded her hands into each other. She looked at the judge and said:

'No, your honour, I do not know him. I have never seen him before.'

Over the years I have tried, but failed to put back together the shattered pieces of my heart. That was the last time I saw my sister Katherine, the last time I spoke to my aunties and uncle. By the time my mother and I left the court and reached the village, the local gossip had carried the news and spread it around. It was a Thursday, market day in our small village and in every doorway, every house, people mocked my mother, people pointed at her, her name was the main topic of the village. I was only seventeen years old but that was the day my soul died, the day that Satan flew away with me and the start of my journey from Cameroon, to Russia and eventually here, to Wales, as a sixty-seven-year-old Zimbabwean.

When I looked at my daughter, she was in tears. We walked on past the Millennium Centre, and jumped on a Number Eight bus via Corporation Road into Grangetown. To cheer her up, I told her the story of the man whose one wish in life is to become the first Welsh astronaut – two unsuccessful attempts so far, but he has not given up.

Brexit has never come up again in our conversation; I am still The Good Migrant, my daughter now speaks English, Welsh, French and, now, a little Russian.

When two elephants fight, it is the grass that suffers
— African proverb

THE WHITE WALL

FROM *LA BLANCHE* BY MAÏ-DO HAMISULTANE

TRANSLATED BY SUZY CEULAN HUGHES

I've hired a convertible and decided to do a trip around the
country before going back to Paris.
I'm no longer afraid of Victor, of life, of myself.
I'm filled with a need to live life, not intensely but to the full.

My fingers grip the Bakelite of the steering wheel, something
tangible that helps me to cope with this new freedom echoing
with loneliness.
Before heading out of Casablanca, I drive past Mira Ventos.
I automatically follow the route I used to take with Grandpa.
The big villas, tended by caretakers, with their beautiful, lush
gardens, line the road. I go beyond the white wall where
Grandpa used to make me turn around.
A few metres further on, the beautiful, wide, tarred avenue
becomes a narrow, unsurfaced track.
The tyres cautiously bump along in the gravel.
The track leads to a neighbourhood that looks like a shantytown.
Children dressed in rags come running towards me.
They hang onto the car. I accelerate, my heart in my mouth. I do
a U-turn.
The narrow, sandy track. The villas barricaded behind brightly
coloured hedges. The caretakers standing outside their respective
properties, exchanging knowing looks.
I understand why Grandpa didn't want to go beyond the white
wall.

I understand that the sunny world of my childhood wasn't
Morocco, it was Mira Ventos.

I had never suffered before my grandfather was murdered.

Mira Ventos – an enchanted place cut off from the rest of the
world.

I think about my grandfather's murderers, who believed the
bust of Juba II was a bust of Christ.

They lived in poverty, with opulence in their faces.

The life we lived at Mira Ventos seems obscene to me.

The sumptuous parties.

The festival of Eid al-Adha, the men full of joy, giving praise.

The warm smell of méchoui, the traditional slow-roasted lamb,
wafting out into the narrow, sandy track and drifting through
the shantytown, where mothers are listening to their children
crying of hunger.

I think about Victor, his beauty – a marble statue falling upon
my body of glass.

Toothless children hanging onto the Bakelite steering wheel.

Mira Ventos, which is no longer Morocco.

Mira Ventos, a world apart.

Mira Ventos and a tragedy waiting to happen.

And us – bathed in sunlight on long summer afternoons, with
the fountain softly singing.

I think of Nan Goldin's photograph.

Look beyond the surface.

Look beyond Victor's appearance.

Beyond intuition.

Look beyond experience.

I think the man in the photo looks kind. Yes, why not the
pleasure of tobacco after the pleasure of the body? He puts
down his cigarette and turns towards the woman lying on the
bed. He kisses her. Nan smiles.

I think of Eduardo Mallea's words: 'Each man's destiny is personal only insofar as it may resemble what is already in his memory.'

I do another U-turn. I don't want my destiny to lie in my memories. I don't want to be a prisoner of my past.

I drive along the narrow, sandy track.

Moving towards the unexpected. Seeing and hearing what we cannot plan out.

A boy asks me where I'm going.

He speaks good French.

I say, 'I don't know.'

In a voice full of life and light-heartedness, he asks me, 'Will you take me home?'

'Where do you live?'

'Taroudant.'

I nod.

He gets in the car.

I wanted an extraordinary, incredible, life-saving, self-confirming adventure.

The hospitality offered by this boy and his family in the mountains.

A climb up to a dam. Golden sunlight.

Palm trees full of dates.

Couscous quite different from any I had had before.

Immersion in a Morocco I didn't know.

They introduce me to a French guy who wants to open an eco-hotel.

They tell me he's someone. That he rubs shoulders with important people in France.

I talk to him.

He's a man with vision who is drawn to Morocco.
At the top of the dam.
In bright sunshine.
Looking across at the mountain, with its red earth.
I close my eyes.
I'm looking for Mira Ventos, Le Mirage Hotel, Tahiti Beach.
I no longer have a home.
Home is with my grandmother, my mother, my grandfather.
Grandma has lost her mind. Mum plunged into chronic
depression after the tragedy. Grandpa is dead and buried.
You can't 'lose the quotidian south', you can't lose your
bearings when you no longer have any bearings to lose.
Before you can escape, you have to be a prisoner.
Make yourself a prisoner of your memories.
I decide to leave.

Mira Ventos.
The images pile one on top of another.
Huge playground of my childhood.
Lunches out in the sun.
Equestrian displays on moonlit summer evenings.
Mirrors covered with white sheets.
Torn Persian carpets.
My grandfather's blood at the foot of the white marble
staircase.
Hassan looking at me with hatred.
The bougainvillea.
The room stinking of conspiracy.
The white wall.
What lies behind it.

◉ GB HAS LEFT THE GROUP ◉

SIÔN TOMOS OWEN

From a joint love of football and setting off fireworks down the back lanes of the terraces, they had forged strong friendships since primary school. A rarity. Like a soap opera, they had seen each others' characters develop over the years; some had left and returned, others were stalwarts of the village. Over three decades the classroom bond had not waned. Initially kept alive through the odd text, birthday night out and annual rugby international tournament weekends, now, thanks to the *group chat* option on WhatsApp, they could be in constant discussion via social media.

The group was originally set up to share a rumoured low resolution homemade porno of someone they once knew. But after hours of 'analysis' they eventually succumbed to the disappointment that it was not the 'Swedish Goddess' who moved to the area for Summer '01 only to disappear by September. They still shared the odd photo and video for mutual appreciation of filth (some sharing more than others) but now it was far more than somewhere to debate the areola colouring of a teenage fantasy from fifteen years ago (regardless of the fact none of them had ever seen her naked, despite claims by one of the group). It was a place to discuss sporting results, national team selections, social events, terrorism, DIY advice, job gripes and career prospects, racism, traffic, philosophical thought, Philistine thought and to swear more than they ever would in person.

For the single men it was a vainglorious chance for bragging rights of their 'totals', for the married men it was an insight to these philandering adventures. They argued, they bantered, they shared, they abused each other's mothers, they left the group, then privately messaged someone to be re-added, then left the group again a few weeks later. The tradesmen laughed at the office workers when they sent inappropriate NSFW (Not Suitable For Work) photos or what looked like a viral prank video only to turn into a man getting his genitals stuck in a mousetrap. Those who worked in schools or offices knew never to open a video with the sound on less their work colleagues raise an eyebrow at the questionable moans, grunts or cursing that would then hastily be muted. Some knew not to even bother opening videos shared by certain members of the group since it would inevitably be followed by the vomiting emoji and comments asking where they even get them from.

The old adage, 'never discuss money or politics at a dinner party' did not apply to this group as this group was not a party, it was a swamp and a paradise. It was a filthy, funny, fickle and unforgiving digital social club in their pockets.

Ceirion, Max, Levi, Dafydd, Neil, Rej, Joe and Gobber were fully fledged members of:

♣ THE HATEFUL 8 ♣

JOE   I'm, on 50K a year now so I'm fuckin rollin in it $ $

LEVI   Fuck off r u! u don't even do nything, u clipboard cunt.

REJ   LOLOL

MAX   🚫 🚫 🚫

NEIL   LOL

CEIRION Haha! Clipboard cunt!

JOE   I'm transitional maintenance foreman u callcenter bitch!📞 📞 📞

LEVI   Basic comeback. I'm no one's bitch, top dog I am. transitional maintenance ain't even a real job title, either

220

JOE   Fuckin is though. I organise the train all the freight and haulage guys now. I'm their king

LEVI   King of the morons more like. U were shunting and grunting last month

JOE   Career progression init, dick head. More than u, chewing off people's arm for their pin numbers and pensions 🙏 😵 😵

LEVI   Salesman of the week for the last two months, I've been, butt!

JOE   You've only been there 3 weeks, Pinocchio … 🤥

DAFYDD Thought u'd only just started, Lev?

GOBBER Billy Bullshit 💩 💩

> Levi Phillip Evans, Leviathan@hotmail.co.uk
> Salesman, Twilight Insurance
> A braggart but an incredible salesman, could sell a steak to a vegan. Had over 50 jobs because of boredom and unprofessionalism but always lands on his feet. The eternal bachelor who's lived with a number of women over the years but none of the relationships ever last and returns to live with his parents for brief periods before moving in with the next poor soul that succumbs to his charms. Most recently living in the capital city with an ex's best friend and working as a salesman for Twilight Insurance selling over 50s life insurance. Doesn't like living in a multicultural city but suits his current lifestyle, until his money or current girlfriend's patience runs out.

LEVI   I was recruited wern I, told u that

GOBBER Recruitment runt. Salesman of the weak. Can't even lift 60K 🏆

LEVI   What the the fuxat got to do with anything?

GOBBER Haven't been to the gym in years. Get the Rocky theme on them headsets u want instead of talking 😤💪💪

CEIRION LOL 😂😂😂

MAX   LOL

LEVI   What does that even mean u meathead?
        Why do i gotto lift weights to be good at my job?
        I'm not a fuckin chippy am I?

GOBBER What u trying to say?! Nothing wrong with being a chippy!

MAX   ☐ *sends gif of Olive Oyl from Popeye with
        flailing arms*

GOBBER I could piss salesman of the week easy

CEIRION I'd fucking pay to c that!

JOE   LOLOLOL 😂

REJ   ☐ *sends a meme of Vladimir Putin with a raised
        eyebrow and the word 'Niet' below*

JOE   Fuck me, that would be gold!

DAFYDD That would b hilarious!

GOBBER What u all fuckin laughin at piss easy job no lifting
        indoors sit on ur fat arse all day and phone grannys
        tellin em to buy coffins before they die fuckin simple

LEVI   Yup, exactly what I do

MAX   'Kinell, lolol 😅😅

REJ   😂😂😂

NEIL   😂

JOE   ☐ *sends a photo of an old woman sunbathing topless*
        Gobber's first customer

MAX   Oh god, who's that?

LEVI   Ur mother!

JOE   Ur mother!!

GOBBER Ur mother

CEIRION LOL

REJ   LOL, too easy

MAX   Walked right into that one

JOE   Schoolboy error

MAX   Gimi a break mun, my head's shot, haven't slept tidy in 4 weeks. Baby keeps screamin all night.

I love her and that but she's a fuckin lunatic 😵

Macsen Raymond Lewis, MaxLew84@gmail.com Production Engineering Assistant, ResCom Contracting. Left school at GCSE with decent grades. Didn't want to stay on at 6th form and went straight in to work at a factory on a production line to save for his first car. Despite the monotony of 6 years punching holes into sheets of aluminium, he worked his way through the floor as far as he could before leaving to a rival company on better pay. Was the first of the group to buy his own home out of the valley nearer the industrial estates in the next county. Met his current girlfriend on a work night out, a few months later she was pregnant. His new pregnant girlfriend moved in 5 months into the pregnancy. Now they have a 2 month old son who is not sleeping well which is beginning to affect Max's shift work.

Can't keep my eyes open in work. Fuckin dick of a boss cautioned me already.

Told him bout the baby. Couldn't give a fuck

LEVI   I'd caution u too, lazy fuck

MAX   Fuck u

GOBBER Just punch him in the face and tell him to fuck off 😖 🗯

Rej   Excellent idea, Gob

Joe   *sends a gif of a UFC fighter being knocked out*

Dafydd Of course, that'd work wouldn't it ... 😑

Max Aye, perfect that would be. I'd b selling my arse down the docks to buy nappies ...

Levi No one would pay to shag that arse

Joe 💣 🙄

Ceirion First ever minimum wage rent boy in a union

Levi Jobsucker's allowance

Joe Down the Blowjob Centre

Rej And what are your skills, sir?

Engineering

Forklifting

Handjobs

Gobber Fisting

Dafydd Fuckin L, bit early for fisting in it, Gob? Not even morning break yet.

Gobber fuck off boring mr pedo

Dafydd Hilarious, every teacher is a paedo

Gobber Nah, just u

Rej LOL

Joe 😂

Gobber ROFL

Dafydd Fuck the lot of u!

Gobber Aw snowflake pedo off back to wank in a store cupboard before assembly

Dafydd Joke's getting old now, butt

Gobber 🙁 🙁 ❄️ ❄️

Levi If u can't take it don't dish it out

Dafydd I never do dish it out, only you ever do it!

Levi ☐ *sends a photo of a handbag*

Calm down, dear

Dafydd I been teaching 7 years now and you still wind me up about it, though. Does my head in!

GB Has Left the Group

GOBBER ☐ *sends a photo of a Jimmy Saville with Dafydd's face photoshopped onto it*

⦿Dafydd left the group⦿

MAX   Oh, Jesus, that's rough

REJ   Nice one, Gob mun

CEIRION I'll re-add him now

LEVI   Don't! Let him pout a bit. Get it out of his system.

MAX   Gob, text him ur sorry and get him back in

GOBBER I'm not texting a pedo it'll b evidence if he gets caught

REJ   What u on about evidence, u mental?

GOBBER If e cant take it fuck him

NEIL   Except Simon's not actually a paedophile though is he?

GOBBER Teacher=pedo SIMPLES

NEIL   How have you even got a job?

GOBBER Wat u mean?

NEIL   Never mind

GOBBER Say it

        say it

LEVI   Calm down, Captain Caveman

GOBBER Fuck off Levi

        wat u mean neil u boring twat?

        wat do u even do dole bum?

MAX   Wow, Gob

REJ   Too far, Gob. Chill out, u dick!

JOE   Faxake, Gob

LEVI   C'mon, Gob butt, bit much

.   Neil Corben Jones, npj19@Aol.com
        Additional Needs Assistant at County Borough
        Council at Abereba Community Centre. After planned
        Council restructuring of four local Communities First

areas, Neil was recently made redundant after two of the four community centres were closed. Neil signed on at the Jobcentre three months ago and was originally eligible for Jobseekers Allowance. On June 22nd 2017 he reached the 3 month threshold without a successful application for gainful employment and is now on intensive Jobmatch, facing sanctions if he is not successful.

To get to the Jobcentre he passes the community project building where someone has spray painted a yellow 'Why?' on the blue shutters. He asks himself the same question every day. His girlfriend asked him the same question when he couldn't find work. He told her he was trying but with no train line in the valley and busses cut to a reduced timetable, competing with other carers without a car was difficult. After a few weeks she told him to move out and they no longer speak. He had to move in with his gran for the past month due to an error in his housing benefit.

NEIL   I just mean, HOW did u get a job? U left school before u even finished GCSEs basically and u always got a job wherever u move to. How?

GOBBER Fuckin work dont i

NEIL   HOW though? I got A-levels and qualifications coming out of my arse! I can't get anything!

JOE   Sumin'll come, butt

GOBBER Just find a job init

NEIL   Not that easy though, Gob, is it?
        Ur on the tools, different type of work init.
        U can just rock up to a site in your van and crack on. I can't do that.

226

GOBBER Be a welder or sumin we always looking for welders

NEIL I'm not a fucking welder though, am I, Gob?
I can look after people, I can use a disability winch in a swimming pool, I can plan activities for OAPs and organise trips for disabled people but they don't seem to want nothing like that. Unless ur a qualified social worker or got a degree in care there's fuckin nothing!

CEIRION Something'll come, butt

REJ U tried going up to all the old people's homes round here, butt? They must need someone every now and then.

NEIL I'm in 2 of em already! But it's fucking zero hours. Barely get a few hours a week so I still gotto sign on cause it's less than 16 hours

LEVI Sounds shit, butt

NEIL It is, I'm literally begging them for more hours but they never give em to me.

GOBBER How u workin and signin on

NEIL U sign on unless u work more than 16 hours a week. Otherwise I'd get bout £50 a week for them care home hours. That's just £200 a month, fuckin rent in Angela's place was £400 a month on it's own!

GOBBER I get £50 for half a day

LEVI Jesus Gob, Shut up

NEIL Fuck me, ur a bellend sometimes

GOBBER Scrounging that is

NEIL If u weren't in Swindon I'd smack u in ur fuckin face

REJ Fuck me, what's wrong with u, Gob

GOBBER DO IT CUNT GO ON

⦿GOBBER was removed from the group⦿

Cerion Sorry, Neil, butt. He's thick as shit

Levi Oh fuck, he's gonna be fuming

Rej Serves him right.

Joe Roid rage ✏️ 👍 😣 😠

Levi He's not all there sometimes

Neil All the fucking times

⦿CEIRION added DAFYDD to the group⦿

Joe Ark at Ceirion, the bouncer deciding who's allowed in or out.

Ceirion Only when people r being dickheads and he's prime dickhead today

Rej Prime

Ceirion I'll re-add him after he calms down.

Dafydd What's he done now, then?

Rej After he had a pop at you and you left, he went off at Neil cause Gob a tactless arsehole

Joe Fuck me he's going apeshit at me
☐ *sends screenshot of messages from Gobber in block capitals threatening to drive back to Abereba to beat Neil up.*
Apparently Neil butt, ur a gypo paki cunt.

Neil 😕?!

Joe Probably cz ur a bit tanned, I dno

Rej Talking shit aint he. Don't take notice Neil, butt

Dafydd Maybe this is the teacher in me, but how come he can't use punctuation but switches to capitals when he's angry?
He's like an illiterate Jekyll and Hyde. I honestly think my year 5s are more switched on than him.

Ceirion LOL

Levi   Tell him he'll have to pay the bridge toll if he's coming home, that'll stop him, the tightarse.

Rej   LOL

Neil   Genuinely though, why is he so angry all the time? Got a job, a flat and a missus and he's always raging about something. Last week it was the Polish for nickin jobs, this week I'm getting it in the neck for NOT having a job. I don't get him

.   Gordon Farr bignobgobber 100kg@aol.com
       Scaffolder for B&P Construction, Swindon
       Moved between family members' homes when growing up due to his parents alcoholism and separation. Left school before completing all of his GCSEs. Expelled twice for fighting. Left to work as a labourer with his uncle then worked as a scaffolder. He became used to travelling long hours for work, mostly along the M4 corridor but worked hard, played harder. Dabbled in drugs but nothing serious. After meeting a girl on a night out, they began seeing each other but it ended badly after Gobber's friends discovered she was a stripper not a waitress and wound him up about it on a night out. Gobber got into a fight and hospitalised someone. He was arrested and spent 18 months in Swansea Prison. During this time his uncle had a heart attack and retired, but to keep him out of trouble, he convinced his mate to offer Gobber work away from the valleys. Gobber moved to Swindon and now only comes home during rugby internationals twice a year and to see his mother at Christmas. Over the years the boys have seen him fluctuate physically so are sure he takes steroids, which

he denies. He is often removed from the group for extreme abuse or being overtly racist.

Levi   He's thick as shit is why. He doesn't mean any harm, though

Joe   ☐ *Posts a screenshot of a message from Gobber saying he's going to rip Neil's head off and shove it up his arse* Aye, totally harmless. LOL

Neil   He's got a screw loose, mun.

Joe   He's probably got blueballs, his missus is away on a hen weekend in Maga.

Max   Lucy hasn't let me near her the last 2 months since the baby was born but I ain't kicking off at everyone like him

Rej   Fuckin L, I haven't had a wank in 3 days but I don't get that fucking angry.

Levi   It's the roids mun, gotto be

Joe   Says he don't take them though. He used to hate needles in school

Neil   Now he just hates the Polish and Asians

Rej   And Gypsies

Levi   And Gays

Joe   Swindon's full of them though

Rej   So. I read somewhere that Swindon's one of the fastest growing cities. It's not just gonna be filled with English is it?

Joe   It's in England though

Rej   Same as this valley. They came from everywhere when there were pits. English, Scottish, Italians, Polish. We're all immigrants

Levi   I'm not

Joe   Swindon's full of Immigrants en is it?

Ceirion including Gobber ...

Levi 😋

Joe How's Gobber an immigrant?

Neil Immigrant just means someone who moves from one place to another to live

◻ *Posts a screenshot of a dictionary description of Immigrant 'A person who leaves one country to settle permanently in another.'*

Ceirion Technically, Gobber's a Welsh immigrant in England. If ur gonna be pedantic, if Cardiff was another country, u'd be an Abereba immigrant in another country

Levi Now ur just making shit up.
Fuck does pedantic mean?

Rej Fussy. Like u and Gobber are fussy who's allowed to be in this country

Levi Don't lump me in with him. I just don't think they should be allowed here unless they got a job

Neil I haven't got a job, does that mean I can't to move to Swindon?

Levi U can't move to Swindon cz Gob will 'Fuckin smash u' LOL

Neil 😅

Rej 😂

Joe Different world living in a city though in it. Changes you.

Max What u defending him for, Joe?

Joe I ain't I'm just saying he's different since moving to England

Levi Fuckin English ruining him

Neil U sound just as racist as him saying that

Ceirion U make it sound like he wasn't always like this, his uncle basically sent him away BECAUSE he was like this

Levi   Sent away? He's not a fuckin refugee

Dafydd   Don't u mean evacuee?

Levi   Fuck me. Now who's fussy?

Dafydd   Evacuees are evacuated for their safety. Refugees escape persecution. He's more like the bloody persecutor! He's like a hate preacher that gets deported

Rej   Oh, the irony

Joe   He'll be tamping if he sees u all slagging him off

Ceirion Today he deserves a bit of slagging off the amount he's doing himself

Neil   Seems like he hates everything though, without reason.

Rej   Definitely hates his exes.

Ceirion Fair play, he does always have a reason to hate his exes though, it's just that they're mental reasons.

Joe   The last one was a bitch to him though, by the sound of it.

Rej   No one ever met her though. We only got his word to go on and he's about as trustworthy as a Tory.

Levi   Oh god, don't start with the politics now Rej

Ceirion How come fisting and topless grannies are fine but it's too early for politics?!

I'll never understand this group

Rej   It's polling day! How can it be too early? Even the polls opened at 7am.

The papers don't stop going on about it and I ain't gonna stop until they stop lying about it.

Joe   What they lying about now en?

Levi   Oh here we fucking go ... 😵

Rej   Joe butt, how many times we gonna go over this?

       ⬜ *sends photo of a bus with a slogan about spending £350M a week on the NHS instead of the EU.*

☐ *sends photo of a fact check disputing the claim*
☐ *sends photo of the Daily Mail front page*
proclaiming the £350M to the NHS
☐ *sends photo of the same page with sections highlighted and*
fact checked as false.

Levi   Don't start this again now. How many times you gonna put these up?

Rej   When UKIP stop lying about immigrants coming and wanting to throw them out. When Tories stop lying about how much money leaving the EU will save us.

Levi   Booooooorrrrrrring L 😵
We're better off out. EU is 💩

Dafydd My father says the same

Neil   I don't know how ur dad can say that, butt. He's worked in the same factory all his working life and it's got a bit sign that says Funded by the EU on the side of the fucking building!
He literally wouldn't have a job without it.

Dafydd I'm not saying I agree with him but I don't disagree either

Rej   What the fuck does that even mean?

Levi   Just cause it's got yellow stars on it doesn't mean he wouldn't still be there doing the same job. Everyone is buying cars. They say it all the time. It's the one part of the economy that's booming.

Rej   That's bollocks though, it's got to be. U can't keep an economy going on cars. How many of us lot have ever bought a brand new car?

Dafydd We do live in a poor area though. Doesn't mean other people don't buy new cars.

Rej   U for leave as well now Daf, r u?

Dafydd I'm just playing devil's advocate.
Still haven't decided 🤷

Levi   Fuckin L, like. Today the vote is, u gutless prick 🗓31

Rej   Ur arse must be killing from sitting on that fuckin fence, Daf.

Neil   We live in a poor area, which is more reason than ever to stay in the EU. It basically funds our entire valley. My project was EU funded.

Joe   Not the best example that ain't, mind, Neil ...

Neil   It's Tory austerity that caused me to lose my fuckin job not the EU Our council's Labour though

Rej   Aye, but we get the money from central government, so we got less because Tories give out less in the budget

Joe   But ain't the Welsh Assembly Labour as well?

Dafydd   Aye, but Council money comes from Parliament

Ceirion   I don't think it does, Daf

Dafydd   Doesn't Westminster give it to the Assembly who then give it to the councils?

Rej   Yes

Max   I'm fuckin confused as fuck now

Neil   What I'm saying is that where we live, we get more out of the EU than we put in BECAUSE we're a poor area. Tories won't give us fuck all if we end up having to rely on them.

Rej   Brexit ain't bout Tory or Labour, it's whether we stay in the EU so we can get the funding allocated to Wales because we're a poorer part of the EU.

    ☐ *posts a colour coded map of Europe from richest to poorest areas based on green, orange and red, Wales is highlighted the only red area in the West of Europe*

Levi   Still don't know if that's true though

Rej   What do u mean, u still don't know? It fuckin IS true. That's a fact. A real one. Not a fake one. That's a European Parliament chart, u tit. We get more funding from the EU because we need it.

That's the whole point of the EU, everyone pays in to improve the areas that need it so they get better.

Levi   Why ain't we better then?

Rej   ...

Neil   Cz we still need it.

Levi   So after 40 odd years of the EU we're still poor 🙁
Shows it ain't working then doesn't it?

Max   U Voted Leave en, Levi?

Levi   ▢ *posts a photo of his voting card with an X in the Leave box*

Taking back control mother fuckers

Neil   Massive error

Ceirion   ▢ *posts a gif of a beautiful woman shaking her head in disappointment*

Rej   Knob.

U sound like fuckin Gobber, u'll be ranting that immigrants are stealing ur job while simultaneously living off benefits next.

Fuckin Schrodinger's immigrant 🐱

Levi   Lost me now

Neil   LOL

Dafydd   LOLOL

Joe   ▢ *posts a photo of his voting card with an X in the Remain box*

Do I get a gold star?

Rej   Fuckin A! U get 12 yellow stars butt! 🏳

Max   Thought you were voting leave, Joe

Joe   I was, but I bin reading all the stuff u all sent and it makes more sense to stay in

Rej   Fuckin right it does! Bewsh! 🙌

Levi   Here we go, jumping on another bandwagon is it Joe?
😳 Like ur fuckin bleach blonde Eminem phase, that

month of crossfit and 2 weeks of being a vegan.
Fuxake like, u shithouse Tryin to be one of the cool
kids

Joe Fuck off! Just makes more sense, economy wise and
that. Plus all our distribution goes to Europe so I'm
keeping jobs ana

Levi Like fuck,
👍voting friends👍
☐*posts gif of a TV show character doing a wanker sign*

Rej Looks like it's just u and Gob that are voting out
anyway Lev, so ...

Max And Daf, he's just too gutless to say ...

Rej Well, Daf?

Dafydd ...

Levi Fuckin right he did, nice one Daf boy!

Dafydd I voted, Just keeping it to myself. It's my right

Rej Oh you fuckin did and all, u stupid twat

Levi Welcome to the team, Daf
☐*posts a gif of two muscular men fist bumping*

Rej Congratulations, Daf, butt. Ur in great company.

Ceirion Speaking of which.

◉CERION added GOBBER to the group◉

Gobber FUCKIN DO THAT AGAIN AND I'LL KILL U

Ceirion Welcome back, behave now ...

Levi Simmer down, Hulk

Gobber U cnt just chuck people out for no reason cause u
fuckin say so

Rej Oh, the irony

Gobber What u sayin now thasorus boy

Dafydd Just that ur timing is impeccable

Neil　　We're talkin bout Brexit

Gobber I'm out!

　　　　☐ *posts a gif of Britain's Got Talent pressing 4 X in a row*

Rej　　Speaking of chucking people out, I was just saying
　　　　something similar Gob

　　　　Tell me

　　　　What would u do with someone with a history of
　　　　violence, who'd say, been to jail in another country and
　　　　was saying he hated and was threatening to kill to
　　　　people in this country?

Dafydd C'mon Rej, he ain't that thick

Gobber Fuckin chuck em out

　　　　send the cunts back to where they come from

Rej　　Perfect answer. Ladies and Gentlemen, I give you the
　　　　Leave Voter in a nutshell

Dafydd Jesus wept

Neil　　🙈

Max　　😂 😂

Gobber ☐ *posts a gif of people waving at an overcrowded boat of*
　　　　black people

Rej　　Oh, and a racist gif as well to back it up. Delightful

　　　　There's ur tag team partner, Daf. Enjoy ur social
　　　　cleansing and economic Armageddon together

Dafydd Don't be so dramatic

Levi　　We'll see tonight now, who's right

Rej　　More like who's right wing

Gobber What u choppsin shit about now

　　　　i was right wing in school

Rej　　Ur answers are becoming beyond satire, butt

　　　　I can't even laugh at them anymore

Gobber Fuck u on about rej

Rej　　Never mind

(22:01)

Rej	Polls have shut, nothing to be done about it now
Neil	U stayin up to watch it roll out?
Rej	Aye, See u tomorrow in the darkness or the light
Levi	This ain't fuckin Star Wars, Yoda

(00:23)

Levi	What they saying en?
Rej	Remain got it so far but only bin a few counties come in
Neil	Guardian blog got pollsters saying it for Remain 55%
Rej	It's looking good so far
Levi	I'm off to bed, c u boring fuckers in the morning

(01:44)

Rej Fuckin L, u seen the most common google search since the polls closed?!

☐ *posts a screenshot of Google search bar with 'What happens if UK leaves the European Union?'*

People are googling it AFTER casting their fucking votes! Fkin unbelievable

Neil U drinking?

Rej 2nd bottle of Black Tower

Neil I'm on my gran's Bristol Cream. Nothing else here. Bad times

Max What happening? Up with the baby. Can't av the telly on tho so just on Twitter. Can't keep up with what's going on. Too much info at the same time. Head's shot

Dafydd Just checked Twitter too. Why is Lindsay Lohan avin a crack at Kettering?

Rej Cause they voted leave
Like u

Neil	Kettering voted out massively
Dafydd	What's it got to do with her though?
Rej	Stop deflecting
Neil	She's doing what UKIP do, trying to force their opinions on something they don't understand

(02:05)

Rej	Fuckin Merthyr voted Leave
Max	Merthyr?!
Rej	They're practically sponsored by the fucking EU the cheeky fucks
Max	Struggling to stay awake now, text me when u know
Neil	This ain't looking good, butt

(03:03)

Neil	Rhondda Cynon Taff voted out
Rej	We're fucked butt
Neil	And Gwent
Rej	All the places in Wales that get the most EU funding voting out. Fuckin stupid. Biting the hand that feeds em
Neil	3 projects I worked for were EU funded. They run out of funding and another project comes along, same thing just different targets. Half my fuckin working life. I'm even more fucked if we vote out
Rej	Not just u butt, we'll all be fucked, fuckin fuckin fucked

(04:16)

| Neil | Almost all of Wales, like |
| Rej | I can't believe it.
I'm so fuckin depressed, it's unreal. |

(04:39)

Neil	They've called it
Rej	...

(06:30)

Gobber WEHEY U FUCKIN CUNTS

Joe   What was the score?

Levi   Only a couple of percent in it. They haven't finished
        but they've said Leave won

Dafydd That's it then

Joe   Rej, u knob, u convinced me it was the right thing to do
        Ended up on the fucking losing side, like, gutted

Gobber WINNER WINNER CHICKEN DINNER

🔒 *Messages to this group are now secured with end-to-end encryption.*
Tap for more info.

⬤EXIT GROUP CHAT⬤

Author Biographies

Albert Forns is a journalist and award-winning Catalan writer. He has published two novels – *Jambalaia* (Anagrama, 2016) which won the Anagrama Prize, and *Albert Serra (la novel·la, no el cineasta)* (Empúries, 2013) which picked up the Documenta Prize. He has also published a volume of poetry *Ultracolors* (LaBreu Edicions, 2013), inspired by the work of contemporary artists. He regularly writes on theatre, literature and visual arts for his blog as well as for *Time Out* magazine and the digital magazine Núvol.com.

Uršul'a Kovalyk is a Slovak poet, fiction writer, playwright and social worker. She has worked for a non-profit organisation focusing on women's rights and currently works for the NGO Against the Current, which helps homeless people. She is the director of the Theatre With No Home, which features homeless and disabled actors. She has published two collections of short stories, and two novels, *Žena zo sekáča*, and *Krasojazdkyňa* shortlisted for Slovakia's most prestigious Anasoft Litera Award, winner of the Bibliotéka Prize 2013 and published in English as *The Equestrienne* by Parthian in 2016.

Raised in Caernarfon, north Wales, **Llŷr Gwyn Lewis** studied at Cardiff and Oxford, before completing a doctorate on the work of T. Gwynn Jones and W.B. Yeats. Following periods as lecturer in Welsh at universities in Swansea and Cardiff University he now works as resource editor at the Welsh Joint Education Committee in Cardiff. His first prose work, *Rhyw Flodau Rhyfel (Some Flowers of War*, 2014), won the Creative Non-Fiction category in the 2015 Wales Book of the Year award, and his poetry collection, *Storm ar Wyneb Haul (Storm on the Face of the Sun*, 2014), was shortlisted in the poetry category. His first short story collection, *Fabula*, was shortlisted for the Wales Book of the Year award 2018. In 2017 Llŷr Gwyn Lewis became one of the Ten New Voices form Europe for 2017, a selection of emerging writers from around Europe made by Literature Across Frontiers' network of European festivals Literary Europe Live.

Lloyd Markham was born in Johannesburg, South Africa, moving to and settling in Bridgend, south Wales when he was thirteen. He spent the rest of his teenage years miserable and strange and having bad nights out before undertaking a BA in Writing at Glamorgan followed by an MPhil. He enjoys noise music, Japanese animation and the documentaries of Adam Curtis. He operates synthesisers in a band called Deep Hum and has less bad nights out these days. His novel, *Bad Ideas\Chemicals* from which 'Mercy' was extracted was shortlisted for the Wales Book of the Year and Betty Trask prizes.

Clare Azzopardi is an award-winning Maltese writer who writes for both children and adults. She is the Head of Department of Maltese at the University of Malta Junior College and for the past several years has been an active member of Inizjamed, an NGO whose mission is to promote literature in Malta and abroad. Azzopardi has also published two books of short stories for adults, both of which won the National Book Prize for Literature and many of her stories were published in literary magazines such as *Words Without Borders* and *Asymptote*. Clare Azzopardi took part in several festivals and in 2016 she was chosen as one of Europe's New Voices.

Alys Conran's first novel, *Pigeon* (Parthian), won the Wales Book of the Year Award 2017 and was shortlisted for the International Dylan Thomas Prize. The first novel to be published simultaneously in English and Welsh, *Pigeon* also won a People's

Choice Award, the Rhys Davies Trust Fiction Award, and was longlisted for the Authors' Society First Novel Award. Her second novel, *Dignity*, will be published in 2019. She lived for several years in first Edinburgh and then Barcelona, and is now Lecturer in Creative Writing in her hometown of Bangor, north Wales.

Oisín Fagan has had short fiction published in *The Stinging Fly*, *New Planet Cabaret* and the anthology *Young Irelanders*, with work featured in the Irish Museum of Modern Art. In 2016, he won the inaugural Penny Dreadful Novella Prize for *The Hierophants*. *Hostages*, his first collection, was also published in 2016 by New Island.

Eluned Gramich is a Welsh-German writer and translator. She won the inaugural People and Places: New Welsh Writing Award with *Woman Who Brings the Rain*, a memoir based on her experiences of Hokkaido, Japan. She was also runner-up in the Terry Hetherington Award 2015 and short-listed for the Bristol Short Story Prize in 2011. She was selected for the Arts Council of Wales' 'Writers at Work' at Hay Festival, and participated in the Jaipur and Hyderabad Literature Festivals in India as part of Literature Across Frontier's commitment to promote European writing abroad.

Karmele Jaio is a Basque author of three books of short stories and two novels. Her short stories have also been published in many anthologies, including the recent *Best European Fiction* 2017. Jaio's debut novel, *Her Mother's Hands*, published in English by Parthian, remains one of the bestselling books on the Basque literary scene and has been adapted for the big screen.

Eddie Matthews is originally from California and currently a PhD in creative writing student at Swansea University. His stories explore how borders influence our behaviour. He aims to use storytelling to create space for positive dialogue about the shared human experience.

Durre Shahwar is a writer and recipient of Literature Wales' Writers' Bursary 2018, which she is using to work towards her short story collection exploring South Asian identities in Wales. This year, Durre was also part of the Hay Writers at Work programme. As of this autumn, she will be undertaking a PhD in Creative Writing at Cardiff University. Durre is an Associate Editor for Wales Arts Review and the co-founder of 'Where I'm Coming From', an open mic that promotes BAME writing in Wales.

Born in Zagreb in 1966, **Zoran Pilić** is a novelist and short-story writer. His first collection of short stories *Doggiestyle* (2007) was turned into a theatre play *Sex, laži i jedan anđeo* (*Sex, Lies and One Angel*) which was performed at the Zagreb Academy of Drama Arts in 2009. His debut novel *Đavli od papira* (*Paper Devils*) was shortlisted for the prestigious Croatian literary award 'Jutarnji list' and listed as one of the best novels in 2012 by the Croatian Ministry of Culture. The Ministry listed Pilic's collection of short stories *Nema slonova u Meksiku* (*There Are No Elephants in Mexico*) as one of the country's best books again in 2014. His short story *Kad su Divovi hodali zemljom* (*When Giants Walked the Earth*) won the European Short Story Festival prize in 2015. He also writes book reviews and publishes fictional editorial on Booksa.hr. Pilić is one of the Ten New Voices from Europe 2016, selected by Literature Across Frontiers' network of European festivals Literary Europe Live.

Marcie Layton was born and raised in Southern California. After living with her husband and two sons in Britain for more than thirty years, she and her husband relocated to Italy, where she now travels, cooks, caters, and revels in all things Italian.

Marcie has worn many hats over the years: actor, director, teacher, musician, caterer and writer.She worked for many years at Drama Studio London, and DSL/USA, teaching, directing, and as an Associate Director and Course Tutor. She founded Ysgol Glan Tegid, providing drama classes for young actors in North Wales. Having arrived in Lazio, south of Rome, Marcie loves to travel, cook, eat, and write about it all on her blog site *Italy Food Traveller.*

Eric Ngalle Charles is a Cameroon-born writer, poet and performer based in Wales. His work with many organizations including Wales PEN Cymru, Displaced People in Action, Exiled Writers and Welsh Refugee Council focuses on issues surrounding immigration, integration and diversity, and the role of storytelling in overcoming the trauma of displacement. He has co-edited several anthologies of writing by refugees in Wales, and his book *Asylum* (2016) is part of a trilogy. His play *My Mouth Brought me Here* was showcased at the Southbank Centre in 2016. His latest publication is an anthology of writing from Cameroon and Wales, *Hiraeth Erzolirzoli* (2018). He has appeared in a number of festivals in Wales, including the Hay Festival of Literature, and recently in SabirFest in Sicily where he collaborated with local musicians during a residency. His most recent collaboration with poet and artist Nicky Arscott resulted in a collection of poetry comics based on the refugee experience, to be published in 2019.

Maï-Do Hamisultane is a Franco-Moroccan writer born in La Rochelle in 1983. After a childhood spent between Cap d'Antibes and Casablanca1, she studied in preparatory classes at the Lycée Janson-de-Sailly in Paris. Then she began studying medicine and specialized in psychiatry. As the literary critic Meriem El Youssoufi points out, the literary works of Maï-Do Hamisultane navigate between the real and the imaginary. She has participated at the first Marrakech book festival, in October 2015, at the Rentrée littéraire du Mali, in February 2016, and at the Tangier Book Fair in May 2016. Maï-Do is a member of the jury of the po science scenario award for the year 2017 and was included in the list of thirty-four authors invited to represent the country in the spotlight, Morocco, at the Paris Book Fair in March 2017.

Siôn Tomos Owen is a Welsh illustrator, bilingual presenter and author. His first book, *Cawl*, an anthology of short stories, poetry, essays and comics was published in 2016 by Parthian and *Y Fawr a'r Fach: Straeon o'r Rhondda*, a book for Foundation Welsh Learners, was published in 2018 by Y Lolfa. He is a part of the presenting team on S4Cs Cynefin, as well as appearing on Jonathan and BBC Wales Scrum V. He holds creative workshops through his company CreaSion and lives in Treorchy, Rhondda with his wife and daughter

Hanan Issa is a mixed-race poet from Wales. Her work has been featured on both ITV Wales and BBC Radio Wales and published in Banat Collective, Hedgehog Press, *Sukoon, Lumin, sister-hood* and *MuslimGirl.com*. Her winning monologue was featured at Bush Theatre's Hijabi Monologues. She is the co-founder of Cardiff's first BAME open mic series 'Where I'm Coming From'. She is also one of the 2018 Hay Festival Writers at Work. Her debut poetry pamphlet will be published by BurningEye Books in October 2019.

Alexandra Büchler is Director of Literature Across Frontiers (LAF). A translator and editor of numerous publications, she was born in Prague and started her career as cultural manager with the Australia Council for the Arts before moving to the UK where she co-founded LAF in 2000 and launched it with support of the then Culture Programme of the European Union. Her interest lies in the area of literature and translation policies, EU external cultural relations, and the role of civil society in international cultural activities and cultural policy development. She has translated more than twenty books of fiction and poetry and publications on visual arts and architecture, and edited six anthologies of short fiction in Czech and English translation. Among the authors she has translated into her native Czech are J.M. Coetzee, David Malouf, Janice Galloway, Gail Jones, Jeanette Turner Hospital and Rhea Galanaki. Her translation into English of the Czech modern classic *The House of a Thousand Floors* by Jan Weiss was published by Central European University Press in 2016.

Alison Evans is a freelance publishing assistant based in south Wales, with experience in book design and editing. She is the editor of Parthian Baltic, a series of translated poetry collections published in 2018.

The cover is designed by Syncopated Pandemonium, the design handle of **Robert Harries**. He is an editor and graphic designer originally from Swansea, but now based in London.

The cover photograph is called *Noir Moods*.

The photographer: **Pekka Keskinen** is a graphic designer and photographer from Finland who's interested in keeping film photography alive, shooting with old mechanical cameras on traditional black and white film. www.pekkakeskinen.com and www.attemptsat35mm.com.

The model: **Eugenia Antinomy** is a Helsinki-based model who specialises in conceptual, documentary and fashion photography. Her emphasis is on avantgarde and alternative, as well as vintage fashion. Besides modelling she is a philosophy student and is involved in a wide range of art, including visual art, music and fashion design, and plays dark electronic music under the name DJ Antinomy.

PARTHIAN

CARNIVALE

2019 / 21

La Blanche
Maï-Do Hamisultane
Translated by Suzy Ceulan Hughes
ISBN 978-1-91-268123-5
£8.99 • Paperback

TRANSLATED BY JULIA AND PETER SHERWOOD
The Night Circus
and Other Stories
Uršuľa Kovalyk

TRANSLATED BY SUZY CEULAN HUGHES
La Blanche
Maï-Do Hamisultane

The Night Circus and Other Stories
Uršuľa Kovalyk
Translated by Julia and Peter Sherwood
ISBN 978-1-91-268104-4
£8.99 • Paperback

Fiction in Translation

The Book of Katerina
Auguste Corteau
Translator TBC
ISBN 978-1-91-268126-6
£8.99 • Paperback

The Book of Katerina
Auguste Corteau

A Glass Eye
Miren Agur Meabe

A Glass Eye
Miren Agur Meabe
Translated by Amaia Gabantxo
ISBN 978-1-91-210954-8
£8.99 • Paperback

Her Mother's Hands
Karmele Jaio
Translated by Kristin Addis
ISBN 978-1-91-210955-5
£8.99 • Paperback

PARTHIAN
CARNIVALE
2 0 1 9 / 2 1

Her Mother's Hands
Karmele Jaio